CONSTANCE DUNLAP

ARTHUR B. REEVE

1st WORLD
LIBRARY
Literary Society

Constance Dunlap

Arthur B. Reeve

© 1st World Library, 2008
PO Box 2211
Fairfield, IA 52556
www.1stworldlibrary.com
First Edition

LCCN: 2007935353

Softcover ISBN: 978-1-4218-9309-9
Hardcover ISBN: 978-1-4218-9409-6
eBook ISBN: 978-1-4218-9209-2

Purchase *"Constance Dunlap"*
as a traditional bound book at:
www.1stWorldLibrary.com/purchase.asp?ISBN=978-1-4218-9309-9

1st World Library is a literary, educational organization
dedicated to:

- Creating a free internet library of downloadable ebooks

- Hosting writing competitions and offering book publishing
scholarships.

Interested in more 1st World Library books? contact:
literacy@1stworldlibrary.com
Check us out at: www.1stworldlibrary.com

1ˢᵗ World Library Literary Society

Giving Back to the World

"If you want to work on the core problem, it's early school literacy."

- James Barksdale, former CEO of Netscape

"No skill is more crucial to the future of a child, or to a democratic and prosperous society, than literacy."

- Los Angeles Times

"Literacy... means far more than learning how to read and write... The aim is to transmit... knowledge and promote social participation."

- UNESCO

"Literacy is not a luxury, it is a right and a responsibility. If our world is to meet the challenges of the twenty-first century we must harness the energy and creativity of all our citizens."

- President Bill Clinton

"Parents should be encouraged to read to their children, and teachers should be equipped with all available techniques for teaching literacy, so the varying needs and capacities of individual kids can be taken into account."

- Hugh Mackay

CONTENTS

CHAPTER I

THE FORGERS

There was something of the look of the hunted animal brought to bay at last in Carlton Dunlap's face as he let himself into his apartment late one night toward the close of the year.

On his breath was the lingering odor of whisky, yet in his eye and hand none of the effects. He entered quietly, although there was no apparent reason for such excessive caution. Then he locked the door with the utmost care, although there was no apparent reason for caution about that, either.

Even when he had thus barricaded himself, he paused to listen with all the elemental fear of the cave man who dreaded the footsteps of his pursuers. In the dim light of the studio apartment he looked anxiously for the figure of his wife. Constance was not there, as she had been on other nights, uneasily awaiting his return. What was the matter? His hand shook a trifle now as he turned the knob of the bedroom door and pushed it softly open.

She was asleep. He leaned over, not realizing that her every faculty was keenly alive to his presence, that she was acting a part.

"Throw something around yourself, Constance," he whispered hoarsely into her ear, as she moved with a little well-feigned start at being suddenly wakened, "and come into the studio. There is something I must tell you tonight, my dear."

"My dear!" she exclaimed bitterly, now seeming to rouse herself with an effort and pretending to put back a stray wisp of her dark hair in order to hide from him the tears that still lingered on her flushed cheeks. "You can say that, Carlton, when it has been every night the same old threadbare excuse of working at the office until midnight?"

She set her face in hard lines, but could not catch his eye.

"Carlton Dunlap," she added in a tone that rasped his very soul, "I am nobody's fool. I may not know much about bookkeeping and accounting, but I can add—and two and two, when the same man but different women compose each two, do not make four, according to my arithmetic, but three, from which,"—she finished almost hysterically the little speech she had prepared, but it seemed to fall flat before the man's curiously altered manner—"from which I shall subtract one."

She burst into tears.

"Listen," he urged, taking her arm gently to lead her to an easy-chair.

"No, no, no!" she cried, now thoroughly aroused, with eyes that again snapped accusation and defiance at him, "don't touch me. Talk to me, if you want to, but don't, don't come near me." She was now facing him, standing in the high-

Arthur B. Reeve

ceilinged "studio," as they called the room where she had kept up in a desultory manner for her own amusement the art studies which had interested her before her marriage. "What is it that you want to say? The other nights you said nothing at all. Have you at last thought up an excuse? I hope it is at least a clever one."

"Constance," he remonstrated, looking fearfully about. Instinctively she felt that her accusation was unjust. Not even that had dulled the hunted look in his face. "Perhaps— perhaps if it were that of which you suspect me, we could patch it up. I don't know. But, Constance, I—I must leave for the west on the first train in the morning." He did not pause to notice her startled look, but raced on. "I have worked every night this week trying to straighten out those accounts of mine by the first of the year and—and I can't do it. An expert begins on them in a couple of days. You must call up the office to-morrow and tell them that I am ill, tell them anything. I must get at least a day or two start before they—"

"Carlton," she interrupted, "what is the matter? What have you—"

She checked herself in surprise. He had been fumbling in his pocket and now laid down a pile of green and yellow banknotes on the table.

"I have scraped together every last cent I can spare," he continued, talking jerkily to suppress his emotion. "They cannot take those away from you, Constance. And—when I am settled—in a new life," he swallowed hard and averted his eyes further from her startled gaze, "under a new name, somewhere, if you have just a little spot in your heart that still responds to me, I—I—no, it is too much even to hope. Constance, the accounts will not come out right because I am—I am an embezzler."

He bit off the word viciously and then sank his head into his hands and bowed it to a depth that alone could express his shame.

Why did she not say something, do something? Some women would have fainted. Some would have denounced him. But she stood there and he dared not look up to read what was written in her face. He felt alone, all alone, with every man's hand against him, he who had never in all his life felt so or had done anything to make him feel so before. He groaned as the sweat of his mental and physical agony poured coldly out on his forehead. All that he knew was that she was standing there, silent, looking him through and through, as cold as a statue. Was she the personification of justice? Was this but a foretaste of the ostracism of the world?

"When we were first married, Constance," he began sadly, "I was only a clerk for Green & Co., at two thousand a year. We talked it over. I stayed and in time became cashier at five thousand. But you know as well as I that five thousand does not meet the social obligations laid on us by our position in the circle in which we are forced to move."

His voice had become cold and hard, but he did not allow himself to be betrayed into adding, as he might well have done in justice to himself, that to her even a thousand dollars a month would have been only a beginning. It was not that she had be accustomed to so much in the station of life from which he had taken her. The plain fact was that New York had had an over-tonic effect on her.

"You were not a nagging woman, Constance," he went on in a somewhat softened tone. "In fact you have been a good wife; you have never thrown it up to me that I was unable to make good to the degree of many of our friends in purely

Arthur B. Reeve

commercial lines. All you have ever said is the truth. A banking house pays low for its brains. My God!" he cried stiffening out in the chair and clenching his fists, "it pays low for its temptations, too."

There had been nothing in the world Carlton would not have given to make happy the woman who stood now, leaning on the table in cold silence, with averted head, regarding neither him nor the pile of greenbacks.

"Hundreds of thousands of dollars passed through my hands every week," he resumed. "That business owed me for my care of it. It was taking the best in me and in return was not paying what other businesses paid for the best in other men. When a man gets thinking that way, with a woman whom he loves as I love you—something happens."

He paused in the bitterness of his thoughts. She moved as if to speak. "No, no," he interrupted. "Hear me out first. All I asked was a chance to employ a little of the money that I saw about me—not to take it, but to employ it for a little while, a few days, perhaps only a few hours. Money breeds money. Why should I not use some of this idle money to pay me what I ought to have?

"When Mr. Green was away last summer I heard some inside news about a certain stock, go it happened that I began to juggle the accounts. It is too long a story to tell how I did it. Anybody in my position could have done it—for a time. It would not interest you anyhow. But I did it. The first venture was successful. Also the spending of the money was very successful, in its way. That was the money that took us to the fashionable hotel in Atlantic City where we met so many people. Instead of helping me, it got me in deeper.

"When the profit from this first deal was spent there was

nothing to do but to repeat what I had done successfully before. I could not quit now. I tried again, a little hypothecation of some bonds. Stocks went down. I had made a bad bet and five thousand dollars was wiped out, a whole year's salary. I tried again, and wiped out five thousand more. I was at my wits' end. I have borrowed under fictitious names, used names of obscure persons as borrowers, have put up dummy security. It was possible because I controlled the audits. But it has done no good. The losses have far outbalanced the winnings and to-day I am in for twenty-five thousand dollars."

She was watching him now with dilating eyes as the horror of the situation was burned into her soul. He raced on, afraid to pause lest she should interrupt him.

"Mr. Green has been talked into introducing scientific management and a new system into the business by a certified public accountant, an expert in installing systems and discovering irregularities. Here I am, faced by certain exposure," he went on, pacing the floor and looking everywhere but at her face. "What should I do? Borrow? It is useless. I have no security that anyone would accept.

"There is just one thing left." He lowered his voice until it almost sank into a hoarse whisper. "I must cut loose. I have scraped together what I can and I have borrowed on my life insurance. Here on the table is all that I can spare.

"To-night, the last night, I have worked frantically in a vain hope that something, some way would at last turn up. It has not. There is no other way out. In despair I have put this off until the last moment. But I have thought of nothing else for a week. Good God, Constance, I have reached the mental state where even intoxicants fail to intoxicate."

He dropped back again into the deep chair and sank his head again on his hands. He groaned as he thought of the agony of packing a bag and slinking for the Western express through the crowds at the railroad terminal.

Still Constance was silent. Through her mind was running the single thought that she had misjudged him. There had been no other woman in the case. As he spoke, there came flooding into her heart the sudden realization of the truth. He had done it for her.

It was a rude and bitter awakening after the past months when the increased income, with no questions asked, had made her feel that they were advancing. She passed her hands over her eyes, but there it was still, not a dream but a harsh reality. If she could only have gone back and undone it! But what was done, was done, She was amazed at herself. It was not horror of the deed that sent an icy shudder over her. It was horror of exposure.

He had done it for her. Over and over again that thought raced through her mind. She steeled herself at last to speak. She hardly knew what was in her own mind, what the conflicting, surging emotions of her own heart meant.

"And so, you are leaving me what is left, leaving me in disgrace, and you are going to do the best you can to get away safely. You want me to tell one last lie for you."

There was an unnatural hollowness in her voice which he did not understand, but which out him to the quick. He had killed love. He was alone. He knew it. With a final effort he tried to moisten his parched lips to answer. At last, in a husky voice, he managed to say, "Yes."

But with all his power of will he could not look at her.

"Carlton Dunlap," she cried, leaning both hands for support on the table, bending over and at last forcing him to look her in the eyes, "do you know what I think of you? I think you are a damned coward. There!"

Instead of tears and recriminations, instead of the conventional "How could you do it?" instead of burning denunciation of him for ruining her life, he read something else in her face. What was it?

"Coward?" he repeated slowly. "What would you have me do—take you with me?"

She tossed her head contemptuously.

"Stay and face it?" he hazarded again.

"Is there no other way?" she asked, still leaning forward with her eyes fixed on his. "Think! Is there no way that you could avoid discovery just for a time? Carlton, you—we are cornered. Is there no desperate chance?"

He shook his head sadly.

Her eyes wandered momentarily about the studio, until they rested on an easel. On it stood a water color on which she had been working, trying to put into it some of the feeling which she would never have put into words for him. On the walls of the apartment were pen and ink sketches, scores of little things which she had done for her own amusement. She bit her lip as an idea flashed through her mind.

He shook his head again mournfully.

"Somewhere," she said slowly, "I have read that clever forgers use water colors and pen and ink like regular artists.

Think—think! Is there no way that we—that I could forge a check that would give us breathing space, perhaps rescue us?"

Carlton leaned over the table toward her, fascinated. He placed both his hands on hers. They were icy, but she did not withdraw them.

For an instant they looked into each other's eyes, an instant, and then they understood. They were partners in crime, amateurs perhaps, but partners as they had been in honesty.

It was a new idea that she had suggested to him. Why should he not act on it? Why hesitate? Why stop at it? He was already an embezzler. Why not add a new crime to the list? As he looked into her eyes he felt a new strength. Together they could do it. Hers was the brain that had conceived the way out. She had the will, the compelling power to carry the thing through. He would throw himself on her intuition, her brain, her skill, her daring.

On his desk in the corner, where often until far into the night he had worked on the huge ruled sheets of paper covered with figures of the firm's accounts, he saw two goose-necked vials, one of lemon-colored liquid, the other of raspberry color. One was of tartaric acid, the other of chloride of lime. It was an ordinary ink eradicator. Near the bottles lay a rod of glass with a curious tip, an ink eraser made of finely spun glass threads which scraped away the surface of the paper more delicately than any other tool that had been devised. There were the materials for his, their rehabilitation if they were placed in his wife's deft artist fingers. Here was all the chemistry and artistry of forgery at hand.

"Yes," he answered eagerly, "there is a way, Constance. Together we can do it."

There was no time for tenderness between them now. It was cold, hard fact and they understood each other too well to stop for endearments.

Far into the night they sat up and discussed the way in which they would go about the crime. They practised with erasers and with brush and water color on the protective coloring tint on some canceled checks of his own. Carlton must get a check of a firm in town, a check that bore a genuine signature. In it they would make such trifling changes in the body as would attract no attention in passing, yet would yield a substantial sum toward wiping out Carlton's unfortunate deficit.

Late as he had worked the night before, nervous and shaky as he felt after the sleepless hours of planning their new life, Carlton was the first at the office in the morning. His hand trembled as he ran through the huge batch of mail already left at the first delivery. He paused as he came to one letter with the name "W. J. REYNOLDS CO." on it.

Here was a check in payment of a small bill, he knew. It was from a firm which habitually kept hundreds of thousands on deposit at the Gorham Bank. It fitted the case admirably. He slit open the letter. There, neatly folded, was the check:

No. 15711. Dec. 27, 191—.

THE GORHAM NATIONAL BANK

Pay to the order of....... Green & Co.......

Twenty-five 00/100 ....Dollars

$25.00/100

W. J. REYNOLDS Co., per CHAS. M. BROWN, Treas.

It flashed over him in a moment what to do. Twenty-five thousand would just about cover his shortage. The Reynolds firm was a big one, doing big transactions. He slipped the check into his pocket. The check might have been stolen in the mail. Why not?

The journey uptown was most excruciatingly long, in spite of the fact that he had met no one he knew either at the office or outside. At last he arrived home, to find Constance waiting anxiously.

"Did you get a check?" she asked, hardly waiting for his reply. "Let me see it. Give it to me."

The coolness with which she went about it amazed him. "It has the amount punched on it with a check punch," she observed as she ran her quick eye over it while he explained his plan. "We'll have to fill up some of those holes made by the punch."

"I know the kind they used," he answered. "I'll get one and a desk check from the Gorham. You do the artistic work, my dear. My knowledge of check punches, watermarks, and paper will furnish the rest. I'll be back directly. Don't forget to call up the office a little before the time I usually arrive there and tell them I am ill."

With her light-fingered touch she worked feverishly, partly with the liquid ink eradicator, but mostly with the spun-glass eraser. First she rubbed out the cents after the written figure "Twenty-five." Carefully with a blunt instrument she smoothed down the roughened surface of the paper so that the ink would not run in the fibers and blot. Over and over she practised writing the "Thousand" in a hand like that on the check. She already had the capital "T" in "Twenty" as a guide. During the night in practising she had found that in raising checks only seven capital letters were used—O in one, T in two, three, ten, and thousand, F in four and five, S in six and seven, E in eight, N in nine and H in hundred.

At last even her practice satisfied her. Then with a coolness born only of desperation she wrote in the words, "Thousand 00/100." When she had done it she stopped to wonder at herself. She was amazed and perhaps a little frightened at how readily she adapted herself to the crime of forgery. She did not know that it was one of the few crimes in which women had proved themselves most proficient, though she felt her own proficiency and native ability for copying.

Again the eraser came into play to remove the cents after the figure "25." A comma and three zeros following it were inserted, followed by a new "00/100." The signature was left untouched.

Erasing the name of "Green & Co.," presented greater difficulties, but it was accomplished with as little loss of the protective coloring on the surface of the check as possible. Then after the "Pay to the order of" she wrote in, as her husband had directed, "The Carlton Realty Co."

Next came the water color to restore the protective tint where the glass eraser and the acids had removed it. There was much delicate matching of tints and careful painting in with a fine camel's hair brush, until at last the color of those parts where there had been an erasure was apparently as good as any other part.

Of course, under the microscope there could have been seen the angry crisscrossing of the fibers of the paper due to the harsh action of the acids and the glass eraser. Still, painting the whole thing over with a little resinous liquid somewhat restored the glaze to the paper, at least sufficiently to satisfy a cursory glance of the naked eye.

There remained the difficulty of the protective punch marks. There they were, a star cut out of the check itself, a dollar sign and 25 followed by another star.

She was still admiring her handiwork, giving it here and there a light little fillip with the brush and comparing this check with some of those which had been practised on last night, to see whether she had made any improvement in her technique of forgery, when Carlton returned with the punch and the blank checks on the Gorham Bank.

From one of the blank checks he punched out a number of little stars until there was one which in watermark and scroll work corresponded precisely with that punched out in the original check.

Constance, whose fingers had long been accustomed to fine work, fitted in the little star after the $25, then took it out, moistened the edges ever so lightly with glue on the end of a toothpick, and pasted it back again. A hot iron completed the work of making the edges smooth and unless a rather powerful glass had been used no one could have seen the pasted-in insertion after the $25.

Careful not to deviate the fraction of a hair's breadth from the alignment Carlton took the punch, added three 0's, and a star after the 25, making it $25,000. Finally the whole thing was again ironed to give it the smoothness of an original. Here at last was the completed work, the first product of their combined skill in crime:

No. 15711. Dec. 27,191—. THE GORHAM NATIONAL BANK

Pay to the order of... The Carlton Realty Co.

Twenty-five Thousand 00/100.........Dollars $25,000.00/100

W. J. REYNOLDS Co., per CHAS. M. BROWN, Treas.

How completely people may change, even within a few hours, was well illustrated as they stood side by side and regarded their work with as much pride as if it had been the result of their honest efforts of years. They were now pen and brush crooks of the first caliber, had reduced forgery to a fine art and demonstrated what an amateur might do. For, although they did not know it, nearly half the fifteen millions or so lost by forgeries every year was the work of amateurs such as they.

The next problem was presenting the check for collection. Of course Carlton could not put it through his own bank, unless he wanted to leave a blazed trail straight to himself. Only a colossal bluff would do, and in a city where only colossal bluffs succeed it was not so impossible as might have been first imagined.

Luncheon over, they sauntered casually into a high-class office building on Broadway where there were offices to rent. The agent was duly impressed by the couple who talked of their large real estate dealings. Where he might have been thoroughly suspicious of a man and might have asked many embarrassing but perfectly proper questions, he accepted the woman without a murmur. At her suggestion he even consented to take his new tenants around to the Uptown Bank and introduce them. They made an excellent impression by a first cash deposit of the money Carlton had thrown down on the table the night before. A check for the first month's rent more than mollified the agent and talk of a big deal that was just being signed up to-day duly impressed the bank.

The next problem was to get the forged check certified. That, also, proved a very simple matter. Any one can walk into a bank and get a check for $25,000 certified, while if he appears, a stranger, before the window of the paying teller to cash a check for twenty-five dollars he would almost be thrown out of the bank. Banks will certify at a glance practically any check that looks right, but they pass on the responsibility of cashing them. Thus before the close of banking hours Dunlap was able to deposit in his new bank the check certified by the Gorham.

Twenty-four hours must elapse before he could draw against the check which he had deposited. He did not propose to waste that time, so that the next day found him at Green & Co.'s, feeling much better. Really he had come prepared now to straighten out the books, knowing that in a few hours he could make good.

The first hesitation due to the newness of the game had worn off by this time. Nothing at all of an alarming nature had happened. The new month had already begun and as most firms have their accounts balanced only once a month, he had, he reasoned, nearly the entire four weeks in which to operate.

Conscience was dulled in Constance, also, and she was now busy with ink eraser, the water colors, and other paraphernalia in a wholesale raising of checks, mostly for amounts smaller than that in the first attempt.

"We are taking big chances, anyway," she urged him. "Why quit yet? A few days more and we may land something worth while."

The next day he excused himself from the office for a while and presented himself at his new bank with a sheaf of new checks which she had raised, all certified, and totaling some thousands more.

His own check for twenty-five thousand was now honored. The relief which he felt was tremendous after the weeks of grueling anxiety. At once he hurried to a broker's and placed an order for the stocks he had used on which to borrow. He could now replace everything in the safe, straighten out the books, could make everything look right to the systematizer, could blame any apparent irregularity on his old system. Even ignorance was better than dishonesty.

Constance, meanwhile, had installed herself in the little office they had hired, as stenographer and secretary. Once having embarked on the hazardous enterprise she showed no disposition to give it up yet An office boy was hired and introduced at the bank.

The mythical realty company prospered, at least if prosperity is measured merely by the bank book. In less than a week the skilful pen and brush of Constance had secured them a balance, after straightening out Carlton's debts, that came well up to a hundred thousand dollars, mostly in small checks, some with genuine signatures and amounts altered, others complete forgeries.

As they went deeper and deeper, Constance began to feel the truth of their situation. It was she who was really at the helm in this enterprise. It had been her idea; the execution of it had been mainly her work; Carlton had furnished merely the business knowledge that she did not possess. The more she thought of it during the hours in the little office while he was at work downtown, the more uneasy did she become.

What if he should betray himself in some way? She was sure of herself. But she was almost afraid to let him go out of her

Arthur B. Reeve

sight. She felt a sinking sensation every time he mentioned any of the happenings in the banking house. Could he be trusted alone not to betray himself when the first hint of discovery of something wrong came?

It was now near the middle of the month. It would not pay to wait until the end. Some one of the many firms whose checks they had forged might have its book balanced at any time now. From day to day small amounts in cash had already been withdrawn until they were twenty thousand dollars to the good. They planned to draw out thirty thousand now at one time. That would give them fifty thousand, roughly half of their forgeries.

The check was written and the office boy was started to the bank with it. Carlton followed him at a distance, as he had on other occasions, ready to note the first sign of trouble as the boy waited at the teller's window. At last the boy was at the head of the line. He had passed the check in and his satchel was lying open, with voracious maw, on the ledge below the wicket for the greedy feeding of stacks of bills. Why did the teller not raise the wicket and shove out the money in a coveted pile? Carlton seemed to feel that something was wrong. The line lengthened and those at the end of the queue began to grow restive at the delay. One of the bank's officers walked down and spoke to the boy.

Carlton waited no longer. The game was up. He rushed from his coign of observation, out of the bank building, and dashed into a telephone booth.

"Quick, Constance," he shouted over the wire, "leave every-thing. They are holding up our check. They have discovered something. Take a cab and drive slowly around the square. You will find me waiting for you at the north end."

That night the newspapers were full of the story. There was the whole thing, exaggerated, distorted, multiplied, until they had become swindlers of millions instead of thousands. But nevertheless it was their story. There was only one grain of consolation. It was in the last paragraph of the news item, and read: "There seems to be no trace of the man and woman who worked this clever swindle. As if by a telepathic message they have vanished at just the time when their whole house of cards collapsed."

They removed every vestige of their work from the apartment. Everything was destroyed. Constance even began a new water color so that that might suggest that she had not laid aside her painting.

They had played for a big stake and lost. But the twenty thousand dollars was something. Now the great problem was to conceal it and themselves. They had lost, yet if ever before they loved, it was as nothing to what it was now that they had tasted together the bitter and the sweet of their mutual crime.

Carlton went down to the office the next day, just as before. The anxious hours that his wife had previously spent thinking whether he might betray himself by some slip were comparative safety as contrasted with the uncertainty of the hours now. But the first day after the alarm of the discovery passed off all right. Carlton even discussed the case, his case, with those in the office, commented on it, condemned the swindlers, and carried it off, he felt proud to say, as well as Constance herself might have done had she been in his place.

Another day passed. His account of the first day, reassuring as it had been to her, did not lessen the anxiety. Yet never before had they seemed to be bound together by such ties as knitted their very souls in this crisis. She tried with a

Arthur B. Reeve

devotion that was touching to impart to him some of her own strength to ward off detection.

It was the afternoon of the second day that a man who gave the name of Drummond called and presented a card of the Reynolds Company.

"Have you ever been paid a little bill of twenty-five dollars by our company?" he asked.

Down in his heart Carlton knew that this man was a detective. "I can't say without looking it up," he replied.

Carlton touched a button and an assistant appeared. Something outside himself seemed to nerve him up, as he asked: "Look up our account with Reynolds, and see if we have been paid—what is it?—a bill for twenty-five dollars. Do you recall it?"

"Yes, I recall it," replied the assistant. "No, Mr. Dunlap, I don't think it has been paid. It is a small matter, but we sent them a duplicate bill yesterday. I thought the original must have gone astray."

Carlton cursed him inwardly for sending the bill. But then, he reasoned, it was only a question of time, after all, when the forgery would be discovered.

Drummond dropped into a half-confidential, half-quizzing tone. "I thought not. Somewhere along the line that check has been stolen and raised to twenty-five thousand dollars," he remarked.

"Is that so?" gasped Carlton, trying hard to show just the right amount of surprise and not too much. "Is that so?"

"No doubt you have read in the papers of this clever realty company swindle? Well, it seems to have been part of that."

"I am sure that we shall be glad to do all in our power to cooperate with Reynolds," put in Dunlap.

"I thought you would," commented Drummond dryly. "I may as well tell you that I fear some one has been tampering with your mail."

"Tampering with OUR mail?" repeated Dunlap, aghast. "Impossible."

"Nothing is impossible until it is proved so," answered Drummond, looking him straight in the eyes. Carlton did not flinch. He felt a new power within himself, gained during the past few days of new association with Constance. For her he could face anything.

But when Drummond was gone he felt as he had on the night when he had finally realized that he could never cover up the deficit in his books. With an almost superhuman effort he gripped himself. Interminably the hours of the rest of the day dragged on.

That night he sank limp into a chair on his return home. "A man named Drummond was in the office to-day, my dear," he said. "Some one in the office sent Reynolds a duplicate bill, and they know about the check."

"Well?"

"I wonder if they suspect me?"

"If you act like that, they won't suspect. They'll arrest," she commented sarcastically.

He had braced up again into his new self at her words. But there was again that sinking sensation in her heart, as she realized that it was, after all, herself on whom he depended, that it was she who had been the will, even though he had been the intellect of their enterprise. She could not overcome the feeling that, if only their positions could be reversed, the thing might even yet be carried through.

Drummond appeared again at the office the next day. There was no concealment about him now. He said frankly that he was from the Burr Detective Agency, whose business it was to guard the banks against forgeries.

"The pen work, or, as we detectives call it, the penning," he remarked, "in the case of that check is especially good. It shows rare skill. But the pitfalls in this forgery game are so many that, in avoiding one, a forger, ever so clever, falls into another."

Carlton felt the polite third degree, as he proceeded: "Nowadays the forger has science to contend with, too. The microscope and camera may come in a little too late to be of practical use in preventing the forger from getting his money at first, but they come in very neatly later in catching him. What the naked eye cannot see in this check they reveal. Besides, a little iodine vapor brings out the original 'Green & Co.' on it.

"We have found out also that the protective coloring was restored by water color. That was easy. Where the paper was scratched and the sizing taken off, it has been painted with a resinous substance to restore the glaze, to the eye. Well, a little alcohol takes that off, too. Oh, the amateur forger may be the most dangerous kind, because the professional regularly follows the same line, leaves tracks, has associates, but," he concluded impressively, "all are caught sooner or later—sooner or later."

Dunlap managed to maintain his outward composure admirably. Still the little lifting of the curtain on the hidden mysteries of the new detective art produced its effect. They were getting closer, and Dunlap knew it, as Drummond intended he should. And, as in every crisis, he turned naturally to Constance. Never had she meant so much to him as now.

That night as he entered the apartment he happened to glance behind him. In the shadow down the street a man dodged quickly behind a tree. The thing gave him a start. He was being watched.

"There is just one thing left," he cried excitedly as he hurried upstairs with the news. "We must both disappear this time."

Constance took it very calmly. "But we must not go together," she added quickly, her fertile mind, as ever, hitting directly on a plan of action. "If we separate, they will be less likely to trace us, for they will never think we would do that."

It was evident that the words were being forced out by the conflict of common sense and deep emotion. "Perhaps it will be best for you to stick to your original idea of going west. I shall go to one of the winter resorts. We shall communicate only through the personal column of the Star. Sign yourself Weston. I shall sign Easton."

The words fell on Carlton with his new and deeper love for her like a death sentence. It had never entered his mind that they were to be separated now. Dissolve their partnership in crime? To him it seemed as if they had just begun to live since that night when they had at last understood each other.

And it had come to this—separation.

"A man can always shift for himself better if he has no impediments," she said, speaking rapidly as if to bolster up her own resolution. "A woman is always an impediment in a crisis like this."

In her face he saw what he had never seen before. There was love in it that would sacrifice everything. She was sending him away from her, not to save herself but to save him. Vainly he attempted to protest. She placed her finger on his lips. Never before had he felt such over-powering love for her. And yet she held him in check in spite of himself.

"Take enough to last a few months," she added hastily. "Give me the rest. I can hide it and take care of myself. Even if they trace me I can get off. A woman can always do that more easily than a man. Don't worry about me. Go somewhere, start a new life. If it takes years, I will wait. Let me know where you are. We can find some way in which I can come back into your life. No, no,"—Carlton had caught her passionately in his arms—"even that cannot weaken me. The die is cast. We must go."

She tore herself away from him and fled into her room, where, with set face and ashen lips, she stuffed article after article into her grip. With a heavy heart Carlton did the same. The bottom had dropped out of everything, yet try as he would to reason it out, he could find no other solution but hers. To stay was out of the question, if indeed it was not already too late to run. To go together was equally out of the question. Constance had shown that. "Seek the woman," was the first rule of the police.

As they left the apartment they could see a man across the street following them closely. They were shadowed. In despair Carlton turned toward his wife. A sudden idea had flashed over her. There were two taxicabs at the station on the corner.

"I will take the first," she whispered. "Take the second and follow me. Then he cannot trace us."

They were off, leaving the baffled shadow only time to take the numbers of the cab. Constance had thought of that. She stopped and Carlton joined her. After a short walk they took another cab.

He looked at her inquiringly, but she said nothing. In her eyes he saw the same fire that blazed when she had asked him if there was no way to avoid discovery and had suggested it herself in the forgery. He reached over and caressed her hand. She did not withdraw it, but her averted eyes told that she could not trust even herself too far.

As they stood before the gateway to the steps that led down into the long under-river tunnel which was to swallow them so soon and project them, each into a new life, hundreds, perhaps thousands of miles apart, Carlton realized as never before what it all had meant. He had loved her through all the years, but never with the wild love of the past two weeks. Now there was nothing but blackness and blankness. He felt as though the hand of fate was tearing out his wildly beating heart.

She tried to smile at him bravely. She understood. For a moment she looked at him in the old way and all the pent-up love that would have, that had done and dared everything for him struggled in her rapidly rising and falling breast.

It was now or never. She knew it, the supreme effort. One word or look too many from her and all would be lost. She flung her arms about him and kissed him. "Remember—one week from to-day—a personal—in the STAR," she panted.

She literally tore herself from his arms, gathered up her grip, and was gone.

A week passed. The quiet little woman at the Oceanview House was still as much a mystery to the other guests as when she arrived, travel-stained and worn with the repressed emotion of her sacrifice. She had appeared to show no interest in anything, to take her meals mechanically, to stay most of the time in her room, never to enter into any of the recreations of the famous winter resort.

Only once a day did she betray the slightest concern about anything around her. That was when the New York papers arrived. Then she was always first at the news-stand, and the boy handed out to her, as a matter of habit, the STAR. Yet no one ever saw her read it. Directly afterward she would retire to her room. There she would pore over the first page, reading and rereading every personal in it. Sometimes she would try reading them backward and transposing the words, as if the message they contained might be in the form of a cryptograph.

The strain and the suspense began to show on her. Day after day passed, until it was nearly two weeks since the parting in New York. Day after day she grew more worn by worry and fear. What had happened?

In desperation she herself wired a personal to the paper: "Weston. Write me at the Oceanview. Easton."

For three days she waited for an answer. Then she wired the personal again. Still there was no reply and no hint of reply. Had they captured him? Or was he so closely pursued that he did not dare to reply even in the cryptic manner on which they had agreed!

She took the file of papers which she kept and again ran through the personals, even going back to the very day after they had separated. Perhaps she had missed one, though she knew that she could not have done so, for she had looked at them a hundred times. Where was he? Why did he not answer her message in some way? No one had followed her. Were they centering their efforts on capturing him?

She haunted the news-stand in the lobby of the beautifully appointed hotel. Her desire to read newspapers grew. She read everything.

It was just two weeks since they had left New York on their separate journeys when, on the evening of another newsless day, she was passing the news-stand. From force of habit she glanced at an early edition of an evening paper.

The big black type of the heading caught her eye:

NOTED FORGER A SUICIDE

With a little shriek, half-suppressed, she seized the paper. It was Carlton. There was his name. He had shot himself in a room in a hotel in St. Louis. She ran her eye down the column, hardly able to read. In heavier type than the rest was the letter they had found on him:

MY DEAREST CONSTANCE,

When you read this I, who have wronged and deceived you beyond words, will be where I can no longer hurt you. Forgive me, for by this act I am a confessed embezzler and forger. I could not face you and tell you of the double life I was leading. So I have sent you away and have gone away myself—and may the Lord have mercy on the soul of

Your devoted husband, CARLTON DUNLAP.

Over and over again she read the words, as she clutched at the edge of the news-stand to keep from fainting—"wronged and deceived you," "the double life I was leading." What did he mean? Had he, after all, been concealing something else from her? Had there really been another woman?

Suddenly the truth flashed over her. Tracked and almost overtaken, lacking her hand which had guided him, he had seen no other way out. And in his last act he had shouldered it all on himself, had shielded her nobly from the penalty, had opened wide for her the only door of escape.

CHAPTER II

THE EMBEZZLERS

"I came here to hide, to vanish forever from those who know me."

The young man paused a moment to watch the effect of his revelation of himself to Constance Dunlap. There was a certain cynical bitterness in his tone which made her shudder.

"If you were to be discovered—what then?" she hazarded.

Murray Dodge looked at her significantly, but said nothing. Instead, he turned and gazed silently at the ruffled waters of Woodlake. There was no mistaking the utter hopelessness and grim determination of the man.

"Why—why have you told so much to me, an absolute stranger?" she asked, searching his face. "Might I not hand you over to the detectives who, you say, will soon be looking for you?"

"You might," he answered quickly, "but you won't."

There was a note of appeal in his voice as he pursued slowly,

Arthur B. Reeve

not as if seeking protection, but as if hungry for friendship and most of all her friendship, "Mrs. Dunlap, I have heard what the people at the hotel say is your story. I think I understand, as much as a man can. Anyhow, I know that you can understand. I have reached a point where I must tell some one or go insane. It is only a question of time before I shall be caught. We are all caught. Tell me," he asked eagerly, bending down closer to her with an almost breathless intensity in his face as though he would read her thoughts, "am I right? The story of you which I have heard since I came here is not the truth, the whole truth. It is only half the truth—is it not?"

Constance felt that this man was dangerously near understanding her, as no one yet had seemed to be. It set her heart beating wildly to know that he did. And yet she was not afraid. Somehow, although she did not betray the answer by a word or a look, she felt that she could trust him.

Through the door of escape from the penalty of her forgeries, which Carlton Dunlap had thrown open for her by the manner of his death, Constance had passed unsuspected. To return to New York, however, had become out of the question. She had plenty of money for her present needs, although she thought it best to say nothing about it lest some one might wonder and stumble on the truth.

She had closed up the little studio apartment, and had gone to a quiet resort in the pines. Here, at least, she thought she might live unobserved until she could plan out the tangled future of her life.

There had seemed to be no need to conceal her identity, and she had felt it better not to do so. She knew that her story would follow her, and it had. She was prepared for that. She was prepared for the pity and condescension of the gossips and had made up her mind to stand aloof.

Then came a day when a stranger had registered at the hotel. She had not noticed him especially, but it was not long before she realized that he was noticing her. Was he a detective? Had he found out the truth in some uncanny way? She felt sure that the name on the hotel register, Malcolm Dodd, was not his real name.

Constance had not been surprised when the head waiter had seated the young man at her table. No doubt he had manoeuvred it so. Nor did she avoid the guarded acquaintance that resulted in the natural course of events.

One afternoon, shortly after his arrival, she had encountered him unexpectedly on a walk through the pines. He appeared surprised to meet her, yet she knew intuitively that he had been following her. Still, it was so different now to have any one seek her company that, in spite of her uncertainty of him, she almost welcomed his speaking.

There was a certain deference in his manner, too, which did not accord with Constance's ideas of a detective. Yet he did know something of her. How much! Was it merely what the rest of the world knew? She could not help seeing that the man was studying her, while she studied him. There was a fascination about it, a fascination that the human mystery always possesses for a woman. On his part, he showed keenly his interest in her.

Constance had met him with more frankness as she encountered him often during the days that followed. She had even tried to draw him out to talk of himself.

"I came here," he had said one day when they were passing the spot where he had overtaken her first, "without knowing a soul, not expecting to meet any one I should care for, indeed hoping to meet no one."

Constance had said nothing, but she felt that at last he was going to crash down the barrier of reserve. He continued earnestly, "Somehow or other I have come to enjoy these little walks."

"So have I," she admitted, facing him; "but, do you know, sometimes I have thought that Malcolm Dodd is not your real name?"

"Not my real name?" he repeated.

"And that you are here for some other purpose than—just to rest. You know, you might be a detective."

He had looked at her searchingly. Then in a burst of confidence, he had replied, "No, my name is not Dodd, as you guessed. But I am not a detective, as you suspected at first. I have been watching you because, ever since I heard your story here, I have been—well, not suspicious, but—attracted. You seem to me to have faced a great problem. I, too, have come to the parting of the ways. Shall I run or shall I fight?"

He had handed her a card without hesitation. It bore the name, "Murray Dodge, Treasurer, Globe Importing Company."

"What do you mean?" she had asked quickly, hardly expecting an answer. "What have you done?"

"Oh, it is the usual trouble, I suppose," he replied wearily, much to her surprise. "I began as a boy in the company and ultimately worked myself up as it grew, until I became treasurer. To cut it short, I have used funds belonging to the company, lost them. I don't need to tell you how a treasurer or a cashier can do that."

Constance was actually startled. Was he what he represented himself to be? Or was he leading her on in this way to a confession of her own part, which she had covered so well, in the forgeries of her dead husband?

"How did you begin?" she asked tentatively.

"A few years ago," he answered with a disconcerting lack of reserve, "the company found that we could beat our competitors by a very simple means. The largest stockholder, Mr. Dumont, was friendly with some of the customs officials and—well, we undervalued our goods. It was easy. The only thing necessary was to bribe some of the officials. The president of the company, Walton Beverley, put the dirty work on me as treasurer. Now you can imagine what that meant."

He had fallen into a cynical tone again.

"It meant that I soon found, or, rather, thought I found, that every man has his price—some higher, some lower, but a price, nevertheless. It was my business to find it, to keep it as low as I could with safety. So it went, from one crooked thing to another. I knew I was crooked, but not as bad, I think, as the rest who put the actual work on me. I was unfortunate, weak perhaps. That is all. I tried to get mine, too. I lost what I meant to put back after I had used it. They are after me now, or soon will be—the crooks! And here I am, momentarily expecting some one to walk up quietly behind me, tap me on the shoulder and whisper, 'You're wanted.'"

Time had not softened the bitterness of Constance's feelings.

Arthur B. Reeve

Somehow she felt that the world, or at least society owed her for taking away her husband. The world must pay. She sympathized with the young man who was appealing to her for friendship. Why not help him?

"Do you really, really want to know what I think?" asked Constance after he had at last told her his wretched story. It was the first time that she had looked at him since she realized that he was unburdening the truth to her.

"Yes," he answered eagerly, catching her eye. "Yes," he urged.

"I think," she said slowly, "that you are running away from a fight that has not yet begun."

It thrilled her to be talking so. Once before she had tasted the sweetness and the bitterness of crime. She did not stop to think about right or wrong. If she had done so her ethics would have been strangely illogical. It was enough that, short as their acquaintance had been, she felt unconsciously that there was something latent in the spirit of this man akin to her own.

Murray also felt rather than understood the bond that had been growing so rapidly between them. His was the temperament that immediately translates feeling into action. He reached into his breast pocket. There was the blue-black glint of a cold steel automatic. A moment he balanced it in his hand. Then with a rapid and decisive motion of the arm he flung it far from him. As it struck the water with a sound horribly suggestive of the death gurgle of a lost man, he turned and faced her.

"There," he exclaimed with a new light in the defiant, desperate smile that she had observed many times before, "there. The curtain rises—instead of falls."

Neither spoke for a few moments. At last he added, "What shall I do next?"

"Do?" she repeated. She felt now the weight of responsibility for interfering with his desperate plans, but it did not oppress her. On the contrary, it was a pleasant burden. "According to your own story," she went on, "they know nothing yet, as far as you can see. You would have forestalled them by taking this little vacation during which you could disappear while they would discover the shortage. Do? Go back."

"And when they discover it?" he asked evidently prepared for the answer she had given and eager to know what she would propose next.

Constance had been thinking rapidly.

"Listen," she cried, throwing aside restraint now. "No one in New York outside my former little circle knows me. I can live there in another circle unobserved. For weeks I have been amusing myself by the study of shorthand. I have picked up enough to be able to carry the thing off. Discharge your secretary. Put an advertisement in the newspapers. I will answer it. Then I will be able to help you. I cannot say at a distance what you should do next. There, perhaps, I can tell you."

What was it that had impelled her to say it? She could not have told. Murray looked at her. Her very presence seemed to infuse new determination into him.

It was strange about this woman, what a wonderful effect she had on him.

A few days before he would have laughed at any one who had suggested that any woman might have aroused in him the passions that were now surging through his heart. Ten thousand years ago, perhaps, he would have seized her and carried her off in triumph to his clan or tribe. To-day he must, he would win her by more subtle means.

His mind was made up. She had pointed the way. That night Dodge left Woodlake hastily for New York.

To Constance a new purpose seemed to have entered into a barren life. She was almost gay as she packed her trunks and grips and quietly slipped into the city a few hours later and registered at a quiet hotel for business women.

Sure enough in the Star the next morning was the advertisement. She wrote in a formal way, giving her telephone number. That afternoon, apparently as soon as the letter had been delivered, a call came. The following morning she was the private secretary of Murray Dodge, sitting unobtrusively before a typewriter desk in a sort of little anteroom that guarded the door to his office.

She took pains to act the part of private secretary and no more. As appeared natural to the rest of the office force at first she was much with Murray, who made the most elaborate explanations of the detail of the business.

"Do they suspect anything?" she asked anxiously as soon as they were absolutely alone.

"I think so," he replied. "They said nothing except that they had not expected me back so soon, I think the 'so soon' was an afterthought. They didn't expect me back at all. For," he added significantly, "I've been in fear and trembling until I could get you. They already have asked the regular audit company to go over the books in advance of the time when we usually employ them. I didn't ask why. I merely accepted it with a nod. It might have meant bringing matters to a crisis now."

He felt safer with Constance installed as his private secretary. True, Beverley and Dumont had viewed her from the start with suspicion.

Constance had been thinking hard out in her little office since she had begun to understand how matters stood. "Well?" she demanded. "What of it? Don't try to conceal it. Let them discover it. Go further. Dare them. Court exposure."

It was bold and ingenious. What a woman she was for meeting emergencies. Murray, who had a will that had been accustomed to bend others to his purposes except in the instance where they had bent him and nearly broken him, recognized the masterful mind of Constance. He was willing to allow her to play the game.

Thus Constance began collecting the very data that would have sent Murray to jail for bribery. Day by day as she worked on, the situation became more and more delicate. They found themselves alone much of the time now. Beverley was, or pretended to be, busy on other matters and avoided Dodge as much as possible. Only the regular routine affairs passed through his hands, but he said nothing. It gave him more time with her. Dumont came in as rarely as it was possible.

And as they worked along gathering the data Constance came to admire Murray more than ever. She worked patiently over the big books, taking only those on which the accountant was not engaged at such times as she could get them without exciting suspicion. Together they dug out the extent of the frauds that had been practiced on the Government for years back. From the letter files they rescued notes and orders and letters, pieced them together into as near a continuous record as they could make. With his own knowledge of the books Dodge could count on making better progress on the essential things than the regular accountant of the audit company. He felt sure that they would finish sooner and that they would have a closer report of the frauds of all kinds than could be uncovered by the man who had been set on the trail of Dodge to discover just how much of the illicit gains he had taken for himself.

Constance became aware soon that whenever she left the office at night she was being followed. She had at first studiously repelled the offers of Murray to see her home. It was not that he had taken advantage of the situation into which she had put herself. He would never have done that. Still, she wished a little more time to analyze her own conflicting feelings toward him. Then, too, several times in the crowded subway cars she had noticed a face that was familiar. It was Drummond, never looking directly at her, always engrossed in something else, yet never failing to note where she was going. That must be, she reasoned, some of the work of Beverley and Dumont.

Murray was now working feverishly. As he worked he found himself feeling differently toward the whole affair. He actually came to enjoy it with all its risks and uncertainty, to enjoy gathering the data which, he should have said, ought really to be destroyed. Often he caught himself wishing that everything had come out all right in the end and that Constance really was his private secretary.

Every moment with her seemed now to pass so quickly that he would willingly have smashed all the clocks and destroyed all the calendars. Association with other women had been tame beside his new friendship with her. She had suffered, felt, lived. She fascinated him, as often over the books they would stop to talk, talk of things the most irrelevant, yet to him the most interesting, until she would bring him back inevitably to the point of their work and start him again with a new power and incentive toward the purpose she had in mind.

To Constance he seemed to fill a blank spot in her empty life. If she had been bitter toward the world for what had happened to her, the pleasure of helping another to beat that harsh world seemed an unspeakably sweet compensation.

At last even Constance herself began to realize it. It was not, after all, merely the bitterness toward society, that lured her on. She was not a woman carved out of a block of stone. There was a sweetness about this association that carried her along as if in a dream. She was actually falling in love with him.

One day she had been working later than usual. The accountant had shown signs of approaching the end of his task sooner than they had expected. Murray was waiting, as was his custom, for her to finish before he left.

There was no sound in the almost deserted office building save the banging of a door echoing now and then, or an insistent ring of the elevator bell as an anxious office boy or stenographer sought to escape after an extra period of work.

Murray stood looking at her admiringly as she deftly shoved the pins into her hat. Then he held her coat, which brought them close together.

"It will soon be time for the final scene," he remarked. His manner was different as he looked down at her. "We must succeed, Constance," he went on slowly. "Of course, after it is over, it will be impossible for me to remain here with this company. I have been looking around. I must—we must clear ourselves. I already have an offer to go with another company, much better than this position in every way— honest, square, with no dirty work, such as I have had here."

It was a moment that Constance had foreseen, without planning what she would do. She moved to the door as if to go.

"Take dinner with me to-night at the Riverside," he went on, mentioning the name of a beautifully situated inn uptown overlooking the lights of the Hudson and thronged by gay parties of pleasure seekers.

Before she could say no, even though she would have said it, he had linked his arm in hers, banged shut the door and they were being whisked to the street in the elevator.

This time, as they were about to go out of the building, she noticed Drummond standing in the shadow of a corner back of the cigar counter on the first floor. She told Murray of the times she had seen Drummond following her. Murray ground his teeth.

"He'll have to hustle this time," he muttered, handing her quickly into a cab that was waiting for a fare.

Before he could give the order where to drive she had leaned out of the window, "To the ferry," she cried.

Murray looked at her inquiringly. Then he understood. "Not to the Riverside—yet," she whispered. "That man has just summoned a cab that was passing."

In her eyes Murray saw the same fire that had blazed when she had told him he was running away from a fight that had not yet begun. As the cab whirled through the now nearly deserted downtown streets, he reached over in sheer admiration and caressed her hand. She did not withdraw it, but her averted eyes and quick breath told that a thousand thoughts were hurrying through her mind, divided between the man in the cab beside her and the man in the cab following perhaps half a block behind.

At the ferry they halted and pretended to be examining a time table, though they bought only ferry tickets. Drummond did the same, and sauntered leisurely within easy distance of the gate. Nothing seemed to escape him, and yet never did he seem to be watching them.

The gateman shouted "All aboard!"

The door began to close.

"Come," she tugged at his sleeve.

They dodged in just in time. Drummond followed. They started across the wagonway to the opposite side of the slip. He kept on the near side. Constance swerved back again to the near side. Drummond had been opposite them and they had now fallen in behind him. He was now ahead, but going slowly. Murray felt her pulling back on his arm. With a little exclamation she dropped her purse, which contained a few coins. She had contrived to open it, and the coins ran in every possible direction. Drummond was now on the boat.

"All aboard," growled the guard surlily. "All aboard."

"Go ahead, go ahead," shouted Murray, trying to pick up the scattered change and scattering it the more. At last he understood. "Go ahead. We'll take the next boat. Can't you see the lady has dropped her purse?"

The gates closed. The warning whistle blew, and the ferryboat, departed, bearing off Drummond alone.

Another cab toot them to the Riverside. A new bond of experience had been established between them. They dined quietly and as the lights grew mellow she told him more of her story than she had ever breathed to any other living soul.

As Murray listened he looked his admiration for the daring of the little woman opposite him at the table.

They drifted. ...

It was the day of the threatened exposure. Curiously enough, Dodge felt no nervousness. The understanding which he had reached or felt that he had reached with Constance made him rather eager than, otherwise to have the whole affair over with at once.

Drummond had been shut up for some time in the office of Beverley with Dumont, going over the report which the accountant had prepared and other matters—He had come in without seeing either Constance or Murray, though they knew he must be nursing his chagrin over the episode of the night before.

"They are waiting to see you," reported Constance to Dodge, half an hour later, after one of the office boys had been sent over as a formal messenger to their office.

"We are ready for them?" he asked, smiling at her.

Constance nodded.

"Then I shall go in. Wait a moment. When they have hurled their worst at me I shall call on you. Have the stuff ready."

There was no hesitation, no misgiving on the part of either, as he strode into Beverley's office. Constance had prepared the record which they had been working on, and for days had been momentarily expecting this crisis. She felt that she was ready.

An ominous silence greeted Dodge as he entered.

"We have had experts on your books, Dodge," began Beverley, clearing his throat, as Murray seated himself, waiting for them to speak first.

"I have seen that," he replied dryly.

"They are fifty thousand dollars short," shot out Dumont.

"Indeed?"

Dumont gasped at the coolness of the man. "Wh—what? You have nothing to say? Why, sir," he added, raising his voice, "you have actually made no effort to conceal it!"

Dodge smiled cynically. "A consultation, will rectify it," was all he said. "A conference will show you that it is all right."

"A consultation?" broke in Beverley in rage. "A consultation in jail!"

Still Dodge merely smiled.

"Then you consider yourself trapped. You admit it," ground out Dumont.

"Anything you please," repeated Dodge. "I am perfectly willing—"

"Let us end this farce—now," cried Beverley hotly. "Drummond!"

The detective had been doing some rapid thinking. "Just a moment," he interrupted. "Don't be too precipitate. Hear his side, if he has any. I can manage him. Besides, I have something else to say about another person that will interest us all."

"Then you are willing to have the consultation!"

Drummond nodded.

"Miss Dunlap," called Murray, taking the words almost from the detective's lips, as he opened the door and held it for her to enter.

"No—no. Alone," almost shouted Beverley.

The detective signaled to him and he subsided, muttering.

As she entered Drummond looked hard at her. Constance met him without wavering an instant.

"I think I've seen you before, MRS. Dunlap," insinuated the detective.

"Perhaps," replied Constance, still meeting his sharp ferret eye squarely, which increased his animosity.

"Your husband was Carlton Dunlap, cashier of Green & Company, was he not?"

She bit her lip. The manner of his raking up of old scores, though she had expected it, was cruel. It would have been cruel in court, if she had had a lawyer to protect her rights. It was doubly cruel, merciless, here. Before Dodge could interrupt, the detective added, "Who committed suicide after forging checks to meet his—"

Murray was at Drummond like a hound. "Another word from you and I'll throttle you," he blurted out.

"No, Murray, no. Don't," pleaded Constance. She was burning with indignation, but it was not by violence that she expected to prevail. "Let him say what he has to say."

Drummond smiled. He had no scruples about a "third degree" of this kind, and besides there were three of them to Dodge.

"You were—both of you—at Woodlake not long ago, were you not?" he asked calmly.

There was no escaping the implication of the tone. Still Drummond was taking no chances of being misunderstood. "There was one man," he went on, "who embezzled for you. Here is another who has embezzled. How will that look when it goes before a jury!" he concluded.

The fight had shifted before it had well begun. Instead of being between Dodge on one side and Beverley and Dumont on the, other, it now seemed to be a clash between a cool detective and a clever woman.

"Mrs. Dunlap," interrupted Murray, with a mocking smile at the detective, "will you tell us what you have found out since you have been my private secretary?"

Constance had not lost control of herself for a moment.

"I have been looking over the books a little bit myself," she began slowly, with all eyes riveted on her. "I find, for instance, that your company has been undervaluing its imported goods. Undervaluing merchandise is considered, I believe, one of the meanest forms of smuggling. The undervaluer has frequently to make a tool of a man in his employ. Then that tool must play on the frailties of an unfortunate or weak examiner at the Public Stores where all invoices and merchandise from foreign countries are examined."

Drummond had been trying to interrupt, but she had ignored him, and was speaking rapidly so that he could get no chance.

"You have cheated the Government of hundreds of thousands dollars," she hurried on facing Beverley and Dumont. "It would make a splendid newspaper story."

Dumont moved uneasily. Drummond was now staring. It was a new phase of the matter to him. He had not counted on handling a woman like Constance, who knew how to take advantage of every weak spot in the armor.

"We are wasting time," he interrupted brusquely. "Get back to the original subject. There is a fifty thousand-dollar shortage on these books."

The attempt clumsily to shift the case away again from Constance to Dodge was apparent.

"Mrs. Dunlap's past troubles," Dodge asserted vigorously, "have nothing to do with the case. It was cowardly to drag that in. But the other matter of which she speaks has much to do with it."

"One moment, Murray," cried Constance. "Let me finish what I began. This is my fight, too, now."

She was talking with blazing eyes and in quick, cutting tone.

"For three years he did your dirty work," she flashed. "He did the bribing—and you saved half a million dollars."

"He has stolen fifty thousand," put in Beverley, white with anger.

"I have kept an account of everything," pursued Constance, without pausing. "I have pieced the record together so that he can now connect the men higher up with the actual acts he had to do. He can gain immunity by turning state's evidence. I am not sure but that he might be able to obtain his moiety of what the Government recovers if the matter were brought to suit and won on the information he can furnish."

She paused. No one seemed to breathe.

"Now," she added impressively, "at ten per cent. commission the half million that he saved for you yields fifty thousand dollars. That, gentlemen, is the amount of the shortage—an offset."

"The deuce it is!" exclaimed Beverley.

Constance reached for a telephone on the desk near her.

"Get me the Law Division at the Customs House," she asked simply.

Dumont was pale and almost speechless. Beverley could ill suppress his smothered rage. What could they do? The tables had been turned. If they objected to the amazing proposal

Constance had made they might all go to jail. Dodge even might go free, rich. They looked at Dodge and Mrs. Dunlap. There was no weakening. They were as relentless as their opponents had been before.

Dumont literally tore the telephone from her. "Never mind about that number, central," he muttered.

Then he started as if toward the door. The rest followed. Outside the accountant had been waiting patiently, perhaps expecting Drummond to call on him to corroborate the report. He had been listening. There was no sound of high voices, as he had expected. What did it mean?

The door opened. Beverley was pale and haggard, Dumont worn and silent. He could scarcely talk. Dodge again held the door for Constance as she swept past the amazed accountant.

All eyes were now fixed on Dumont as chief spokesman.

"He has made a satisfactory explanation," was all he said.

"I would lock all that stuff up in the strongest safe deposit vault in New York," remarked Constance, laying the evidence that involved them all on Murray's desk. "It is your only safeguard."

"Constance," he burst forth suddenly, "you were superb."

The crisis was past now and she felt the nervous reaction.

"There is one thing more I want to say," he added in a low tone.

He had crossed to where she was standing by the window,

and bent over, speaking with great emotion.

"Since that afternoon at Woodlake when you turned me back again from the foolish and ruinous course on which I had decided you—you have been more to me than life. Constance, I have never loved until now. Nothing has ever mattered except money. I never had any one else to think of, care for, except myself. You have changed everything."

She was gazing out of the window at the tall buildings. There, in a myriad of offices, lay wealth untold, opportunity as yet untasted to seize that wealth. Only for an instant she turned and looked at him, then dropped her eyes. What lay that way?

"You are clear now, respected, respectable," she said simply.

"Yes, thank God. Clear and with a new ambition, thanks to you."

She had been expecting this ever since that last night. The relief of Murray to feel that the old score that would have ruined him was now wiped off the slate was precisely what she had anticipated.

Yet, somehow, it disappointed her. She felt instinctively that her triumph was burning fast to ashes.

"Keep clear," she faltered.

"Constance," he urged, approaching closer and taking her cold hand.

Was she to be the one to hold him back in any way from the new life that was now before him? What if Drummond, in his animosity, ever got the truth? She gently unclasped her

Arthur B. Reeve

hand from his. No, that happiness was not for her.

"I am afraid I am a crook at heart, Murray," she said sadly. "I have gone too far to turn back. The brand is on me. But I am not altogether bad—yet. Think of me always with charity. Yes," she cried wildly, "I must return to my loneliness. No, do not try to stop me, you have no right," she added bitterly as the reality of her situation burned itself into her heart.

She broke away from him wildly, but with set purpose. The world had taken away her husband; now it was a lover; the world must pay.

CHAPTER III

THE GUN RUNNERS

"We'll land here, Mrs. Dunlap."

Ramon Santos, terror of the Washington State Department and of a half dozen consulates in New York, stuck a pin in a map of Central America spread out on a table before Constance.

"Insurrectos will meet us," he pursued, then added, "but we must have money, first, my dear Senora, plenty of money."

Dark of eye and skin, with black imperial and mustache, tall, straight as an arrow, Santos had risen and was now gazing down with rapt attention, not at the map, but at Constance herself.

Every curve of her face and wave of her hair, every line of her trim figure which her filmy gown seemed to accentuate rather than conceal added fire to his ardent glances.

He touched lightly another pin sticking in a little, almost microscopic island of the Caribbean.

"Our plan, it is simple," he continued with animation in spite of his foreign accent. "On this island a plant to print paper money, to coin silver. With that we shall land, pay our men as they flock to us, collect forces, seize cities, appropriate the customs. Once we start, it is easy."

Constance looked up quickly. "But that is counterfeiting," she exclaimed.

"No," rejoined Santos, "it is a war measure. We—the provisional government—merely coin our own money. Besides, it will not be done in this country. It will not come under your laws."

There was a magnetism about the man that fascinated her, as he stood watching the effect of his words. Instinctively she knew that it was not alone enthusiasm over his scheme that inspired his confidences.

"Though we are not counterfeiters," he went on, "we do not know what moment our opponents may set your Secret Service to destroy all our hopes. Besides, we must have money—now—to buy machinery, arms, ammunition. We must find some one," he lowered his voice, "who can persuade American bankers and merchants to take risks to gain valuable concessions in the new state."

Santos was talking rapidly and earnestly, urging his case on her.

"We are prepared," he hurried on confidentially, "to give you, Senora, half the money that you can raise for these purposes."

He paused and stood before her. He was certainly a handsome figure, this soldier of fortune, and he was at his best now.

Constance looked out of the window of her sitting room. This was a business proposition, not to be influenced by any sentiment.

She watched the lights moving up and down the river and bay. There were craft from the ends of the earth. She speculated on the romantic secrets hidden in liner and tramp. Surely they could scarcely be more romantic than the appeal Santos was making.

"Will you help us?" urged Santos, leaning further over the map to read her averted face.

In her loneliness after she had given up Murray Dodge, life in New York had seemed even more bitter to Constance than before. Yet the great city cast a spell over her, with its countless opportunities for adventure. She could not leave it, but had taken a suite in a quiet boarding house overlooking the bay from the Heights in Brooklyn.

One guest in particular had interested her. He was a Latin American, Ramon Santos. She noticed that he seldom appeared at breakfast or luncheon. But at dinner he often, ordered much as if it were seven o'clock in the morning instead of the evening. He was a mystery and mysteries interested her. Did he work all night and sleep all day? What was he doing?

She was astonished a few nights after her arrival to receive a call from the mysterious evening breakfaster.

"Pardon—I intrude," he began gracefully, presenting his card. "But I have heard how clever you are, Senora Dunlap. A friend, in an importing firm, has told me of you, a Mr. Dodge."

Constance was startled at the name. Murray had indeed written a little note expressing his entire confidence in Mr. Santos. Formal as it was, Constance thought she could read between the lines the same feeling toward her that he had expressed at their parting.

Santos gave her no time to live over the past.

"You see, Mrs. Dunlap," he explained, as he led up to the object of his visit, "the time has come to overthrow the regime in Central America—for a revolution which will bring together all the countries in a union like the old United States of Central America."

He had spread out the map on the table.

"Only," he added, "we would call the new state, Vespuccia."

"We?" queried Constance.

"Yes—my—colleagues-you call it in English! We have already a Junta with headquarters in an old loft on South Street, in New York."

Santos indicated the plan of campaign on the map.

"We shall strike a blow," he cried, bringing his fist down on the table as if the blow had already fallen, "that will paralyze the enemy at the very start!"

He paused.

"Will you help us raise the money?" he repeated earnestly.

Constance had been inactive long enough. The appeal was romantic, almost irresistible. Besides—no, at the outset she put out of consideration any thought of the fascinating young soldier of fortune himself.

The spirit of defiance of law and custom was strong upon her. That was all.

"Yes," she replied, "I will help you."

Santos leaned over, and with a graceful gesture that she could not resent, raised her finger tips gallantly to his lips.

"Thank you," he said with, a courtly smile. "We have already won!"

The next day Ramon introduced her to the other members of the Junta. It was evident that he was in fact as well as name their leader, but they were not like the usual oily plotters of revolution who congregate about the round tables in dingy back rooms of South Street cafes, apportioning the gold lace, the offices, and the revenues among themselves. There was an "air" about them that was different.

"Let me present Captain Lee Gordon of the Arrayo," remarked Santos, coming to a stockily-built, sun-burned man with the unmistakable look of the Anglo-Saxon who has spent much time in the neighborhood of the tropical sun. "The Arroyo is the ship that is to carry the arms and the plant to the island—from Brooklyn. We choose Brooklyn because it is quieter over there—fewer people late at night on the streets."

Captain Gordon bowed, without taking his eyes off Constance.

"I am, like yourself, Mrs. Dunlap, a recent recruit," he explained. "It is a wonderful plan," he added enthusiastically.

"We shall sweep the country with it."

He flicked off the ash of his inevitable cigarette, much as if it were the opposition of the governments they were to encounter.

It was evident that the Captain was much impressed by Constance. Yet she instinctively disliked the man. His cameraderie had something offensive about it, as contrasted with the deferential friendship of Santos.

With all her energy, however, Constance plunged directly into her work. Indeed, even at the start she was amazed to find that money for a revolution could be raised at all. She soon, found that it could be done more easily in New York than anywhere else in the world.

There seemed to be something about her that apparently appealed to those whom she went to see. She began to realize what a tremendous advantage a woman of the world had in presenting the case and convincing a speculator of the rich returns if the revolution should prove successful. More than that, she quickly learned that it was best to go alone, that it was she, quite as much as the promised concessions for tobacco, salt, telegraph, telephone monopolies, that loosed the purse strings.

Her first week's report of pledges ran into the thousands with a substantial immediate payment of real dollars.

"How did you do it?" asked Santos in undisguised admiration, as she was telling him one night of her success, in the dusty, cobwebbed little ship chandlery on South Street where the Junta headquarters had been established.

"Dollar diplomacy," she laughed, not displeased at his

admiration. "We shall soon convert American dollars into Vespuccian bullets."

They were alone, and a week had made much difference in the fascinating friendship to Constance.

"Let me show you what I have done," Ramon confided. "Already, I have started together the 'counterfeiting plant,' as you call it."

Piece by piece, as he had been able to afford them, he had been ordering the presses, the stamping machine, and a little "reeding" or milling machine for the edges of the coins.

"The paper, the ink, and the bullion, we shall order now as we can," he explained, resting his head on his elbow at the table beside her. "Everything will be secured from firms which make mint supplies for foreign governments. A photo-engraver is now engaged on the work of copying the notes. He is making the plates by the photo-etching process—the same as that by which the real money plates are made. Then, too, there will be dies for the coins. Coined silver will be worth, twice the cost of the bullion to us. Why," he added eagerly, "a few more successful days, Senora, and we shall have even arms and ammunition."

A key turned in the door. Santos sprang to his feet. It was Gordon.

"Ah, good evening," the Captain greeted them. The fact that they had been talking so earnestly alone was not lost on him. "May I join the conspiracy?" he smiled. "What luck to-day? By the way, I have just heard of a consignment of a thousand rifles as good as new that can be bought for a song."

Santos, elated at the progress so far, told hastily of

Constance's success. "Let us get an option on them for a few days," he cried.

"Good," agreed Gordon, "only," he added, shaking his finger playfully at Constance, as the three left the headquarters, "don't let the commander-in-chief monopolize ALL your time, Remember, we all need you now. Santos, that was an inspiration to get Mrs. Dunlap on our side."

Somehow she felt uncomfortable. She half imagined that a frown had flitted over Santos' face.

"Are you going to Brooklyn?" she asked him.

"No, we shall be working at the Junta late to-night," he replied, as they parted at the subway, he and Gordon to secure the option on the guns, she to plan for the morrow.

"I have made a good beginning," she congratulated herself, when, later in her rooms, she was going over the list of names of commission merchants who handled produce of South American countries.

There was a tap on the door.

Quickly, she shoved the list into the drawer of the table.

"A gentleman to see you, downstairs, ma'am," announced the maid.

As she pushed aside the portieres, her heart gave a leap—it was Drummond.

"Mrs. Dunlap," began the wily detective, seeming to observe everything with eyes that seldom had the appearance of looking at anything, "I think you will recall that we have met before."

Constance bit her lip. "And why again?" she queried curtly.

"I am informed," he went on coolly ignoring her curtness, "that there is a guest in this house named Santos—Ramon Santos."

He said it in a half insinuating, half questioning tone.

"You might inquire of the landlady," replied Constance, now perfectly composed.

"Mrs. Dunlap," he burst forth, exasperated, "what is the use of beating about? Do you know the real character of this Santos!"

"It is a matter of perfect indifference," she returned.

"Then you do not think a warning from me worth troubling about?" demanded the detective.

Constance continued to stand as if to terminate the interview.

"I came here," continued the detective showing no evidence of taking the hint, "to make a proposition to you. Mrs. Dunlap, you are in bad again. But this time there is a chance for you to get out without risk. I—I think I may talk plainly? We understand each other!"

His manner had changed. Constance could not have described to herself the loathing she felt for the man as it suddenly flashed over her what he was after. If she had resented his familiarity before, it brought the stinging blood to her cheeks now to realize that he was actually seeking to persuade her to betray her friends.

"Do you want to know what I think?" she scorned, then

without waiting added, "I think you are a crook—a black-mailer,—that's what I think of a private detective like you."

The defiance of the little woman amazed even Drummond. Instead of fear as of the pursued, Constance Dunlap showed all the boldness of the pursuer.

"You have got to stop this swindling," the detective raged, taking a step closer to her. "I know the bankers you have fooled. I know how much you have worked them for."

"Swindling?" she repeated coolly, in assumed surprise. "Who says I am swindling?"

"You know well enough what I mean—this revolution that is being planned to bring about the new state of Vespuccia, as your friends Santos and Gordon call it."

"Vespuccia—Santos—Gordon?"

"Yes," he shouted, "Vespuccia—Santos—Gordon. And I'll go further. I'll tell you something you may not care to hear."

Drummond leaned over closer to her in his favorite bulldozing manner when he dealt with a woman. All the malevolence of the human bloodhound seemed concentrated in his look.

"Who forged those Carlton Realty checks?" he hissed. "Who played off the weakness of Dumont and Beverley against the clever thefts of Murray Dodge! Who is using a counterfeiter and a soldier of fortune and swindling honest American bankers and business men as no man crook—you seem to like that word—crook—could ever do?"

Constance met him calmly. "Oh," she laughed airily, "I

suppose you mean to imply that it is I."

"I don't imply," he ground out, "I assert—accuse."

Constance shrugged her pretty shoulders.

"I want to tell you that I am employed by the Central American consulates in this city," blustered Drummond. "And I am waiting only for one thing. The moment an order is given for the withdrawal of that stuff from the little shop in South Street—you know what I mean—I am ready. I shall not be alone, then. You will have the power of the United States Secret Service to deal with, this time, my clever lady."

"Well, what of that?"

"There is this much of it. I warn you now against working with this Santos. He—you—can make no move that we do not know."

Why had Drummond come to see her? Constance was asking herself. The very insolence of the man seemed to arouse all the combativeness of her nature. The detective had thought to "throw a scare into" her. She turned suddenly and swept out of the room.

"I thank you for your kindness," she said icily. "It is unnecessary. Good-night."

In her own room she paced the floor nervously, now that the strain was off. Should she desert Santos and save herself? He had more need of her help now than ever before. She did not stop to analyze her own feelings. She knew he had been making love to her during the past week as only a Spaniard could. It fascinated her without blinding her. Yes, she would match her wits against this detective, clever though she knew he was. But Santos must be warned.

Santos and Gordon were alone when she burst in on them, breathlessly, an hour later at the Junta.

"What is the matter?" inquired Ramon quickly, placing a chair for her.

Gordon looked his admiration for the little woman, though he did not speak it. She saw him cast a sidewise glance at Santos and herself.

Though the three were friends, it was evident to her that Gordon did not trust Santos any further than the suspicious Anglo-Saxon trusts a foreigner usually when there is a woman in the case.

"The Secret Service!" exclaimed Constance. "I have just had a visit from a private detective employed by one of the consulates. They know too much. He has threatened to tell all to the Secret Service, has even had the effrontery to ask me to betray you."

"The scoundrel," burst out Santos impulsively.

"You are not frightened?" Gordon asked quickly.

"On the contrary, I expected something of the sort soon, but not from this man. I can meet him!"

"Good," exclaimed the Captain.

There was that in his voice that caused her to look at him quickly. Santos had noticed it, too, and a sullen scowl spread over his face.

Intuitively Constance read the two men before her. She had fled from one problem to a greater. Both Santos and Gordon were in love with her.

In the whirl of this new discovery, two things alone crowded all else from her mind. She must contrive to hold off Drummond until that part of the expedition which was ready could be got off. And she must play the jealous rivals against each other with such finesse as to keep them separated.

Far into the night after she had left the Junta she debated the question with herself. She could not turn back now. The attentions of Gordon were offensive. Yet she could have given no other reason than that she liked Santos the better. Yet what was Santos to her, after all? Once she had let herself go too far. She must be careful in this case. She must not allow this to be other than a business proposition.

The crisis for her came sooner than she had anticipated. It was the day after the visit of Drummond. She was waiting at the Junta alone for Santos when Gordon entered. She had dreaded just that. There was no mistaking the man.

"Mrs. Dunlap," began Gordon bending down close over her.

She was almost trembling with emotion, and he saw it.

"You can read me like a book," he hurried on, mistaking her feelings. "I can see that you know how much I think of you—how much I—"

"No, no," she implored. "Don't talk to me that way. Remember—there is work to do. After it is over—then—"

"Work!" he scorned. "What is the whole of Central America to me compared to you?"

"Captain Gordon!" she stood facing him. "You must not. Listen to me. You do not know—I—please, please leave me. Let me think."

She did not dare accept him; she could not reject him. It seemed that with an almost superhuman effort Gordon gripped himself. But he did not go.

Constance was distracted, what if Santos with his fiery nature should find Gordon talking to her alone? She must temporize.

"One week," she murmured. "When the Arroyo sails—that night—I shall give you my answer."

Gordon shot a peculiar glance at her—half doubt, half surprise. But she was gone. As she hurried unexpectedly out of the Junta she fancied she caught a glimpse of a familiar figure. It must have been Drummond. Every move at the Junta was being watched.

At the boarding house all night she waited. She must see Santos. Plan after plan whirled through her brain as the hours dragged.

It was not until almost morning that, seeing a light, he tapped cautiously at her door.

"You were not at the Junta to-night," he remarked.

There was something of jealousy in the tone.

"No. There is something I wanted to say to you where we should not be interrupted," she answered as he sat down.

A fold of her filmy house dress fluttered near him. Involuntarily he moved closer. His eyes met hers. She could feel the passions surging in the man beside her.

"I saw Drummond again, to-day," she began. "Captain Gordon—"

The intense look of hatred that blazed in the eyes of Santos frightened her. What might have happened if he instead of Gordon had met her at the Junta she could not have said. But now she must guard against it. If flashed over her that there was only one thing to be done.

She rose and laid her hand on his arm. As quickly the look changed. There was only one way to do it; she must make this man think they understood each other without saying so.

"You must get the counterfeiting plant down on the island—immediately—alone. Don't tell any of the others until it is there safely. You were going to send it down on the Arroyo next week. It must not go from New York at all. It must be shipped by rail, and then from New Orleans. You must—"

"But—Gordon?" His voice was hoarse.

She looked at Santos long and earnestly. "I will take care of him," she said in a tone that Santos could not mistake. "No—Ramon, no. After the revolution—perhaps—who shall say? But now—to work!"

It was with a sigh of relief that she sank to rest at last when he had gone. For the moment she had won.

Piece by piece, Santos and she secretly carried out the goods that had already been collected at the Junta, during the next few days. Without a word to a soul they were shipped south. The boxes and barrels remained in the musty shop, apparently undisturbed.

Next the order for the arms and ammunition was quietly diverted so that they, too, were on their way to New Orleans. Instead, cases resembling them were sent to the Junta headquarters. Drummond, least of all, must be allowed to think that there was any change in their plans.

While Santos was at work gathering the parts, the stamping machine, the press, the dies, the plates, and the rest of the counterfeiting plant which had not yet been delivered, Constance, during the hours that she was not collecting money from the concession-grabbers, haunted the Junta. There was every evidence of activity there as the week advanced.

She was between two fires, yet never had she enjoyed the tang of adventure more than now. It was a keen pleasure to feel that she was outwitting Drummond when, as some apparently insurmountable difficulty arose, she would overcome it. More delicate was it, however, to preserve the balance between Santos and Gordon. In fact it seemed that the more she sought to avoid Gordon, the more jealously did he pursue her. It was a tangled skein of romance and intrigue that Constance was weaving.

At last all was ready. It was the night before the departure of Santos for the south. Constance had decided on the last interview in her own rooms where the first had been.

"I shall go ahead preparing as if to ship the things on the Arroyo," she said. "Let me know by the code the moment you are ready."

Santos was looking at her, oblivious of everything else.

He reached over and took her hand. She knew this was the moment against which she had steeled herself.

"Come with me," he asked suddenly.

She could feel his breath, hotly, on her cheek.

It was the final struggle. If she let go of herself, all would be lost.

"No, Ramon," she said softly, but without withdrawing her hand. "It can never be—listen."

It was terrific, to hold in cheek a nature such as his.

"I went into this scheme for—for money. I have it. We have raised nearly forty thousand dollars. Twenty thousand you have given me as my share."

She paused. He was paying no attention to her words. His whole self was centered on her face.

"With me," she continued, half wearily withdrawing her hand as she assumed the part she had decided on for herself, "with me, Ramon, love is dead—dead. I have seen too much of the world. Nothing has any fascination for me now except excitement, money—"

He gently leaned over and recovered the hand that she had withdrawn. Quickly he raised it to his lips as he had done that first night.

"You are mine," he whispered, "not his."

She did not withdraw the hand this time.

"No—not his—nobody's."

For a moment the adventurers understood each other.

"Not his," he muttered fiercely as he threw his arms about her wildly, passionately.

"Nobody's," she panted as she gave one answering caress, then struggled from him.

She had conquered not only Ramon Santos but Constance Dunlap.

Early the next morning he was speeding southward over the clicking rails.

Every energy must be bent toward keeping the new scheme secret until it was carried out successfully. Not a hint must get to Drummond that there was any change in the activities of the Junta. As for the Junta itself, there was no one of those who believed implicitly in Santos whom Constance need fear, except Gordon. Gordon was the bete noire.

Two days passed and she was able to guard the secret, as well as to act as though nothing had happened. Santos had left a short note for the Junta telling them that he would be away for a short time putting the finishing touches on the purchase of the arms. The arrival of a cartload of cases at the Junta, which Constance arranged for herself, bore out the letter. Still, she waited anxiously for word from him.

The day set for the sailing of the Arroyo arrived and with it at last a telegram: "Buy corn, oats, wheat. Sell cotton."

It was the code, telling of the safe arrival of the rifles, cartridges and the counterfeiting plant in New Orleans, a little late, but safe. "Sell cotton," meant "I sail to-night."

On the way over to the Junta, she had noticed one of Drummond's shadows dogging her. She must do anything to keep the secret until that night.

She hurried into the dusty ship chandlery. There was Gordon.

"Good morning, Mrs. Dunlap," he cried. "You are just the person I am looking for. Where is Santos? Has the plan been changed?"

Constance thought she detected a shade of jealousy in the tone. At any rate, Gordon was more attentive than ever.

"I think he is in Bridgeport," she replied as casually as she could. "Your ship, you know, sails to-night. He has sent word to me to give orders that all the goods here at the Junta be ready to cart over by truck to Brooklyn. There has been no change. The papers are to be signed during the day and she is to be scheduled to sail late in the afternoon with the tide. Only, as you know, some pretext must delay you. You will hold her at the pier for us. He trusts all that to you as a master hand at framing such excuses that seem plausible."

Gordon leaned over closer to her. He was positively revolting to her in the role of admirer. But she must not offend him—yet.

"And my answer!" he asked.

There was something about him that made Constance almost draw away involuntarily.

"To-night—at the pier," she murmured forcing a smile.

Shortly after dark the teams started their lumbering way across the city and the bridge. Messengers, stationed on the way, were to report the safe progress of the trucks to Brooklyn.

Constance slipped away from the boardinghouse, down through the deserted streets to the waterfront, leaving word at home that any message was to be sent by a trusty boy to the pier.

It was a foggy and misty night on the water, an ideal night for the gun-runner. She was relieved to learn that there had been not a hitch so far. Still, she reasoned, that was natural. Drummond, even if he had not been outwitted, would scarcely have spoiled the game until the last moment.

On the Arroyo every one was chafing. Below decks, the engineer and his assistants were seeing that the machinery was in perfect order. Men in the streets were posted to give Gordon warning of any danger.

In the river a tug was watching for a possible police boat. On the wharf the only footfalls were those of Gordon himself and an assistant from the Junta. It was dreary waiting, and Constance drew her coat more closely around her, as she shivered in the night wind and tried to brace herself against the unexpected.

At last the welcome muffled rumble of heavily laden carts disturbed the midnight silence of the street leading to the river.

At once a score of men sprang from the hold of the ship, as if by magic. One by one the cases were loaded. The men were working feverishly by the light of battle lanterns—big lamps with reflectors so placed as to throw the light exactly where it was needed and nowhere else. They were taking aboard the Arroyo dozens of coffin-like wooden cases, and bags and boxes, smaller and even heavier. Silently and swiftly they toiled.

It was risky work, too, at night and in the tense haste. There was a muttered exclamation—a heavy case had dropped! a man had gone down with a broken leg.

It was a common thing with the gun-runners. The crew of the Arroyo had expected it. The victim of such an accident could not be sent to a hospital ashore. He was carried, as gently as the rough hands could carry anything, to one side, where he lay silently waiting for the ship's surgeon who had been engaged for just such an emergency. Constance bent over and made the poor fellow as comfortable as she could. There was never a whimper from him, but he looked his gratitude.

Scarcely a fraction of a minute had been lost. The last cases were now being loaded. The tug crawled up and made fast. Already the empty trucks were vanishing in the misty darkness, one by one, as muffled as they came.

Suddenly lights flashed through the fog on the river.

There was a hurried tread of feet on the land from around the corner of a bleak, forbidding black warehouse.

They were surrounded. On one side was the police boat Patrol. On the other was Drummond. With both was the Secret Service. The surprise was complete.

Constance turned to Gordon. He was gone.

Before she could move, some one seized her.

"Where's Santos?" demanded a hoarse voice in her ear. She looked up to see Drummond.

She shut her lips tightly, secure in the secret that Ramon was at the moment or soon would be on the Gulf, out of reach.

Across in the fog she strained her eyes. Was that the familiar figure of Gordon moving in the dim light?

There he was, now,—with Drummond, the police, and the Secret Service. It was exactly as she had suspected to herself, and a smile played over her face.

All was excitement, shouts, muttered imprecations. Constance was the calmest in the crowd—deaf to even Drummond's "third degree."

They had begun to break open the boxes marked "salt" and "corn."

A loud exclamation above the sharp crunching of the axes escaped Gordon. "Damn them! They've put one across on us!"

The boxes of "salt" and "corn" contained—salt and corn.

Not a stock of a rifle, not a barrel, not a cartridge was in any of them as the axes crashed in one case after another.

A boy with a telegram emerged indiscreetly from the misty shadows. Drummond seized it, tore it open, and read, "Buy cotton."

It was the code: "I am off safely."

The double cross had worked. Constance was thinking, as

she smiled to herself, of the money, her share, which she had hidden. There was not a scrap of tangible evidence against her, except what Santos had carried with him in the filibustering expedition already off from New Orleans. Her word would stand against that of all of the victims combined before any jury that could be empaneled.

"You thought I needed a warning," she cried, facing Drummond with eyes that flashed scorn at the skulking figure of Gordon behind him. "But the next time you employ a stool-pigeon to make love," she added, "reckon in that thing you detectives scorn—a woman's intuition."

CHAPTER IV

THE GAMBLERS

"Won't you come over to see me to-night? Just a friendly little game, my dear—our own crowd, you know."

There was something in the purring tone of the invitation of the woman across the hall from Constance Dunlap's apartment that aroused her curiosity.

"Thank you. I believe I will," answered Constance. "It's lonely in a big city without friends."

"Indeed it is," agreed Bella LeMar. "I've been watching you for some time and wondering how you stand it. Now be sure to come, won't you?"

"I shall be glad to do so," assured Constance, as they reached their floor and parted at the elevator door.

She had been watching the other woman, too, although she had said nothing about it.

"A friendly little game," repeated Constance to herself. "That sounds as if it had the tang of an adventure in it. I'll go."

The Mayfair Arms, in which she had taken a modest suite of rooms, was a rather recherche apartment, and one of her chief delights since she had been there had been in watching the other occupants.

There had been much to interest her in the menage across the hall. Mrs. Bella LeMar, as she called herself, was of a type rather common in the city, an attractive widow on the safe side of forty, well-groomed, often daringly gowned. Her brown eyes snapped vivacity, and the pert little nose and racy expression of the mouth confirmed the general impression that Mrs. LeMar liked the good things of life.

Quite naturally, Constance observed, her neighbor had hosts of friends who often came early and stayed late, friends who seemed to exude, as it were, an air of prosperity and high living. Clearly, she was a woman to cultivate. Constance felt even more interest in her, now that Mrs. LeMar had pursued a bowing acquaintance to the point of an unsolicited invitation.

"A friendly little game," she speculated. "What IS the game?"

That night found Constance at the buzzer beside the heavy mahogany door across the hall. She wore a new evening gown of warm red. Her face glowed with heightened color, and her nerves were on the qui vive for the unlocking at last of the mystery of the fascinating Mrs. LeMar.

"So glad to see you, my dear," smiled Bella, holding out her hand engagingly. "You are just in time."

Already several of the guests had arrived. There was an air of bonhomie as Bella presented them to Constance—a stocky, red-faced man with a wide chest and narrow waist,

Arthur B. Reeve

Ross Watson; a tall, sloping-shouldered man who inclined his head forward earnestly when he talked to a lady and spoke with animation, Haddon Halsey; and a fair-haired, baby-blue eyed little woman gowned in becoming pink, Mrs. Lansing Noble.

"Now we're all here—just enough for a game," remarked Bella in a business-like tone. "Oh, I beg pardon—you play, Mrs. Dunlap?" she added to Constance.

"Oh, yes," Constance replied. "Almost anything—a little bit."

She had already noted that the chief object in the room, after all, appeared to be a round table. About it the guests seemed naturally to take their places.

"What shall it be to-night—bridge?" asked Watson, nonchalantly fingering a little pack of gilt-edged cards which Bella had produced.

"Oh, no," cried Mrs. Noble. "Bridge is such a bore."

"Rum?"

"No—no. The regular game—poker."

"A dollar limit?"

"Oh, make it five," drawled Halsey impatiently.

Watson said nothing, but Bella patted Halsey's hand in approval, as if all were on very good terms indeed. "I think that will make a nice little game," she cut in, opening a drawer from which she took out a box of blue, red and white chips of real ivory. Watson seemed naturally to assume the role of banker.

"Aren't you going to join us?" asked Constance.

"Oh, I seldom play. You know, I'm too busy entertaining you people," excused Bella, as she bustled out of the room, reappearing a few minutes later with the maid and a tray of slender hollow-stemmed glasses with a bottle wrapped in a white napkin in a pail of ice.

Mrs. Noble shuffled the cards with practiced hand and Watson kept a calculating eye on every face. Luck was not with Constance on the first deal and she dropped out.

Mrs. Noble and Halsey were betting eagerly. Watson was coolly following along until the show-down—which he won.

"Of all things," exclaimed the little woman in pink, plainly betraying her vexation at losing. "Will luck never turn?"

Halsey said nothing.

Constance watched in amazement. This was no "friendly little game." The faces were too tense, too hectic. The play was too high, and the desire to win too great. Mrs. LeMar was something more than a gracious hostess in her solicitude for her guests.

All the time the pile of chips in front of Watson kept building up. At each new deal a white chip was placed in a little box—the kitty—for the "cards and refreshments."

It was in reality one of the new style gambling joints for men and women.

The gay parties of callers on Mrs. LeMar were nothing other

than gamblers. The old gambling dens of the icebox doors and steel gratings, of white-coated servants and free food and drink, had passed away with "reform." Here was a remarkable new phase of sporting life which had gradually taken its place.

Constance had been looking about curiously in the meantime. On a table she saw copies of the newspapers which published full accounts of the races, something that looked like a racing sheet, and a telephone conveniently located near writing materials. It was a poolroom, too, then, in the daytime, she reasoned.

Surely, in the next room, when the light was on, she saw what looked like a miniature roulette wheel, not one of the elaborate affairs of bright metal and ebony, but one of those that can almost be packed into a suitcase and carried about easily.

That was the secret of the flashily dressed men and women who called on Bella LeMar. They were risking everything, perhaps even honor itself, on a turn of a wheel, the fall of a card, a guess on a horse.

Why had Bella LeMar invited her here? she asked herself.

At first Constance was a little bit afraid that she might have plunged into too deep water. She made up her mind to quit when her losses reached a certain nominal point. But they did not reach it. Perhaps the gamblers were too clever. But Constance seemed always to keep just a little bit ahead of the game.

One person in particular in the group interested her as she endeavored intuitively to take their measure. It was Haddon Halsey, immaculately garbed, with all those little touches of smartness which women like to see.

Once she caught Halsey looking intently at her. Was it he who was letting her win at his expense! Or was his attention to her causing him to neglect his own game and play it poorly?

She decided to quit. She was a few dollars ahead. For excuse she pleaded a headache.

Bella accepted the excuse with a cordial nod and a kind inquiry whether she might not like to lie down.

"No, thank you," murmured Constance. "But the cards make me nervous to-night. Just let me sit here. I'll be all right in a minute."

As she lolled back on a divan near the players Constance noted, or thought she noted, now and then exchanges of looks between Bella and Watson. What was the bond of intimacy between them? She noted on Mrs. Noble's part that she was keenly alive to everything that Halsey did. It was a peculiar quadrangle.

Halsey was losing heavily in his efforts to retrieve his fortunes. He said nothing, but accepted the losses grimly. Mrs. Noble, however, after each successive loss seemed more and more nervous.

At last, with a hasty look at her wrist watch, she gave a little suppressed scream.

"How the time flies!" she cried. "Who would have thought it as late as that? Really I must go. I expect my husband back from a director's meeting at ten, and it's much easier to be home than to have to think up an excuse. No, Haddon, don't

disturb yourself. I shall get a cab at the door. Let me see—
two hundred and twenty-eight dollars." She paused as if the
loss staggered her. "I'll have to sign another I O U for it,
Bella. There!"

She left in a flutter, as if some one had winked out the light
by which she, poor little butterfly, had singed her wings, and
there was nothing for her but to fly away alone in the
darkness with her secret.

Halsey accompanied her to the door. For a moment she
raised a questioning face to his, and shot a half covert glance
at Constance. Then, as if with an effort, adhering to her first
resolution to go alone, she whispered earnestly, "I hope you
win. Luck MUST turn."

Halsey plunged back into the game, now with Bella holding
a hand. He played recklessly, then conservatively. It made no
difference. The cards seemed always against him. Constance
began really to feel alarmed at his manner.

Once, however, he chanced to look up at her. Something in
her face must have impressed him. Turning, he flung down
the cards in disgust. "That's enough for to-night," he
exclaimed, rising and draining another glass on the tray.

"Luck will come your way soon again," urged Bella. "It all
averages up in the end, you know. It has to."

"How did you enjoy the evening!" insinuated Bella.

"Very much," replied Constance enthusiastically. "It is so
exciting, you know."

"You must come again when more of my friends are here."

"I should like to. But to-night was very nice."

Halsey looked at her contemplatively. She had risen to go. As she took a step or two toward the door, still facing them, she found Halsey at her side.

"Shall we go over to Jack's for a bite to eat?" he whispered.

There was as much of appeal in his undertone as of invitation.

"Thank you. I shall be glad to go," Constance assented quickly.

There was something about Haddon Halsey that interested her. Perhaps Bella and Watson exchanged a knowing glance as she crossed the hall for her wraps. Whatever it was, Constance determined to see the thing through to a finish, confident that she was quite able to take care of herself.

Outside the raw night air smote dankly on their fevered faces. As they walked along briskly, too glad to get into the open to summon a car, Constance happened to turn. She had an uncomfortable feeling. She could have sworn some one was following them. She said nothing about a figure a few feet behind them.

The lively, all-night restaurant was thronged. Halsey seemed to throw himself into the gayety with reckless abandon, ordering about twice as much as they could eat and drink. But in spite of the fascination of the scene, Constance could not forget the dark figure skulking behind them in the shadow of the street.

Once she looked up. At another table she could just catch a glimpse of Drummond, of the Burr Detective Agency, alone, oblivious.

Never did he look at them. There was nothing to indicate that he was even interested. But Constance knew that that was the method of his shadowing. Never for a moment, she knew, did he permit himself to look into the eyes of his quarry, even for the most fleeting glance.

She knew, too, that there must be some psychological reason for his not looking at them, as he otherwise must have done, if only by chance. It was the method followed by the expert modern trailer. She knew that if one looks at a person intently while in a public place, for instance, it will not be long before the gaze will be returned. Try as she would, she could not catch Drummond's eye, however.

Halsey, now that the strain of the game was off, was rattling along about his losses in an undertone to her.

"But what of it?" he concluded. "Any day luck may change. As for myself, I go always on the assumption that I am the one exception—unlucky both at cards and love. If the event proves I am right, I am not disappointed. If I am wrong, then I am happy."

There was something in the tone of the whimsicality that alarmed her. It covered a desperation which she felt instinctively.

Why was he talking thus to her, almost a stranger? Surely it could not have been for that that Bella LeMar had brought them together.

Gradually it came to her. The man had really, honestly been struck by her from the moment of their introduction. Instead of allowing others, to say nothing of himself, to lead her on in the path he and Mrs. Noble and the others had entered, he was taking the bit in his teeth, like a high-strung race horse, and was running away, now that Bella LeMar for the moment did not hold the reins. He was warning her openly against the game!

Somehow the action appealed to Constance. It was genuine, disinterested. Secretly, it was flattering. Still, she said nothing about Bella, nor about Mrs. Noble. Halsey seemed to appreciate the fact. His face showed plainly as if he had said it that here, at least, was one woman who was not always talking about others.

There had been a rapid-fire suddenness about his confidences which had fascinated her.

"Are you in business?" she ventured.

"Oh, yes," he laughed grimly. "I'm in business—treasurer of the Exporting & Manufacturing Company."

"But," she pursued, looking him frankly in the face, "I should think you'd be afraid to—er—become involved—"

"I know I am being watched," he broke in impatiently. "You see, I'm bonded, and the bonding companies keep a pretty sharp lookout on your habits. Oh, the crash will come some day. Until it does—let us make the most of it—while it lasts."

He said the words bitterly. Constance was confirmed in her original suspicion of him now. Halsey was getting deeper and deeper into the moral quagmire. She had seen his interest in Mrs. Noble. Had Bella LeMar hoped that she, too, would play will-o '-the-wisp in leading him on?

Over the still half-eaten supper she watched Halsey keenly. A thousand questions about himself, about Mrs. Noble, rushed through her mind. Should she be perfectly frank?

"Are you—are you using the company's money!" she asked at length pointedly.

He had not expected the question, and his evident intention was to deny it. But he met her eye. He tried to escape it, but could not. What was there about this little woman that had compelled his attention and interest from the moment he had been introduced?

Quickly he tried to reason it out in his heart. It was not that she was physically attractive to him. Mrs. Noble was that It was not that fascination which Bella aroused, the adventuress, the siren, the gorgon. In Constance there was something different. She was a woman of the world, a man's woman. Then, too, she was so brutally frank in inviting his confidences.

Over and over he turned the answer he had intended to make. He caught her eye again and knew that it was of no use.

"Yes," he muttered, as a cloud spread over his face at not being able, as usual, to let the gay life put the truth out of his mind. "Yes, I have been using—their funds."

As if a switch had been turned, the light broke on Constance. She saw herself face to face with one of the dark shadows in the great city of high lights.

"How?" she asked simply, leaning forward over the table.

There was no resisting her. Quickly he told her all.

"At first with what little money of my own I had I played. Then I began to sign I O U's and notes. Now I have been taking blank stock certificates, some of those held as treasury stock in the company's safe. They have never been issued, so that by writing in the signatures of myself and the other officers necessary, I have been able to use it to pay off my losses in gambling."

As he unfolded to her the plan which he had adopted, Constance listened in amazement.

"And you know that you are watched," she repeated, changing the subject, and sensing rather than seeing that Drummond was watching them then.

"Yes," he continued freely. "The International Surety, in which I'm bonded, has a sort of secret service of its own, I understand. It is the eye that is never closed, but is screened from the man under bond. When you go into the Broadway night life too often, for instance," he pursued, waving his hand about at the gay tables, "run around in fast motors with faster company—well, they know it. Who is watching, I do not know. But with me it will be as it has been when others came to the end. Some day they will come to me, and they are going to say, 'We don't like your conduct. Where do you get this money?' They will know, then, too. But before that time comes I want to win, to be in a position to tell them to go—"

Halsey clenched his fist. It was evident that he did not intend to quit, no matter what the odds against him.

Constance thought of the silent figure of Drummond at the other table—watching, watching. She felt sure that it was to him that the Surety Company had turned over the work of shadowing Halsey. Day after day, probably, the unobtrusive detective had been trailing Halsey from the moment he left his apartment until the time when he returned, if he did return. There was nothing of his goings and comings that was not already an open book to them. Of what use was it, then, for Halsey to fight!

It was a situation such as she delighted in. She had made up her mind. She would help Haddon Halsey to beat the law.

Already it seemed as if he knew that their positions had been reversed. He had started to warn her; she now was saving him.

Yet even then he showed the better side of his nature.

"There is some one else, Mrs. Dunlap," he remarked earnestly, "who needs your help even more than I do."

It had cost him something to say that. He had not been able to accept her help, even under false pretenses. Eagerly he watched to see whether jealousy of the other woman played any part with her.

"I understand," she said with a hasty glance at her watch and a covert look at Drummond. "Let us go. If we are to win we must keep our heads clear. I shall see you to-morrow."

For hours during the rest of the night Constance tossed fitfully in half sleep, thinking over the problem she had assumed.

How was she to get at the inside truth of what was going on across the hall? That was the first question.

In her perplexity, she rose and looked out of the window at the now lightening gray of the courtyard. There dangled the LeMar telephone wire, only a few feet from her own window.

Suddenly an idea flashed over her. In her leisure she had read much and thought more. She recalled having heard of a machine that just fitted her needs.

As soon as she was likely to find places of business open Constance started out on her search. It was early in the forenoon before she returned, successful. The machine which she had had in mind proved to be an oak box, perhaps eighteen inches long, by half the width, and a foot deep. On its face it bore a little dial. Inside there appeared a fine wire on a spool which unwound gradually by clockwork, and, after passing through a peculiar small arrangement, was wound up on another spool. Flexible silk-covered copper wires led from the box.

Carefully Constance reached across the dizzy intervening space, and drew in the slack LeMar telephone wires. With every care she cut into them as if she were making an extension, and attached the wires from the box.

Perhaps half an hour later the door buzzer sounded. Constance could scarcely restrain her surprise as Mrs. Lansing Noble stepped in quickly and shut the door herself.

"I don't want her to know I'm here," she whispered, nodding across the hall.

"Won't you take off your things?" asked Constance cordially.

"No, I can't stay," returned her visitor nervously, pausing.

Constance wondered why she had come. Was she, too, trying to warn a newcomer against the place!

She said nothing, but now that the effort had been made and the little woman had gone actually so far, she felt the reaction. She sank down into an easy chair and rested her pretty head on her delicately gloved hand.

"Oh, Mrs. Dunlap," she began convulsively, "I hope you will pardon an entire stranger for breaking in on you so informally—but—but I can't—I can't help it. I must tell some one."

Accustomed as she was now to strange confidences, Constance bent over and patted the little hand of Mrs. Noble comfortingly.

"You seemed to take it so coolly," went on the other woman. "For me the glamour, the excitement are worse than champagne. But you could stop, even when you were winning. Oh, my God! What am I to do? What will happen when my husband finds out what I have done!"

Tearfully, the little woman poured out the sordid story of her fascination for the game, of her losses, of the pawning of her jewels to pay her losses and keep them secret, if only for a few days, until that mythical time when luck would change.

"When I started," she blurted out with a bitter little laugh, "I thought I'd make a little pin money. That's how I began— with that and the excitement. And now this is the end."

She had risen and was pacing the floor wildly.

"Mrs. Dunlap," she cried, pausing before Constance, "to-day I am nothing more nor less than a 'capper,' as they call it, for a gambling resort."

She was almost hysterical. The contrast with the gay, respectable, prosperous-looking woman at Bella's was appalling. Constance realized to the full what were the tragedies that were enacted elsewhere.

As she looked at the despairing woman, she could reconstruct the terrible situation. Cultivated, well-bred, fashionably gowned, a woman like Mrs. Noble served admirably the purpose of luring men on. If there had been only women or only men involved, it perhaps would not have been so bad. But there were both. Constance saw that men were wanted, men who could afford to lose not hundreds, but thousands, men who are always the heaviest players. And so Mrs. Noble and other unfortunate women no doubt were sent out on Broadway to the cafes and restaurants, sent out even among those of their own social circle, always to lure men on, to involve themselves more and more in the web into which they had flown. Bella had hoped even to use Constance!

Mrs. Noble had paused again. There was evident sincerity in her as she looked deeply into the eyes of Constance.

Nothing but desperation could have wrung her inmost secrets from her to another woman.

"I saw them trying to throw you together with Haddon Halsey," she said, almost tragically. "It was I who introduced Haddon to them. I was to get a percentage of his losses to pay off my own—but"—her feelings seemed to overcome her and wildly, desperately, she added—"but I can't—I can't. I—I must rescue him—I must."

It was a strange situation. Constance reasoned it out quickly. What a wreck of life these two were making! Not only they were involved, but others who as yet knew nothing, Mrs. Noble's husband, the family of Halsey. She must help.

"Mrs. Noble," said Constance calmly, "can you trust me?"

She shot a quick glance at Constance. "Yes," she murmured.

"Then to-night visit Mrs. LeMar as though nothing had happened. Meanwhile I will have thought out a plan."

It was late in the afternoon when Constance saw Halsey again, this time in his office, where he had been waiting impatiently for some word from her. The relief at seeing her showed only too plainly on his face.

"This inaction is killing me," he remarked huskily. "Has anything happened to-day!"

She said nothing about the visit of Mrs. Noble. Perhaps it was better that each should not know yet that the other was worried.

"Yes," she replied, "much has happened. I cannot tell you now. But to-night let us all go again as though nothing had occurred."

"They have twenty-five thousand dollars in stock certificates already which I have given them," he remarked anxiously.

"Some way—any way, you must get them back for a time. Let me see some of the blanks."

Halsey shut the door. From a secret drawer of his desk he drew a package of beautifully engraved paper.

Constance looked at it a moment. Then with a fountain pen, across the front of each, she made a few marks. Halsey looked on eagerly. As she handed them back to him, not a sign showed on any part of them.

"You must tell them that there is something wrong with the

others, that you will give them other certificates of your own about which there is no question. Tell them anything to get them back. Here—take this other fountain pen, sign the new certificates with that, in their presence so that they will suspect nothing. To-night I shall expect you to play up to the limit, to play into Mrs. Noble's hand and assume her losses, too. I shall meet you there at nine.'"

Constance had laid her plans quickly. That night she waited in her own apartment until she heard Halsey enter across the hall. She had determined to give him plenty of time to obtain the old forged certificates and substitute for them the new forgeries.

Perhaps half an hour later she heard Mrs. Noble enter. As Constance followed her in, the effusive greeting of Bella LeMar showed that as yet she suspected nothing. A quick glance at Halsey brought an answering nod and an unconscious motion toward his pocket where he had stuffed the old certificates carelessly.

A moment later they had plunged into the game. The play that night was spirited. Soon the limit was the roof.

From the start things seemed to run against Halsey and Mrs. Noble even worse than before. At the same time fortune seemed to favor Constance. Again and again she won, until even Watson seemed to think there was something uncanny about it.

"Beginner's luck," remarked Bella with a forced laugh.

Still Constance won, not much, but steadily, though not enough to offset the larger winnings of Watson.

Fast and furious became the play and as steadily did it go

against Halsey. Mrs. Noble retired, scarcely repressing the tears. Constance dropped out. Only Halsey and Watson remained, fighting as if it were a duel to the death.

"Please stop, Halsey," pleaded Mrs. Noble. "What is the use of tempting fortune?"

An insane half light seemed to glow in his eyes as, with a quick glance at Constance and a covert nod of approval from her, he forced a smile and playfully laid his finger on Mrs. Noble's lips.

"Double or quits, Watson," he cried. "Return the new certificates or take others for twice the amount. Are you game?"

"I'm on," agreed Watson coolly.

Halsey laid down his hand in triumph. There were four kings.

"I win," ground out Watson viciously, as he tossed down four aces.

Constance was on her feet in a moment.

"You are a lot of cheats and swindlers," she cried, seizing the cards before any one could interfere.

Deftly she laid out the four aces beside the four deuces, the four kings beside the four queens. It was done so quickly that even Halsey, in his amazement, could find nothing to say. Mrs. Noble paled and was speechless. As for Bella and Watson, nothing could have aroused them more than the open charge that they were using false devices.

Yet never for a moment did Watson lose his iron cynicism.

"Prove it," he demanded. "As for Mr. Halsey, he may pay or I'll show the stock I already hold to the proper people."

Constance was facing Watson, as calm as he.

"Show it," she said quietly.

There was a knock at the door.

"Don't let any one in," ordered Bella of the maid, who had already opened the door.

A man's foot had been inserted into the opening. "What's the matter, Chloe?"

"Good Lawd, Mis' Bella—we done been raided!" burst out the maid as the door flew wholly open.

Halsey staggered back. "A detective!" he exclaimed.

"Oh, what shall I do!" wailed Mrs. Noble. "My husband will never forgive me if this becomes known."

Bella was as calm as a good player with a royal straight flush.

"I've caught you at last," fairly hissed Drummond. "And you, too, Mrs. Dunlap. Watson, I overheard something about some stock. Let me see it. I think it will interest International Surety as well as Exporters and Manufacturers."

Through the still open door Constance had darted across the hall to her apartment.

"Not so fast," cried Drummond. "You can't escape. The front door is guarded. You can't get out."

She was gone, but a moment later emerged from the darkness of her rooms, carrying the oak box.

As she set it down on the card table, no one said a word. Deliberately she opened the box, disclosing two spools of wire inside. To the machine she attached several head pieces such as a telephone operator wears. She turned a switch and the wire began to unroll from one spool and wind up on the other again.

A voice, or rather voices, seemed to come from the box itself. It was uncanny.

"Hello, is this Mrs. LeMar?" came from it.

"What is it?" whispered Halsey, as if fearful of being overheard.

"A telegraphone," replied Constance, shutting it off for a moment.

"A telegraphone? What is that?"

"A machine for registering telephone conversations, dictation, anything of the sort you wish. It was invented by Valdemar Poulsen, the Danish Edison. This is one of his new wire machines. The record is made by a new process, localized charges of magnetism on this wire. It is as permanent as the wire itself. There is only one thing that can destroy them—rubbing over the wire with this magnet. Listen."

She had started the machine again. Whose voice it was calling Bella? Constance was looking fixedly at Drummond.

He shifted uneasily.

"How much is he in for now?" pursued the voice.

Halsey gasped. It was Drummond's own voice.

"Two hundred and fifty shares," replied Bella's voice.

"Good. Keep at him. Don't lose him. To-night I'll drop in."

"And your client will make good?" she anxiously.

"Absolutely. We will pay five thousand dollars for the evidence that will convict him."

Constance's little audience was stunned. But she did not let the telegraphone pause. Skipping some unimportant calls, she began again.

This was a call from Bella to Watson.

"Ross, that fellow Drummond called up to-day."

"Yes?"

"He is going to pull it off to-night. His client will make good—five thousand if they catch Halsey with the goods. How about it?"

"Pretty soft—eh, Bella?" came back from Watson.

"My God! it's a plant!" exclaimed Halsey, staggering and dropping heavily into a chair. "I'm ruined. There is no way out!"

"Wait," interrupted Constance. "Here's another call. It may

serve to explain why luck was with me to-night. I came prepared."

"Yes, Mrs. LeMar," came another strange voice from the machine. "We'd do anything for Mr. Watson. What is it—a pack of strippers?"

"Yes. The aces stripped from the ends, the kings from the sides."

The group looked eagerly at Constance.

"From the maker of fake gambling apparatus, I find," she explained, shutting off the machine. "They were ordering from him cards cut or trimmed so that certain ones could be readily drawn from the deck, or 'stripped.' Small wedge-shaped strips are trimmed off the edges of all the other cards, leaving the aces, say, projecting just the most minute fraction of an inch beyond the others. Everything is done carefully. The rounded edges at the corners are recut to look right. When the cards are shuffled the aces protrude a trifle over the edges of the other cards. It is a simple matter for the dealer to draw or strip out as many aces as he wants, stack them on the bottom of the pack as he shuffles the cards, and draw them from the bottom whenever he wants them. Strippers are one of the newest things in swindling. Marked cards are out of date. But some decks have the aces stripped from the ends, the kings from the sides. With this pack, as you can see, a sucker can be dealt out the kings, while the house player gets the aces."

Drummond brazened it out. With a muttered oath he turned to Watson again. "What rot is this? The stock, Watson," he repeated. "Where is that stock I heard them talking about?"

Mrs. Noble, forgetting all now but Halsey, paled. Bella

LeMar was fumbling at her gold mesh bag. She gave a sudden, suppressed little scream.

"Look!" she cried. "They are blank—those stock certificates he gave me."

Drummond seized them roughly from her hands.

Where the signatures should have been there was nothing at all!

Across the face of the stock were the words in deep black, "SAMPLE CERTIFICATE," written in an angular, feminine hand.

What did it mean? Halsey was as amazed as any of them. Mechanically he turned to Constance.

"I didn't say anything last night," she remarked incisively. "But I had my suspicions from the first. I always look out for the purry kind of 'my dear' woman. They have claws. Last night I watched. To-day I learned—learned that you, Mr. Drummond, were nothing but a blackmailer, using these gamblers to do your dirty work. Haddon, they would have thrown you out like a squeezed lemon as soon as the money you had was gone. They would have taken the bribe that Drummond offered for the stock—and they would have left you nothing but jail. I learned all that over the telegraphone. I learned their methods and, knowing them, even I could not be prevented from winning to-night"

Halsey moved as if to speak. "But," he asked eagerly, "the stock certificates—what of them!"

"The stock?" she answered with deliberation. "Did you ever hear that writing in quinoline will appear blue, but will soon fade away, while other writing in silver nitrate and ammonia, invisible at first, after a few hours appears black? You wrote on those certificates in sympathetic ink that fades, I in ink that comes up soon."

Mrs. Noble was crying softly to herself. They still had her notes for thousands.

Halsey saw her. Instantly he forgot his own case. What was to be done about her? He telegraphed a mute appeal to Constance, forgetful of himself now. Constance was fingering the switch of the telegraphone.

"Drummond," remarked Constance significantly, as though other secrets might still be contained in the marvelous little mechanical detective, "Drummond, don't you think, for the sake of your own reputation as a detective, it might be as well to keep this thing quiet?"

For a moment the detective gripped his wrath and seemed to consider the damaging record of his conversation with Bella LeMar.

"Perhaps," he agreed sullenly.

Constance reached into her chatelaine. From it she drew an ordinary magnet, and slowly pulled off the armature.

"If I run this over the wires," she hinted, holding it near the spools, "the record will be wiped out." She paused impressively. "Let me have those I O U's of Mrs. Noble's. By the way, you might as well give me that blank stock, too. There is no use in that, now."

As she laid the papers in a pile on the table before her she added the old forged certificates from Halsey's pocket. There it lay, the incriminating, ruining evidence.

Deliberately she passed the magnet over the thin steel wire, wiping out what it had recorded, as if the recording angel were blotting out from the book of life.

"Try it, Drummond," she cried, dropping on her knees before the open fireplace. "You will find the wire a blank."

There was a hot, sudden blaze as the pile of papers from the table flared up.

"There," she exclaimed. "These gambling debts were not even debts of honor. If you will call a cab, Haddon, I have reserved a table at Jade's for you and Mrs. Noble. It is a farewell. Drummond will not occupy his place in the corner to-night. But—after it—you are to forget—both of you—forever. You understand?"

CHAPTER V

THE EAVESDROPPERS

"I suppose you have heard something about the troubles of the Motor Trust? The other directors, you know, are trying to force me out."

Rodman Brainard, president of the big Motor Corporation, searched the magnetic depths of the big brown eyes of the woman beside his desk. Talking to Constance Dunlap was not like talking to other women he had known, either socially or in business.

"A friend of yours, and of mine," he added frankly, "has told me enough about you to convince me that you are more than an amateur at getting people out of tight places. I asked you to call because I think you can help me."

There was a directness about Brainard which Constance liked.

"It's very kind of you to place such confidence in me—on such short acquaintance," she returned pointedly, searching his face.

Brainard laughed.

"I don't need to tell you, Mrs. Dunlap, that anything I have said so far is an open secret in Wall Street. They have threatened to drag in the Sherman law, and in the reorganization that will follow the investigation, they plan to eliminate Rodman Brainard—perhaps set in motion the criminal clauses of the law. It's nothing, Mrs. Dunlap, but a downright hypocritical pose. They reverse the usual process. It is doing good that evil may result."

He watched her face intently. Something in her expression seemed to please him. "By George," he thought to himself, "this is a man's woman. You can talk to her."

Brainard, accustomed to quick decisions, added aloud, "Just now they are using Mrs. Brainard as a catspaw. They are spreading that scandal about my acquaintance with Blanche Leblanc, the actress. You have seen her? A stunning woman—wonderful. But I long ago saw that such a friendship could lead to nothing but ruin." He met Constance's eye squarely. There was nothing of the adventuress in it as there had been in Blanche Leblanc. "And," he finished, almost biting off the words, "I decided to cut it out."

"How does Blanche Leblanc figure in the Motor Trust trouble?" asked Constance keenly.

"They had been shadowing me a long time before I knew it, ferreting back into my past. Yesterday I learned that some one had broken into Miss Leblanc's apartments and had stolen a package of letters which I wrote to her. It can't hurt her. People expect that sort of thing of an actress. But it can hurt the president of the Motor Trust—just at present."

"Who has been doing the shadowing?"

"Worthington, the treasurer, is the guiding spirit of the

'insurgents' as they call themselves—it sounds popular, like reform. I understand they have had a detective named Drummond working for them."

Constance raised her eyes quickly at the name. "Was Drummond always to cross her trail?

"This story of the letters," he went on, "puts on the finishing touch. They have me all right on that. I can tell by the way that Sybil—er, Mrs. Brainard—acts, that she has read and reread those letters. But, by God," he concluded, bringing down his fist on the desk, "I shall fight to the end, and when I go down,"—he emphasized each word with an additional blow,—"the crash will bring down the whole damned structure on their own heads, too."

He was too earnest even to apologize to her. Constance studied the grim determination in the man's face. He was not one of those destined to fail.

"All is not lost that is in peril, Mr. Brainard," she remarked quietly. "That's one of the maxims of your own Wall Street."

"What would you do?" he asked. It was not an appeal; rather it was an invitation.

"I can't say, yet. Let me come into the office of the Trust. Can't I be your private secretary?"

"Consider yourself engaged. Name your figure—after it is over. My record on the Streets speaks for how I stand by those who stand by me. But I hate a quitter."

"So do I," exclaimed Constance, rising and giving him her hand in a straight-arm shake that made Brainard straighten himself and look down into her face with unconcealed admiration.

The next morning Constance became private secretary to the president of the Motor Trust.

"You will be 'Miss' Dunlap," remarked Brainard. "It sounds more plausible."

Quietly he arranged her duties so that she would seem to be very busy without having anything which really interfered with the purpose of her presence.

She had been thinking rapidly. Late in the forenoon she reached a decision. A little errand uptown kept her longer than she expected, but by the late afternoon she was back again at her desk, on which rested a small package which had been delivered by messenger for her.

"I beg you won't think as badly of me as it seems on the surface, Miss Dunlap," remarked Brainard, stopping beside her desk.

"I don't think badly of you," she answered in a low voice. "You are not the only man who has been caught with a crowd of crooks who plan to leave him holding the bag."

"Oh, it isn't that," he hastened, "I mean this Blanche Leblanc affair. May I be frank with you?"

It was not the first time Constance had been made a confidante of the troubles of the heart, and yet there was something fascinating about having a man like Brainard consider her worthy of being trusted with what meant so much to him.

"I'm not altogether to blame." he went on slowly. "The estrangement between my wife and myself came long before that little affair. It began over—well—over what they call a

Arthur B. Reeve

serious difference in temperament. You know a man—an ambitious man—needs a partner, a woman who can use the social position that money gives not alone for pleasure but as a means of advancing the partnership. I never had that. The more I advanced, the more I found her becoming a butterfly—and not as attractive as the other butterflies either. She went one way—I, another. Oh well—what's the use? I wont too far—the wrong way. I must pay. Only let me save what I can from the wreck."

It was not Constance, the woman, to whom he was talking. It was Constance, the secretary. Yet it was the woman, not the secretary, who listened.

Brainard stopped again beside her desk.

"All that is neither here nor there," he remarked, forcing a change in his manner. "I am in for it. Now, the question is—what are we going to do about it!"

Constance had unwrapped the package on her desk, disclosing an oblong box.

"What's that?" he asked curiously.

"Mr. Brainard," she answered tapping the box, "there's no limit to the use of this little machine for our purposes. We can get at their most vital secrets with it. We can discover every plan which they have against us. We may even learn the hiding place of those letters Why, there is no limit. This is one of those new microphone detectives."

"A microphone?" he repeated as he opened the box, looked sharply at the two black little storage batteries inside, the coil of silk-covered wire, a little black rubber receiver and a curious black disc whose face was pierced by a circular row of holes.

"Yes. You must have heard of them. You hide that transmitter behind a picture or under a table or desk. Then you run the wire out of the room and by listening in the receiver you can hear everything!"

"But that is what detectives use—"

"Well?" she interrupted coolly, "what of it? If it is good for them, is it not just as good for us?"

"Better!" he exclaimed. "By George, you ARE the goods."

It was late before Constance had a chance to do anything with the microphone. It seemed as if Worthington were staying, perversely, later than usual. At last, however, he left with a curt nod to her.

The moment the door was closed she stopped the desultory clicking of her typewriter with Which she had been toying in the appearance of being busy. With Brainard she entered the board room where she had noticed Worthington and Sheppard often during the day.

It was, without exaggeration, one of the most plainly furnished rooms she had ever seen. A long mahogany table with eight large mahogany chairs, a half inch pile of velvety rug on the floor and a huge chandelier in the middle of the ceiling constituted the furniture. Not a picture, not a cabinet or filing case broke the blankness of the brown painted walls.

For a moment she stopped to consider. Brainard waited and watched her narrowly.

"There isn't a place to put this transmitter except up above that chandelier," she said at length.

He gave her his hand as she stepped on a chair and then on the table. There was a glimpse of a trim ankle. The warmth and softness of her touch caused him to hold her hand just a moment longer than was absolutely necessary. A moment later he was standing on the table beside her.

"This is the place, all right," she said, looking at the thick scum of dust on the top of the reflector.

Quickly she placed the little black disc close to the center on the top of the reflector. "Can you see that from the floor?" she asked.

"No," he answered, walking about the room, "not a sign of it."

"I'll sit here," she said in just a tremor of excitement over the adventure, "and listen while you talk in the board room."

Brainard entered. It seemed ridiculous for him to talk to himself.

"If the microphone works," he said at length, "rap on the desk twice." Then he added, half laughing to himself, "If it doesn't, rap once—Constance."

A single rap came in answer.

"If you couldn't hear," he smiled entering her office, "why did you rap once!"

"It didn't work smoothly on that last word."

"What—Constance?"

He thought there was a subtle change in their relations since the microphone incident. At any rate she was not angry. Were they not partners?

"I think it will be better if I turn that microphone around," she remarked. "I placed it face downwards. Let me change it."

Again he helped her as she jumped up on the board room table. This time his hand lingered a little longer in hers and she did not withdraw it so soon. When she did there was a quick twinkle in her eyes as she straightened the microphone and offered her hand to him again.

"Jump!" he said, as if daring her.

A moment she paused. "I never could take a dare," she answered.

She leaped lightly to the floor. For just a moment she seemed about to lose her balance. Then she felt an arm steadying her. He had caught her and for an instant their eyes met.

"Well, Rodman—I scarcely thought it was as brazen as this!"

They turned in surprise.

Mrs. Brainard was standing in the doorway.

She was a petite blonde little woman of the deceptive age which the beauty parlors convey to thousands of their assiduous patrons.

For a moment she looked coldly from one to the other.

"To what am I indebted for the pleasure of this unexpected visit, Sybil?" asked Brainard with sarcastic emphasis. "I shall

Arthur B. Reeve

finish those letters to-morrow, Miss Dunlap. You need not wait for them."

He held the door to his own office open for Mrs. Brainard.

Sybil Brainard shot a quick glance at Constance. "Well, young lady," she said haughtily, "do you realize what you are doing and with whom you are?"

"It isn't necessary, Sybil, to bother about Miss Dunlap. The lights were out of order and I found Miss Dunlap standing on the table trying to fix them. You came just in time to see her jump down. By the way, Worthington seems to be another who works late. He left only a few minutes ago."

Constance passed a restless night. To have got wrong at the very start worried her. Over and over she thought of what had happened. And always she came back to one question. What had Brainard meant by that reference to Worthington?

He came in late the next day, however. Still, there was no change in his manner as he greeted her. The incident had not affected him, as it had her. Neither of them said anything about it.

A young man had been waiting to see Brainard and as he entered he asked him in.

Just then Sheppard walked casually through the reception room and into the board room.

Constance quickly closed her door. She heard the young man leave Brainard's office but she was too engrossed to pay attention to anything but the voices that were coming through the microphone. She was writing feverishly what she heard.

"Yes, Sheppard, I saw her again last night."

"Where?"

"She was to meet me here, but he stayed later than usual with that new secretary of his. So I cut out and met her at the street entrance."

"And?"

"I told her of the new secretary. She did just what I wanted—came up here—and, say Sheppard—what do you think? They were in this room and he had his arms about her!"

"The letters are all right, are they? How much did you have to pay the Leblanc girl?"

"Twenty thousand. That's all charged up against the pool. Say, Leblanc is—well—give you my word, Sheppard—I can hardly blame Brainard after all."

"You ARE the last word in woman haters, Lee."

Both men laughed.

"And the letters?"

"Don't worry. They are where they'll do the most good. Sybil has them herself. Now, what have you to report? You saw the district attorney?"

"Yes. He is ready to promise us all immunity if we will go on the stand for the state. The criminal business will come later. Only, you have to play him carefully. He's on the level. A breath of what we really want and it will be all off."

"Then we'll have to hold the stock up, as though nothing was going to happen."

They had left the board room.

Constance hurried into Brainard's office. He was sunk deep in his chair reading some papers.

"What's the matter?" she asked.

"She has entered a suit for divorce. That young man was a process server."

"Yes."

"You are named as co-respondent along with Blanche Leblanc."

"I?"

"Yes. It must have been an afterthought. Everything is going—fortune, reputation—even your friendship, now, Constance—"

"Going? Not yet."

She read hastily what she had overheard.

"Devil take Worthington," ground out Brainard, gripping the arms of his chair. "For weeks I have suspected him. They have been too clever for me. Constance, while I have been going around laying myself open to discovery, Sybil has played a cool and careful game."

He was pacing the floor.

"So—that's the plan. Hold back, keep the stock up until they get started. Then let it go down until I'm forced to sell out at a loss, buy it back cheap, and control the reorganization. Well, I haven't control now, alone. I wish I did have. But neither have they. The public owns the stock now. I need it. Who'll get it first—that's the question!"

He was thinking rapidly.

"If you could do a little bear manipulation yourself," she suggested. "That might get the public scared. You could get enough to control, perhaps, then. They wouldn't dare sell—or if they did they would weaken their own control. Either way, you get them, going or coming."

"Exactly what I was thinking. Play their own game—ahead of them—accelerate it."

It was just after the lunch hour that Constance resumed her place at her desk with the receiver at her ear.

There were voices again in the board room.

"My God, Sheppard, what do you think? Someone is selling Motors—five points off and still going down."

"Who is it? What shall we do?"

"Who! Brainard, of course. Some one has peached. What are you going to do?"

"Wait. Let's call up the News Agency. Hello—yes—what? Unofficial rumor of prosecution of Motors by the government—large selling orders placed in advance. The deuce—say, we'll have to meet this or—"

"Meet nothing. It's Brainard. He's going down in a big crash. We pour our money into his pockets now and let him sell at the top and grab back control with OUR money? Not much. I sell, too."

Already boys were on the street with extras crying the great crash in Motors. It was only a matter of minutes before all the news reading public were thoroughly scared at the apparently bursting bubble. Shares were dug up in small lots, in huge blocks and slammed on the market for what they would bring. All day the pounding went on. Thousands of shares were poured out until Motors which had been climbing toward par in the neighborhood of 79 had declined forty points. Brainard had jumped in first and had realized the top price for his holdings.

Yet during all the wild scenes when the telephone was ringing insistently for him, Brainard, having set the machinery in motion and having been ostentatiously in the office when it started in order to avert suspicion, could not now be found.

The market had closed and Constance was reading the account of the collapse as it was interpreted in the Wall Street editions of the papers, when the door opened and Brainard entered.

"This has been a good day's work, Constance," he said, flinging himself into a chair.

"Yes, I was just reading of it in the papers. The little microphone has put an entirely new twist on affairs. And the best of it is that the financial writers all seem to think it was planned by Worthington and the rest."

"Oh, hang Worthington—hang Motors. THAT is what

I meant."

He slapped down a packet of letters on the desk.

"You—you found them?" gasped Constance. She looked at him keenly. It was evident that a great weight had been taken off his mind.

"Yes indeed. I knew there was only one place where she would put them—in her safe with her jewels. She would think I would never suspect that she had them and, besides, she had the combination changed. I went up to the house this afternoon when she was out. I had an expert with me. He worked two hours, steady,—but he opened it. Here they are. Now for the real game."

"What do you mean?"

"I mean that I noticed the name of the manufacturer on your microphone. I have had one installed in the room which she uses most of all. The wires run to the next house where I've hired an apartment. I intend to 'listen in' there. I'll get this Worthington—yet!"

That night Constance and Brainard sat for hours in the empty apartment patiently waiting for word over the microphone.

At last there was a noise as of a door opening.

"Show them in here."

"Sybil," whispered Brainard as if perhaps she might even hear.

Then came more voices.

"Worthington and Drummond," he added. "They suspect nothing yet."

"Drummond knows this Dunlap woman," said Worthington.

The detective launched forth in a tirade against Constance.

"But she is clever, Drummond. You admit that."

"Clever as they make 'em."

"You will have her shadowed?"

"Every moment, Mrs. Brainard." "What's all this about the panic in Motors, Lee?"

"Some other time, Sybil, not now. Drummond, what do people say?"

Drummond hesitated.

"Out with it, man."

"Well, Mr. Worthington, it is said you started it."

"The deuce I did. But I guess Sheppard and I helped it along. We'll go the limit, too. After all, it had to come. We'll load up after it reaches the bottom."

The voices trailed off.

"Good night, Mrs. Brainard."

"Good night, Mr. Drummond. That was what I wanted to know." A pause.

"Lee, how can I ever thank you?"

A sound suspiciously like a kiss came over the wire. Brainard clenched his fist.

"Good night, Sybil. I must go now—" Again the voices trailed off.

It was several minutes before Brainard spoke. Then it was that he showed his wonderful power of concentration.

"I have a conference in half an hour, Constance," he remarked, looking at his watch. "It is very important. It means getting money to support Motors on the opening tomorrow after I have gathered in again what I need. I think I can come pretty near doubling my holdings if I play it right. That's important. But so is this."

"I will listen," put in Constance. "Trust me. If anything else occurs I will tell you."

She was at the office early the next day, but not before Brainard who, bright and fresh, even though he had been up all night, was primed for the battle of his life at the opening of the market.

Brainard had swung in at the turn and had quietly accumulated the stock control which he needed. He was now bulling the market by matching orders, pyramiding stock which he owned, using every device that was known to his astute brain.

On up went Motors, recovering the forty points, gradually, and even going beyond in the reaction. Worthington and Sheppard had been squeezed out. Not for a moment did he let up.

As the clock on Trinity church struck three, the closing hour, Brainard wheeled suddenly in his chair.

"Miss Dunlap," he said quietly. "I wish that you would tell Worthington and Sheppard that I should like to see them in the board room at four."

Constance looked at her watch. There was time also to execute a little scheme of her own.

Four o'clock came. Brainard lounged casually across to the board room. Instantly Constance had the receiver of the microphone at her ear, straining to catch every word, and to make notes of the stormy scene, if necessary.

Her door opened. It was Sybil Brainard.

The two women looked at each other coldly.

Constance was the first to speak.

"Mrs. Brainard," she began, "I asked you to come down here—not Mr. Worthington. More than that, I asked the office boy to direct you here instead of to his office. Do you see that machine?"

Sybil looked at it without a sign of recognition.

"It is a microphone detective. It was the installing of that machine in the board room which you interrupted the other night."

"Was it necessary that Mr. Brainard should put his arm around you for that?" inquired Mrs. Brainard with biting sarcasm.

"I had just jumped down from the table and had almost lost my balance—that was all," pursued Constance imperturbably.

"Another of these microphone eavesdroppers told me of a conversation last night in your own apartment, Mrs. Brainard."

Her face blanched. "You—have one—there?"

"Yes. Mr. Brainard heard the first conversation, when Drummond and Mr. Worthington were there. After they left he had to attend a conference himself. I alone heard what passed when Mr. Worthington returned."

"You are at liberty to—"

"Mrs. Brainard. You do not understand. I have no reason to want to make you—"

An office boy tapped on the door and entered. "Mr. Brainard wants you, Miss Dunlap."

"I cannot explain now," resumed Constance. "Won't you sit here at my desk and listen over the microphone to what happens!"

She was gone before Mrs. Brainard could reply. What did it all mean? Sybil put the black disc receiver to her ear as she had seen Constance do. Her hand trembled. "Why did she tell me that?" she murmured.

"You can't prove it," shouted a voice through the black disc at her ear. She was startled. It was the voice of Worthington.

"Miss Dunlap—have you that notebook?" came the deep

tones of her husband.

Constance read from her first notes that part relating to the conspiracy to control Motors, carefully omitting the part about the Leblanc letters.

"It's a lie—a lie."

"No, it is not a lie. It is all good legal evidence, the record taken over the new microphone detective. Look up there over the chandelier, Worthington. The other end is In the top drawer of Miss Dunlap's desk."

"I'll fight that to a finish, Brainard. You are clever but there are other things besides Motors that you have to answer for."

"No. Those letters—that is what you mean—are in my possession now. You didn't know that? All the eaves-dropping, if you choose to call it that, was not done here, either, by a long shot, Worthington. I had one of these machines in my wife's reception room. I have all sorts of little scraps of conversation," he boasted. "I also have an account of a visit there from two—er—scoundrels—"

"Mrs. Brainard to see you, sir," announced a boy at the door.

Constance had risen. Her face was flushed and her breast rose and fell with excitement.

"Mr. Brainard," she interrupted. "I must explain—confess. Mrs. Brainard has been sitting in my office listening to us over the microphone. I arranged it. I asked her to come down, using another name as a pretext. But I didn't think she would interrupt so soon. Before you see her—let me read this. It was a conversation I got after you had left last night and so far I have had no chance to tell you of it. Some one," she laid particular stress on the word, "came back after that first interview. Listen."

"No, Lee," Constance read rapidly from her notes, "no. Don't think I am ungrateful. You have been one friend in a thousand through all this. I shall have my decree-soon, now. Don't spoil it-"

"But Sybil, think of Mm. What did he ever care for you! He has made you free already."

"He is still my husband."

"Take this latest escapade with this Miss Dunlap."

"Well, what do I really know about that?"

"You saw him."

"Yes, but maybe it was as he said."

The door was flung open, interrupting Constance's reading, and Sybil Brainard entered. The artificiality of the beauty parlor was all gone. She was a woman, who had been wronged and deceived.

"Next friend—a true next friend—fiend would be better, Lee Worthington," she scorned. "How can you stand there and look me in the face, how could you tell me of your love for me, when all the time you cared no more for me or for any other woman than for that—that Leblanc! You knew that I, who was as jealous as I could be of Rodman, had heard a little—you added more. Yet when you had played on my feelings, you would have cast me off, too—I know it; I know your kind."

She paused for breath, then turned slowly to Brainard with a note of pathos in her voice.

"Our temperaments may have been different, Rodman. They were not when we were poor. Perhaps I have not developed with you, the way you want of me. But, Rodman, did you ever stop to think that perhaps, perhaps if I had ever had the chance to be taken into your confidence more often—"

"Will you—forgive me?" Brainard managed to blurt out.

"Will you forgive me?" she returned frankly.

"I—forgive? I have nothing to forgive."

"I could have understood, Rodman, if it had been Miss Dunlap. She is clever, wonderful. But that Leblanc—never!"

Sybil Brainard turned to Constance.

"Miss Dunlap—Mrs. Dunlap," she sobbed, "forgive me. You—you are a better woman than I am."

CHAPTER VI

THE CLAIRVOYANTS

"Do you believe in dreams?" Constance Dunlap looked searchingly at her interrogator, as if her face or manner betrayed some new side of her character.

Mrs. deForest Caswell was an attractive woman verging on forty, a chance acquaintance at a shoppers' tea room downtown who had proved to be an uptown neighbor.

"I have had some rather strange experiences, Mildred," confessed Constance tentatively. "Why!"

"Because—" the other woman hesitated, then added, "why should I not tell you! Last night, Constance, I had the strangest dream. It has left such an impression on me that I can't shake it off, although I have tried all day."

"Yes? Tell me about it."

Mildred Caswell paused a moment, then began slowly, as if not to omit anything from her story.

"I dreamt that Forest was dying. I could see him, could see the doctor and the nurse, everything. And yet somehow I could not get to him. I was afraid, with such an oppressive fear. I tried—oh, how I tried! I struggled, and how badly I felt!" and she shuddered at the very recollection.

"There seemed to be a wall," she resumed, "a narrow wall in the way and I couldn't get over it. As often as I tried, I fell. And then I seemed to be pursued by some kind of animal, half bull, half snake. I ran. It followed closely. I seemed to see a crowd of people and I felt that if I could only get to that crowd, somehow I would be safe, perhaps might even get over the wall and—I woke up—almost screaming."

The woman's face was quite blanched.

"My dear," remonstrated Constance, "you must not take it so. Remember—it was only a dream.

"I know it was only a dream," she said, "but you don't know what is back of it."

Mildred Caswell had from time to time hinted to Constance of the growing incompatibility of her married life, but as Constance was getting used to confidences, she had kept silent, knowing that her friend would tell her in time.

"You must have guessed," faltered Mrs. Caswell, "that Forest and I are not—not on the best of terms, that we are getting further and further apart."

It rather startled Constance to hear frankly stated what she already had observed. She wondered how far the estrangement had gone. The fact was that she had rather liked deForest Caswell, although she had only met her friend's husband a few times. In fact she was surprised that momentarily there flashed through her mind the query as to whether Mildred herself might be altogether blameless in the growing uncongeniality.

Mildred Caswell had drawn out of her chatelaine a bit of newspaper and handed it to Constance, not as if it was of any importance to herself but as if it would explain better than she could tell what she meant.

Constance read:

MME. CASSANDRA,
THE VEILED PROPHETESS

Born with a double veil, educated in occult mysteries in Egypt and India. Without asking a question, tells your name and reads your secret troubles and the remedy. Reads your dreams. Great questions of life quickly solved. Failure turned to success, the separated brought together, advice on all affairs of life, love, marriage, divorce, business, speculation, and investments. Overcomes all evil influences. Ever ready to help and advise those with capital to find a safe and paying investment. No fee until it succeeds. Could anything be fairer?

THE RETREAT, —
W. 47th Street.

"Won't you come with me to Madame Cassandra?" asked Mrs. Caswell, as Constance finished reading. "She always seems to do me so much good."

"Who is Madame Cassandra?" asked Constance, rereading the last part of the advertisement.

"I suppose you would call her a dream doctor," said Mildred.

It was a new idea to Constance, this of a dream doctor to settle the affairs of life. Only a moment she hesitated, then she answered simply, "Yes, I'll go."

"The retreat" was just off Longacre Square among quite a nest of fakers. A queue of automobiles before the place testified, however, to the prosperity of Madame Cassandra, as they entered the bronze grilled plate glass door and turned on the first floor toward the home of the Adept. Constance had an uncomfortable feeling as they entered of being watched behind the shades of the apartment. Still, they had no trouble in being admitted, and a soft-voiced colored attendant welcomed them.

The esoteric flat of Madame Cassandra was darkened except for the electric lights glowing in amber and rose-colored shades. There were several women there already. As they entered Constance had noticed a peculiar, dreamy odor. There did not seem to be any hurry, any such thing as time here, so skilfully was the place run. There was no noise; the feet sank in half-inch piles of rugs, and easy-chairs and divans were scattered about.

Once a puff of light smoke appeared, and Constance awoke to the fact that some were smoking little delicately gold-banded cigarettes. Indeed it was all quite recherche.

Mrs. Caswell took one from a maid. So did Constance, but after a puff or two managed to put it out and later to secure another which she kept.

Madame Cassandra herself proved to be a tall, slender, pale woman with dark hair and a magnetic eye, an eye that probably accounted more than anything else for her success. She was clad in a house gown of purplish silk which clung tightly to her, and at her throat a diamond pendant sparkled, as well as other brilliants on her long, slender fingers.

She met Mildred and Constance with outstretched hands.

"So glad to see you, my dears," purred Madame, leading the way into an inner sanctum.

Mrs. Caswell had seated herself with the air of one who worshiped at the shrine, while Constance gazed about curiously.

"Madame," she began a little tremulously, "I have had another of those dreadful dreams."

"You poor dear soul," soothed Madame, stroking her hand. "Tell me of it—all."

Quickly Mrs. Caswell poured forth her story as she had already told it to Constance.

"My dear Mrs. Caswell," remarked the high priestess slowly, when the story was complete, "it is all very simple. His love is dead. That is what you fear and it is the truth. The wall is the wall that he has erected against you. Try to forget it—to forget him. You would be better off. There are other things in the world—"

"Ah, but I cannot live as I am used to without money," murmured Mrs. Caswell.

"I know," replied Madame. "It is that that keeps many a woman with a brute. When financial and economic independence come, then woman will be free and only then. Now, listen. Would you like to be free—financially? You remember that delightful Mr. Davies who has been here? Yes? Well, he is a regular client of mine, now. He is a broker and never embarks in any enterprise without first consulting me. Just the other day I read his fortune in United Traction. It has gone up five points already and will go fifteen more. If you want, I will give you a card to him. Let me see—yes, I can do that. You too will be lucky in speculation."

Constance, with one ear open, had been busy looking about the room. In a bookcase she saw a number of books and paused to examine their titles. She was surprised to see among the old style dream books several works on modern psychology, particularly on the interpretation of dreams.

"Of course, Mrs. Caswell, I don't want to urge you," Madame was saying. "I have only pointed out a way in which you can be independent. And, you know, Mr. Davies is a perfect gentleman, so courteous and reliable. I know you will be successful if you take my advice and go to him."

Mildred said nothing for a few moments, but as she rose to go she remarked, "Thank you very much. I'll think about it. Anyhow, you've made me feel better."

"So kind of you to say it," murmured the Adept. "I'm sorry you must go, but really I have other appointments. Please come again—with your friend. Good-bye."

"What do you think of her?" asked Mrs. Caswell on the street.

"Very clever," answered Constance dubiously.

Mrs. Caswell looked up quickly. "You don't like her?"

"To tell the truth," confessed Constance quietly, "I have had too much experience in Wall Street myself to trust to a clairvoyant."

They had scarcely reached the corner before Constance again had that peculiar feeling which some psychologists have noted, of being stared at. She turned, but saw no one. Still the feeling persisted. She could stand it no longer.

"Don't think me crazy, Mildred," she said, "but I just have a desire to walk back a block."

Constance had turned suddenly. As she glanced keenly about she was aware of a familiar figure gazing into the window of an art store across the street. He had stopped so that although his back was turned he could, by a slight shift of his position, still see by means of a mirror in the window what was going on across the street behind him.

One look was enough. It was Drummond, the detective. What did it mean?

Neither woman said much as they rode uptown, and parted on the respective floors of their apartment house. Still Constance could not get out of her head the recollection of the dream doctor and of Drummond.

Restless, she determined that night to go down to the Public Library and see whether any of the books at the clairvoyant's were on the shelves. Fortunately she found some, found indeed that they were not all, as she had half suspected, the works of fakers but that quite a literature had been built up around the new psychology of dreams.

Deeply she delved into the fascinating subjects that had been opened by the studies of the famous Dr. Sigmund Freud of Vienna, and as she read she found that she began to understand much about Mrs. Caswell—and, with a start, about her own self.

At first she revolted against the unpleasant feature of the new dream philosophy—the irresistible conclusion that all humanity, underneath the shell, is sensuous or sensual in nature, that practically all dreams portray some delight of the senses and that sexual dreams are a large proportion of all visions. But the more she thought of it, the more clearly was she able to analyze Mrs. Caswell's dream and to get back at the causes of it, in the estrangement from her husband and perhaps the brutality of his ignorance of woman. And then, too, there was Drummond. What was he doing in the case?

She did not see Mildred Caswell again until the following afternoon. But then she seemed unusually bright in contrast with the depression of the day before. Constance was not surprised. Her intuition told her that something had happened and she hardly needed to guess that Mrs. Caswell had followed the advice of the clairvoyant and had been to see the wonderful Mr. Davies, to whom the mysteries of the stock market were an open book.

"Have you had any other dreams?" asked Constance casually.

"Yes," replied Mildred, "but not like the one that depressed me. Last night I had a very pleasant dream. It seemed that I was breakfasting with Mr. Davies. I remember that there was a hot coal fire in the grate. Then suddenly a messenger came in with news that United Traction had advanced twenty points. Wasn't it strange?"

Constance said nothing. In fact it did not seem strange to her at all. The strange thing to her, now that she was a sort of amateur dream reader herself, was that Mrs. Caswell did not seem to see the real import of her own dream.

"You have seen Mr. Davies to-day?" Constance ventured.

Mrs. Caswell laughed. "I wasn't going to tell you. You seemed so set against speculating in Wall Street. But since you ask me, I may as well admit it."

"When did you see him before?" went on Constance. "Did you have much invested with him already?"

Mrs. Caswell glanced up, startled. "My—you are positively uncanny, Constance. How did you know I had seen him before?"

"One seldom dreams," said Constance, "about anything unless it has been suggested by an event of the day before. You saw him today. That would not have inspired the dream of last night. Therefore I concluded that you must have seen him and invested before. Madame Cassandra's mention of him yesterday caused the dream of last night. The dream of last night probably influenced you to see him again to-day, and you invested in United Traction. That is the way dreams work. Probably more of conduct than we know is influenced by dream life. Now, if you should get fifteen or twenty points you would be in a fair way to join the ranks of those who believe that dreams do come true."

Mrs. Caswell looked at her almost alarmed, then attempted to turn it off with a laugh, "And perhaps breakfast with him?"

"When I do set up as interpreter of dreams," answered Constance simply, "I'll tell you more."

On one point she had made up her mind. That was to visit Mr. Davies herself the next day.

She found his office a typical bucket shop, even down to having a section partitioned off for women clients of the firm. She had not intended to risk anything, and so was prepared when Mr. Davies himself approached her courteously. Instinctively Constance distrusted him. He was too cordial, too polite. She could feel the claws hidden in his velvety paw, as it were. There was a debonnaire assurance about him, the air of a man who thought he understood women, and indeed did understand a certain type. But to Constance, who was essentially a man's woman, Davies was only revolting.

She managed to talk without committing herself, and he in his complacency was glad to hope that he was making a new customer. She had to be careful not to betray any of the real and extensive knowledge about Wall Street which she actually possessed. But the glib misrepresentations about United Traction quite amazed her.

When she rose to go, Davies accompanied her to the door, then out into the hall to the elevator. As he bent over to shake hands, she noted that he held her hand just a little longer than was necessary.

"He's a swindler of the first water," she concluded as she was whisked down in the elevator. "I'm sure Mildred is in badly with this crowd, one urging her on in her trouble, the other making it worse and fleecing her into the bargain."

At the entrance she paused, undecided which was the quickest route home. As by chance she turned just for a moment she thought she caught a fleeting glimpse of Drummond dodging behind a pillar. It was only for an instant but even that apparition was enough.

"I WILL get her out of this safely," resolved Constance. "I WILL keep one more fly from his web."

Constance felt as if, even now, she must see Mildred and, although she knew nothing, at least put her on her guard. She did not have long to wait for her chance. It was late in the afternoon when her door buzzer sounded.

"Constance, I've been looking for you all day," sighed Mildred, dropping sobbing into a chair. "I am—distracted."

"Why, my dear, what's the matter?" asked Constance. "Let me make you a cup of coffee."

Over the steaming little cups Mildred grew more calm.

"Forest has found out in some way that I am speculating in Wall Street," she confided at length. "I suppose some of his friends—he has lots down there—told him."

Momentarily the picture of Drummond back of the post in Davies' building flashed over Constance.

"And he is awfully angry. Oh, I never knew him to be so angry—and sarcastic, too."

"Was it wholly over your money?" asked Constance. "Was there nothing else?"

Mrs. Caswell started. "You grow more weird, every day, Constance. Yes—there was something else."

"Mr. Davies?"

Mildred had risen. "Don't—don't—" she cried.

"Then you do really—care for him!" asked Constance mercilessly.

"No—no, a thousand times—no. How can I? I have put all such thoughts out of my mind—long ago." She paused, then went on more calmly, "Constance, believe me or not—I am just as good a woman to-day as I was the day I married Forest. No—I would not even let the thought enter my head—never!"

For perhaps an hour after her friend had gone, Constance sat thinking. What should she do? Something must be done and soon. As she thought, suddenly the truth flashed over her.

Caswell had employed Drummond to shadow his wife in the hope that he might unearth something that might lead to a divorce. Drummond, like so many divorce detectives, was not averse to guiding events, to put it mildly. He had Ingratiated himself, perhaps, with the clairvoyant and Davies. Constance had often heard before of clairvoyants and brokers who worked in conjunction to fleece the credulous. Now another and more serious element than the loss of money was involved. Added to them was a divorce detective—and honor itself was at stake. She remembered the doped cigarettes. She had heard of them before at clairvoyants'. She saw it all—Madame Cassandra playing on Mildred's wounded affections, the broker on both that and her desire to be independent—and Drummond pulling the wires that all might take advantage of her woman's frailty.

That moment Constance determined on action.

First she telephoned to deForest Caswell at his office. It was an unconventional thing to do to ask him to call, but she made some plausible pretext. She was surprised to find that he accepted it without hesitating. It set her thinking. Drummond must have told him something of her and he had thought this as good a time as any to face her. In that case Drummond would probably come too. She was prepared.

She had intended to have one last talk with Mildred, but had no need to call her. Utterly wretched, the poor little woman came in again to see her as she had done scores of times before, to pour out her heart. Forest had not come home to dinner, had not even taken the trouble to telephone. Constance did not say that she herself was responsible.

"Do you really want to know the truth about your dreams?" asked Constance, after she had prevailed upon Mildred to eat a little.

"I do know," she returned.

"No, you don't," went on Constance, now determined to tell her the truth whether she liked it or not. "That clairvoyant and Mr. Davies are in league, playing you for a sucker, as they say."

Mrs. Caswell did not reply for a moment. Then she drew a long breath and shut her eyes. "Oh, you don't know how true what she says is to me. She—"

"Listen," interrupted Constance. "Mildred, I'm going to be frank, brutally frank. Madame Cassandra has read your character, not the character as you think it is, but your unconscious, subconscious self. She knows that there is no better way to enter into the intimate life of a client, according to the new psychology, than by getting at and analyzing the dreams. And she knows that you can't go far in dream analysis without finding sex. It is one of the strongest natural impulses, yet subject to the strongest repression, and hence one of the weakest points of our culture.

"She is actually helping along your alienation for that broker. You yourself have given me the clue in your dreams. Only I am telling you the truth about them. She holds it back and tells you plausible falsehoods to help her own ends. She is trying to arouse in you those passions which you have suppressed, and she has not scrupled to use drugged cigarettes with you and others to do it. You remember the breakfast dream, when I said that much could be traced back to dreams? A thing happens. It causes a dream. That in turn sometimes causes action. No, don't interrupt. Let me finish first.

"Take that first dream," continued Constance, rapidly thrusting home her interpretation so that it would have its full effect. "You dreamed that your husband was dying and you were afraid. She said it meant love was dead. It did not. The fact is that neurotic fear in a woman has its origin in repressed, unsatisfied love, love which for one reason or another is turned away from its object and has not succeeded in being applied. Then his death. That simply means that you have a feeling that you might be happier if he were away and didn't devil you. It is a survival of childhood, when death is synonymous with absence. I know you don't believe it. But if you had studied the subject as I have in the last few days you'd understand. Madame Cassandra understands.

"And the wall. That was Wall Street, probably, which does divide you two. You tried to get over it and you fell. That means your fear of actually falling, morally, of being a fallen woman."

Mildred was staring wildly. She might deny but in her heart she must admit.

"The thing that pursued you, half bull, half snake, was Davies and his blandishments. I have seen him. I know what he is. The crowd in a dream always denotes a secret. He is pursuing you, as in the dream. But he hasn't caught you. He thinks there is in you the same wild demimondaine instinct that with many an ardent woman, slumbers unknown in the back of her mind.

"Whatever you may say, you do think of him. When a woman dreams of breakfasting cozily with some one other than her husband it has an obvious meaning. As for the messenger and the message about the United Traction, there, too, was a plain wish, and, as you must see, wishes in one form or another, disguised or distorted, lie at the basis of dreams. Take the coal fire. That, too, is susceptible of interpretation. I think you must have heard the couplet:

"'No coal, no fire so hotly glows As the secret love that no one knows.'"

Mildred Caswell had risen, an indignant flush on her face.

Constance put her hand on her arm gently to restrain her, knowing that such indignation was the first sign that she had struck at the core of truth in her interpretation.

"My dear," she urged, "I'm only telling you the truth, for your own sake, and not to take advantage of you as Madame Cassandra is doing. Please—remember that the best evidence of your normal condition is just what I find, that absence of love would be abnormal. My dear, you are what the psychologists call a consciously frigid, unconsciously passionate woman. Consciously you reject this Davies; unconsciously you accept him. And it is the more dangerous, although you do not know it, because some one else is watching. It was not one of his friends who told your husband—"

Mrs. Caswell had paled. "Is—is there a—detective?" she faltered.

Constance nodded.

Mildred had collapsed completely. She was sobbing in a chair, her head bowed in her hands, her little lace handkerchief soaked. "What shall I do? What shall I do?"

There was a sudden tap at the door.

"Quick—in there," whispered Constance, shoving her through the portieres into the drawing room.

It was Forest Caswell.

For a moment Constance stood irresolute, wondering just how to meet him, then she said, "Good evening, Mr. Caswell. I hope you will pardon me for asking you to call on me, but, as you know, I've come to know your wife—perhaps better than you do."

"Not better," he corrected, seeming to see that it was directness that she was aiming at. "It is bad enough to get mixed up badly in Wall Street, but what would you yourself say—you are a business woman—what would you say about getting into the clutches of a—a dream doctor—and worse?"

He had put Constance on the defensive in a sentence.

"Don't you ever dream?" she asked quietly.

He looked at her a moment as if doubting even her mentality.

"Lord," he exclaimed in disgust, "you, too, defend it?"

"But, don't you dream?" she persisted.

"Why, of course I dream," he answered somewhat petulantly. "What of it? I don't guide my actions by it."

"Do you ever dream of Mildred?" she asked.

"Sometimes," he admitted reluctantly.

"Ever of other—er—people?" she pursued.

"Yes," he replied, "sometimes of other people. But what has that to do with it? I cannot help my dreams. My conduct I can help and I do help."

Constance had not expected him to be frank to the extent of taking her into his confidence. Still, she felt that he had told her just enough. She discerned a vague sense of jealousy in his tone which told her more than words that whatever he might have said or done to Mildred he resented, unconsciously, the manner in which she had striven to gain sympathy outside.

"Fortunately he knows nothing of the new theories," she said to herself.

"Mrs. Dunlap," he resumed, "since you have been frank with me, I must be equally frank with you. I think you are far too sensible a woman not to understand in just what a peculiar position my wife has placed me."

He had taken out of his pocket a few sheets of closely typewritten tissue paper. He did not look at them. Evidently he knew the contents by heart. Constance did not need to be told that this was a sheaf of the daily reports of the agency for which Drummond worked.

He paused. She had been watching him searchingly. She was determined not to let him justify himself first.

"Mr. Caswell," she persisted in a low, earnest tone, "don't be so sure that there is nothing in this dream, business. Before you read me those reports from Mr. Drummond, let me finish."

Forest Caswell almost dropped them in surprise.

"Dreams," she continued, seeing her advantage, "are wishes, either suppressed or expressed. Sometimes the dream is frank and shows an expressed wish. Other times it shows a suppressed wish, or a wish which in its fulfilment in the dream is disguised or distorted.

"You are the cause of your wife's dreams. She feels in them anxiety. And, according to the modern psychologists who have studied dreams carefully and scientifically, fear and anxiety represent love repressed or suppressed."

She paused to emphasize the point, glad to note that he was following her.

"That clairvoyant," she went on, "has found out the truth. True, it may not have been the part of wisdom for Mildred to have gone to her in the first place. I pass over that. I do not know whether you or she was most to blame at the start. But that woman, in the guise of being her friend, has played on every string of your wife's lonely heart, which you have wrung until it vibrates.

"Then," she hastened on, "came your precious friend Drummond, Drummond who has, no doubt, told you a pack of lies about me. You see that!"

She had flung down on the table a cigarette which she had managed to get at Madame Cassandra's.

"Smoke it."

He lighted it gingerly, took a puff or two, puckered his face, frowned, and rubbed the lighted end on the fireplace to extinguish it.

"What is it?" he asked suspiciously.

"Hashish," she answered tersely. "Things were not going fast enough to suit either Madame Cassandra or Drummond. Madame Cassandra helped along the dreams by a drug noted for its effect on the passions. More than that," added Constance, leaning over toward him and catching his eye, "Madame Cassandra was working in league with a broker, as so many of the fakers do. Drummond knew it, whether he told you the truth about it or not. That broker was a swindler named Davies."

She was watching the effect on him. She saw that he had been reserving this for a last shot at her, that he realized she had stolen his own ammunition and appropriated it to herself.

"They were only too glad when Drummond approached them. There you are, three against that poor little woman—no, four, including yourself. Perhaps she was foolish. But it was not so much to her discredit as to those who cast her adrift when she had a natural right to protection. Here was a woman with passions which she herself did not understand, and a little money—alone. Her case appealed to me. I knew her dreams. I studied them."

Caswell was listening in amazement. "It is dangerous to be with a person who pays attention to such little things," he said.

Evidently Drummond himself must have been listening. The door buzzer sounded and he stepped in, perhaps to bolster up his client in case he should be weakening.

As he met Constance's eye he smiled superciliously and was about to speak. But she did not give him time even to say good evening.

"Ask him," she cried, her eyes flashing, for she realized that it had been part of the plan to confront her, perhaps worm out of her just enough to confirm Drummond's own story to Caswell, "ask him to tell the truth—if he is capable of it—not the truth that will make a good daily report of a hired shadow who colors his report the way he thinks his client desires it, but the real truth."

"Mr. Caswell," interrupted Drummond, "this woman—"

"Mr. Drummond," cried Constance, rising and shaking the burnt stub of the little gold-banded cigarette at him to impress it on his mind, "Mr. Drummond, I don't care whether I am a—a she-devil"—she almost hissed the words at him—"but I have evidence enough to go before the district attorney of this city and the grand jury and get indictments for conspiracy against a certain clairvoyant and a bucket shop operator. To save themselves, they will probably tell all they know about a certain crook who has been using them."

Caswell looked at her, amazed at her denunciation of the detective. As for Drummond, he turned his back on her as if to ignore her utterly.

"Mr. Caswell," he said bitterly, "in those reports—"

"Forest Caswell," insisted Constance, rising and facing him, "if you have in that heart of yours one shred of manhood it should move you. You—this man—the others—have placed in the path of a woman every provocation, every temptation for financial, physical, and moral ruin. She has consulted a clairvoyant—yes. She has speculated—yes. Yet she was proof against something greater than that. And I know—because I know her unconscious self which her dreams reveal, her inmost soul—I know her better than you do, better than she does herself. I know that even now she is as good and true and would be as loving as—"

Constance had paused and taken a step toward the drawing room. Before she knew it, the portieres flew apart and an eager little woman had rushed past her and flung her arms about the neck of the man.

Caswell's features were working, as he gently disengaged her arms, still keeping one hand. Half shoving her aside, ignoring Constance, he had faced Drummond. For a moment the brazen detective flinched.

As he did so, deForest Caswell crumpled up the mass of tissue paper reports and flung them into the fireplace.

"Get out!" he said, suppressing his voice with difficulty. "Send me—your bill. I'll pay it—but, mind, if it is one penny more than it should be, I'll—I'll fight if it takes me from the district attorney and the grand jury to the highest court of the State. Now—go!"

Caswell turned slowly again toward his wife.

"I've been a brute," he said simply.

Something almost akin to jealousy rose in Constance's heart as she saw Mildred, safe at last.

Then Caswell turned slowly to her. "You," he said, stroking his wife's hand gently but looking at Constance, "you are a REAL clairvoyant."

CHAPTER VII

THE PLUNGERS

"They have the most select clientele in the city here."

Constance Dunlap was sitting in the white steamy room of Charmant's Beauty Shop. Her informant, reclining dreamily in a luxurious wicker chair, bathed in the perspiring vapor, had evidently taken a fancy to her.

"And no wonder, either; they fix you up so well," she rattled on; then confidingly, "Now, last night after the show a party of us went to supper and a dance—and it was in the wee small hours when we broke up. But Madame here can make you all over again. Floretta," she called to an attendant who had entered, "if Mr. Warrington calls up on the 'phone, say I'll call him later."

"Yes, Miss Larue."

Constance glanced up quickly as Floretta mentioned the name of the popular young actress. Stella Larue was a pretty girl on whom the wild dissipation of the night life of New York was just beginning to show its effects. The name of Warrington, too, recalled to Constance instantly some gossip she had heard in Wall Street about the disagreement in the board of directors of the new Rubber Syndicate and the effort to oust the president whose escapades were something more than mere whispers of scandal.

This was the woman in the case. Constance looked at Stella now with added interest as she rose languidly, drew her bathrobe about her superb figure carelessly in such a way as to show it at best advantage.

"I've had more or less to do with Wall Street myself," observed Constance.

"Oh, have you? Isn't that interesting," cried Stella.

"I hope you're not putting money in Rubber?" queried Constance.

"On the contrary," rippled Stella, then added, "You're going to stay? Let me tell you something. Have Floretta do your hair. She's the best here. Then come around to see me in the dormitory if I'm here when you are through, won't you?"

Constance promised and Stella fluttered away like the pretty butterfly that she was, leaving Constance to wonder at the natural gravitation of plungers in the money market toward plungers in the white lights.

Charmant's Beauty Parlor was indeed all its name implied, a temple of the cult of adornment, the last cry in the effort to satisfy what is more than health, wealth, and happiness to some women—the fundamental feminine instinct for beauty.

Constance had visited the beauty specialist to have an incipient wrinkle smoothed out. Frankly, it was not vanity. But she had come to realize that her greatest asset was her personal appearance. Once that had a chance to work, her native wit and keen ability would carry her to success.

Madame Charmant herself was a tall, dark-skinned, dark-haired, dark-eyed, well-groomed woman who looked as if she had been stamped from a die for a fashion plate—and then the die had been thrown away. All others like her were spurious copies, counterfeits. More than that, she affected the name of Vera, which in itself had the ring of truth.

And so Charmant had prevailed on Constance to take a full course in beautification and withhold the wrinkle at the source.

"Besides, you know, my dear," she purred, "there's nothing discovered by the greatest minds of the age that we don't apply at once."

Constance was not impervious to feminine reason, and here she was.

"Has Miss Larue gone?" she asked when at last she was seated in a comfortable chair again sipping a little aromatic cup of coffee.

"No, she's resting in one of the little dressing rooms."

She followed Floretta down the corridor. Each little compartment had its neat, plain white enameled bed, a dresser and a chair.

Stella smiled as Constance entered. "Yes," she murmured in response to the greeting, "I feel quite myself now."

"Mr. Warrington on the wire," announced Floretta a moment later, coming down the corridor again with a telephone on a long unwinding wire.

"Hello, Alfred—oh, rocky this morning," Constance overheard. "I said to myself, 'Never again—until the nest time. Vera? Oh, she was as fresh as a lark. Can I lunch with you downtown? Of course.'" Then as she hung up the receiver she called, "Floretta, get me a taxi."

"Yes, Miss Larue."

"I always have a feeling here," whispered Stella, "that I am being listened to. I mean to speak to Vera about it some time. By the way, wouldn't you like to join us to-night? Vera will be along and Mr. Warrington and perhaps 'Diamond Jack' Braden—you know him?"

Constance confessed frankly that she did not have the pleasure of the acquaintance of the well-known turfman and first nighter.

She hesitated. Perhaps it was that that Stella liked. Almost any one else would have been overeager to accept. But to Constance, sure of herself now, nothing of the sort was worth scrambling for. Besides, she was wondering how a man with the fight of his life on his hands could find time to lunch downtown even with Stella.

"I've taken quite a fancy to you," pressed Stella.

"Thank you, it's very kind of you," Constance answered. "I shall try very hard to be there."

"I'll leave a box for you at the office. Come around after the performance to my dressing room."

"Miss Larue, your taxi's waiting," announced Floretta.

"Thanks. Are you going now, Mrs. Dunlap? Yes? Then ride

down in the elevator with me."

They parted at the foot of the elevator and Constance walked through the arcade of the office building in which the beauty parlor occupied the top floor. She stopped at a florist's stand to admire the flowers, but more for an excuse to look back at Stella.

As Stella stepped into a taxicab, showing a generous wealth of silken hosiery beneath the tango gown, Constance was aware that the driver of another cab across the street was also interested. She noticed that he turned and spoke to his fare through the open window.

The cab swung around to follow the other and Constance caught a fleeting glimpse of a familiar face.

"Drummond," she exclaimed almost aloud.

What did it mean? Why had the detective been employed to follow Stella? Instinctively she concluded that he must be engaged by Mrs. Warrington.

"I must accept Stella's invitation," she said to herself excitedly. "At least, she should be put on her guard."

That evening, as she was looking over the newspapers, her eye caught the item in the Wall Street edition:

RUBBER SYNDICATE DISSENSION

Break in Stock Follows Effort of Strong Minority to Oust Warrington from Presidency

Then followed a brief account of the struggle of a powerful group of directors to force Warrington, Braden, and the rest out, with a hint at the scandal of which every one now was talking.

"I never yet knew a man who went in for that sort of thing that lasted long in business," she observed. "This is my chance—a crowd riding for a fall."

Constance chose a modest orchestra seat in preference to the place in a box which Stella had reserved for her at the office, and, aside from the purpose which was rapidly taking shape in her mind, she enjoyed the play very much. Stella Larue, as the "Grass Widow," played her part with a piquancy which Constance knew was not wholly a matter of book knowledge.

As the curtain went down, the audience, its appetite for the risque whetted, filed out on Broadway with its myriad lights and continuous film of motion. Constance made her way around to Stella's dressing room.

She had scarcely been welcomed by Stella, whose cheeks beneath the grease paint were now genuinely ablaze with excitement, when a man entered. He was tall, spare, the type whose very bow is ingratiating and whose "delighted, I assure you" is suave and compelling.

Alfred Warrington seemed to be on very good terms indeed with Stella as she introduced him to Constance.

"You will join us, Mrs. Dunlap?" he asked, throwing an opera cloak over Stella's shoulders. "Vera Charmant and Jack Braden are waiting for us at the Little Montmartre."

As he mentioned the famous cabaret, Constance took a little tighter grip on herself and decided to take the plunge and see the affair out, although that sort of thing had very little attraction for her.

They were leaving the theater when she saw lurking in the crowd the familiar figure of Drummond. She turned her head quickly and sank back into the dark recesses of the limousine.

Should she tell them now about him?

She leaned over to Warrington. "I saw a man in the crowd just now who seemed to be quite interested in us," she said quickly. "Can't we drive around a bit to throw him off if he should get into a cab?"

Warrington looked at her keenly. It was quite evident that he thought it was Constance who was being followed, not Stella or himself. Constance decided quickly to say nothing more that would prejudice Stella, but as Warrington directed his driver to run up through the park she saw that, far from alarming him, the words had only added a zest of mystery about herself.

They left the Park and the car jolted them quickly now over the uneven asphalt to the palace of pleasure, where already the two advance guards were holding one of the best tables in a house crowded with all classes from debutantes to debauchees.

"Diamond Jack" Braden was a heavy-set man with a debonnaire, dapper way about him. He wore a flower in his buttonhole, a smart touch which seemed very fetching, evidently, to the artistic Vera.

Constance fell to studying him, as she did all men and women. "His hands betray him," she said to herself, as she was introduced.

They were in fact shielded from view as he bowed, one with the thumb tucked in the corner of his trousers pocket, the other behind his back.

"He is hiding something," flashed through her mind intuitively. And, when she analyzed it, she felt still that there was nothing fanciful about the idea. It was simply a little unconscious piece of evidence.

From the start the cabaret was pretty rapid. When they entered, two of the performers were rendering the Apache dance with an abandon that improved on its namesake. Scarcely had they finished when the orchestra began all over again, and a couple of diners from the tables glided past them on the dancing floor, then another couple and another.

"Tanguez-vous?" bowed Braden, leaning over to Stella.

"Oui, je tanguerai," she nodded, catching the spirit of the place.

It left Warrington and Constance at the table with Vera, and as Constance looked eagerly after the graceful form of the little actress, Warrington asked, "Will you dance!"

"No, thank you," she said, trying him out. "I haven't had time to learn these new steps. And, besides, I have had a bad day in the market. Steel, Reading, everything is off. Not that I have lost much—but it's what I haven't made."

Warrington, who had been about to repeat his question to Vera, turned suddenly. This was something new to him, to meet a woman like Constance. If she knew about other stocks, she must know about the Syndicate. Already he had felt an attraction toward Constance physically, an attraction of maturity which somehow or other seemed more satisfying, at least novel, in contrast with, the gay butterfly talk of Stella.

He did not ask Vera to dance. Instead he began banteringly to discuss Wall Street and in five minutes he found out that she really knew as much about certain features of the game as he did. She did not need to be told that Alfred Warrington, plunger, man about town, was quite unexpectedly struck by her personality.

Now and then she could see Stella eyeing her covertly. The little actress had had, like many another, a few dollars to invest or rather with which to speculate. Her method had been usually to make a quick profit on a tip from some Wall Street friend. Often, if the tip went wrong, the friend would return the money to the unsuspecting little girl, with some muttered apology about having been unable to get it placed in time, and then, as the market went down or up, seeing that it was too late, adding a congratulation that at least the principal was saved if there was no profit.

The little actress was plainly piqued. She saw, though she did not understand, that Constance was a different kind of plunger from what she had thought at first up at Charmant's. Instead of trying to compete with Constance in her field, she redoubled her efforts in her own. Was Warrington, a live spender, to slip through her grasp for a chance acquaintance?

Another dance. This time it was Stella and Warrington. Braden, who had served excellently as a foil to lead Warrington on when he had eyes for no one else, not even Vera, was left severely alone. Nothing was said, not an action done openly, but Constance, woman-like, could feel the contest in the air. And she felt just a little quiver when they sat down and Warrington resumed the conversation with her where he had left it. Even the daring cut of Stella's gown and the exaggerated proximity of her dainty person had failed this time.

As they chatted gaily, Constance enjoyed her triumph to the full. Yes, she could see that Stella was violently jealous. But she intended that she should be. That was now a part of her plan as it shaped itself in her mind, since she had plunged or, perhaps better, had been dragged into the game.

As the evening wore on and the dancing became more furious, Warrington seemed to catch the spirit of reckless-ness that was in the very air. He talked more recklessly, once in a while with a bitterness not aimed at any one in particular, which passed among the others as blase sarcasm of one who had seen much and to whom even the fastest was slow.

But to Constance, as she tried to fathom him, it presented an entirely different interpretation. For example, she asked herself, why had he been so ready, apparently, to transfer his interest from Stella? Was it because, having cut loose from the one feminine tie that morally bound him, he no longer felt any restraint in cutting loose from others? Was it the same spirit that had carried him on in the money game, having cut loose from one financial principle, to let all go and to guide his course as close to the edge of things as he dared? There had been the same reckless bravado in the way he had urged on the driver of his car in the wild ride of the earlier evening, violating the speed laws yet succeeding in escaping the traffic squad.

Warrington was a plunger. Yet there was something about him that was different from others she had seen. Perhaps it was that he had a conscience, even though he had succeeded in detaching himself from it.

And Stella. There was something different about her, too. Constance more than once was on the point of revising her estimate of the little actress. Was she, after all, wholly mercenary in her attitude toward Warrington? Was he merely a live spender whom she could not afford to lose? Or was she merely a beautiful, delicate creature caught in the merciless maelstrom of the life into which she had been thrown? Did she realize the perilous position this all was placing her in?

They were among the last to leave and Vera and Braden offered to take Constance to her apartment in Braden's car, while Stella contrived prettily to take so much of Warrington's time with the wraps that by the time they were ready to go the manner of the breaking up of the party was as she wanted it. In her final triumph she could not help just an extra inflection on, "I hope I'll see you again at Vera's soon, my dear."

All night, or at least all that was left of it, Constance tried to straighten out the whirl of her thoughts. With the morning she had an idea. Now, in a moment when the exhilaration of the gay life was at low ebb, she must see Stella.

It was early yet, but Stella was not at her hotel when Constance cautiously called up the office to find out. Where was she? Constance drove around to Charmant's on the chance that she might be there. Vera greeted her a trifle coldly, she thought, but then this was not midnight at the Montmartre. No, Stella was not there, she said, but nevertheless Constance decided to wait.

"I'm all unstrung," confided Constance, with an assumed air of languor, as she dropped into a chair.

Charmant, as fresh as if she had just emerged from the

proverbial bandbox, nodded knowingly. "A Turkish bath, massage, something to tone you up," she advised.

With alert eyes Constance went patiently through the process of freshening, first in the steamy hot room where she had met Stella the day before, then the deliciously cool shower, gentle massage, and all the rest.

At one of the little white tables of the manicures she noticed a pretty, rather sad-faced little woman. There was something about her that attracted Constance's attention, although she could not have told exactly what it was.

"You know her?" whispered Floretta, bursting with excitement. "No? Why,—" and here she paused and dropped her voice even lower,—"that's Mrs. Warrington."

"Not the—"

"Yes," she nodded, "his wife. You know, she comes here twice a week. We have to do some tall scheming to keep them apart. No, it's not vanity, either. It's—well—you see, she's trying to get him back, to look like a sport."

Constance thought of the hopeless fight so far which the little woman was waging to keep up with the dashing actress. Then she thought of Warrington, of last night, of how he had sought her, so ready, it seemed, to leave even the "other woman." Then Floretta's remark repeated itself mechanically. "We have to do some tall scheming to keep them apart." Was Stella here, after all?

Mrs. Warrington was not a bad looking woman and in fact it was difficult to see how she expected to be improved by cosmetics that would lighten her complexion, bleaches that would flaxen her hair, tortures for this, that, and the other defect, real or imagined.

Now, however, she was a creature of reinforcements, from her puffy masses of light hair to her French heels and embroidered stockings that showed through the slash in the drapery of her gown.

Constance felt sorry for her, deeply sorry. The whole thing seemed not in keeping with her. She was a home-maker, not a butterfly. Was Warrington worth it all? asked Constance of herself. "At least she thinks so," flashed over her, as Mrs. Warrington rose, and left the room, watchfully guided by Floretta to the next process in her course in beautification.

Constance sank back luxuriously on the cushions of her chaise longue. She longed to explore the beauty parlor, to leave the rest room and go down the narrow corridor, prying into the secrets of the little dressing rooms that opened into it. What did they conceal? Why had Vera seemed so distant? Was it the natural reaction of the "morning after," or was Stella really there and was she keeping her away from Mrs. Warrington to prevent friction between two clients that would have been annoying to all?

She could reach no conclusion, except that there was a feeling of luxurious well-being as she lolled back into the deep recesses of the lounge in the corner of the room separated from the next room by a thin board partition.

Suddenly her attention was arrested by muffled voices on the other side of the partition. She strained her ears. She could not, of course, see the speakers, or even recognize their voices, but they were a man and a woman.

"We must get the thing settled right away," she overheard the man's voice. "You see how he is? Every new face attracts him. See how he took to that new one last night. Who knows what may happen? By and by some one may come along and spoil all."

"Couldn't we use her?" asked the woman.

"No, you can't use that woman. She's too clever. But we must do something, right away—to-night if possible."

A pause. "How, then?"

Another pause and the whispered monosyllable, "Dope!"

"What?"

"I have it here. Use a dozen of them. They can be snuffed as a powder, or it can be put in a drink. If you want more—see, I will put the bottle on this shelf—'way back. No one will see it."

"Don't you think I ought to write a note, something that will be sure to get him up here?"

"Yes—just a line or two—as if in haste."

There was a sound as if of tearing a sheet of note paper from a pad.

"Is that all right?"

"Yes. As soon as the market closes. There will be nothing done to-day. To-morrow's the day. To-night we must get him going and in the meantime a meeting will be held, the plan arranged at the Prince Henry to-night—and then the smash. Between them all, he won't know what has struck him."

"All right. You had better go out as you came in. It's better that no one up here should suspect anything."

The voices ceased.

What did it mean! Constance rose and sauntered around into the next room. It was empty, but when she looked hastily up on the shelf there was a bottle of white tablets and on a table a pad of note paper from which a sheet had been torn.

She picked up the bottle gingerly. Who had touched it? Her mind was working quickly. Somewhere she had read of finger prints and the subject had interested her because the system had been introduced in banks and she saw that it was going to become more and more important.

But how did they get them in a case like this? She had read of some powder that adhered to the marks left by the sweat glands of the fingers. There was the talcum powder. Perhaps it would do.

Quickly she shook the box gently over the glass. Then she blew it off carefully.

Clear, sharp, distinct, there were the imprints of fingers!

But the paper. Talcum powder would not bring them out on that. It must be something black.

A lead pencil! Eagerly she seized it and with, a little silver pen-knife whittled off the wood. Scrape! scrape! until she had a neat little pile of finely powdered graphite.

Then she poured it on the paper and taking the sheet daintily by the edges, so that she would not mix her own finger prints with the others, she rolled the powder back and forth. As she looked anxiously she could see the little grains adhering to the paper.

A fine camel's hair brush lay on the table, for penciling. She took it deftly. It made her think of that first time when she painted the checks for Carlton. A lump came into her throat.

There they were, the second pair of telltale prints. But what tale did they tell? Whose were they?

Her reading on finger prints had been very limited but, like everything she did, to the point. She studied those before her, traced out as best she could the loops, whorls, arches, and composites, even counted the ridges on some of them. It was not so difficult, after all.

She stopped in an uptown branch of her brokers in one of the hotels. The market was very quiet, and even the Rubber Syndicate seemed to be marking time. As she went out she passed the telephone booths. Should she call up Warrington? Would he misinterpret it? What if he did? She was mistress of her own tongue. She need not say too much. Besides, if she were going on a fishing expedition, a telephone line was as good as any other—better than a visit.

"This is Mrs. Dunlap," she said directly.

"Oh, how do you do, Mrs. Dunlap. I have been intending to call you up, but," he paused, and added, "you know we are having a pretty strenuous time down here."

There was a genuine ring to the first part of his reply. But the rest of it trailed off into the old blase tone.

"I'm sorry," she replied. "I enjoyed last night so much."

"Did you?" came back eagerly.

Before he could add anything she asked, "I suppose you are going to see Stella again this afternoon."

"Why—er—yes," he hesitated. "I think so."

"Where? At Vera's?" she asked, adopting a tone not of curiosity but of chiding him for seeing Stella instead of herself.

The moment of hesitation, before he said that he didn't know, told her the truth. It was as good as a plain, "Yes."

For a few moments they chatted. As she hung up the receiver after his deferential goodbye, Constance knew that she had gained a new angle from which to observe Warrington's character. He was intensely human and he was "in wrong." Here was a mess, all around.

The day wore on, yet brought no indecision as to what she would do, though it brought no solution as to how to do it. The inaction was worse than anything else. The last quotations had come in over the ticker, showing the Syndicate stocks still unchanged. She left her brokers and sat for a few moments in the rotunda of the hotel, considering. She could stand it no longer. Whatever happened, she would run around to Charmant's. Some excuse would occur when she got there.

As Constance alighted from the private elevator, a delicate scent as of attar of roses smote lightly on her, and there was, if anything, a greater air of exotic warmth about the place. Everything, from the electric bulbs buried deep in the clusters of amber artificial flowers to the bright green leaves on the dainty trellises, the little square-paned windows and white furniture, bespoke luxury. There was an inviting "tone" to it all.

"I'm glad I've found you," began Constance to Stella, as though nothing had happened. "There is something I'd like to say to you besides thanking you most kindly for the good time last—"

"Is there anything I can do for you?" interrupted Madame Charmant in a business like tone. "I am sure that Miss Larue invited you last night because she thought you were lonely. She and Mr. Warrington, you know, are old friends."

Charmant emphasized the remark to mean, "You trespassed on forbidden ground, if you thought you could get him away."

Constance seemed not to notice the implication.

"There is something I'd like to say," she repeated gently.

She picked up a little inking pad which lay on a mahogany secretary which Vera used as an office desk.

"If you will be so kind, Stella, as to place your fingers flat on this pad-never mind about the ink; call Floretta; she will wipe them off afterwards-and then on this piece of paper, I won't bother you further."

Almost before she knew it, the little actress had placed her dainty white hand on the pad and then on the paper.

Constance did the same, to illustrate, then called Floretta. "If Vera will do as I have done," she said, offering her the pad, and taking her hand. Charmant complied, and when Floretta arrived her impressions were added to the others.

"There's a man wishes to see you, outside, Madame," said Floretta, wiping off the soiled finger tips.

"Tell him to wait—in the little room."

Floretta opened the door to go out and through it Constance caught sight of a familiar face.

A moment later the man was in the room with them. It was Drummond, the same sneer, the same assurance in his manner.

"So," he snarled at Constance. "You here?"

"I seem to be here," she answered calmly. "Why?"

"Never mind why," he blustered. "I knew you saw me the other night. I heard you tell 'em to hit it up so as to shake me. But I found out all right."

"Found out what?" asked Constance coldly.

"Say, that's about your style, isn't it? You always get in when it comes to trimming the good spenders, don't you?"

"Mr. Drummond," she replied, "I don't care to talk to you."

"You don't, hey? Well, perhaps, when the time comes you'll have to talk. How about that?"

She was thinking rapidly. Was Mrs. Warrington preparing to strike a blow that would be the last impulse necessary to send the plunger down for the last time? She decided to take a chance, to temporize until some one else made a move.

"I'd thank you to place your fingers on this pad," said Constance quietly. "I'm making a collection of these things."

"You are, are you?"

"Yes," she cut short. "And if my collection isn't large enough I shall call up Mrs. Warrington and ask her to come over, too," she added significantly.

Floretta entered again. "Please wipe the ink off Mr. Drummond's fingers," ordered Constance quietly, still holding out the pad.

"Confound your impudence," he ground out, seizing the pad. "There! What do you mean by Mrs. Warrington? What has she to do with this? Have a care, Mrs. Dunlap—you're on the wrong track here, and going the wrong way."

"Mr. Warrington is—" began Floretta.

"Show him in—quick," demanded Constance, determined to bring the affair to a show-down on the spot.

As the door swung open, Warrington looked at the group in unfeigned surprise.

"Mr. Warrington," greeted Constance without giving any of the others a chance, "this morning, I heard a little conversation up here. Floretta, will you go into the little room, and on the top shelf you will find a bottle. Bring it here carefully. I have a sheet of paper, also, which I am going to show you. I had already seen the little woman, Mr. Warrington, whom you have treated so unjustly. She was here trying vainly to win you back by those arts which she thinks must appeal to you."

Floretta returned with the bottle and placed it on the secretary beside Constance.

"Some one took some tablets from this bottle and gave them to some one else who wrote on this paper," she resumed, bending first over the paper she had torn from the pad. "Ah, a loop with twelve ridges, another loop, a whorl, a whorl, a loop. The marks on this paper correspond precisely with those made here just now by—Vera Charmant herself!"

"You get out of here—quick," snarled Drummond, placing himself between the now furious Vera and Constance.

"One minute," replied Constance calmly. "I am sure Mr. Warrington is a gentleman, if you are not. Perhaps I have no finger prints to correspond with those on the bottle. If not, I am sure that we can send for some one whose prints will do so."

She was studying the bottle.

"The other, however," she said slowly to conceal her own surprise, "was a person who has been set to trail you and Stella, Mr. Warrington, a detective named Drummond!"

Suddenly the truth flashed over her. Drummond was not employed by Mrs. Warrington at all. Then by whom? By the directors. And the rest of these people? Grafters who were using Stella to bait the hook. Braden had gone over to them, had aided in plunging Warrington into the wild life until he could no longer play the business game as before. Charmant was his confederate, Drummond his witness.

"Stella," said Constance, turning suddenly to the little actress, "Stella, they are using you, 'Diamond Jack' and Vera, using you to lead him on, playing the game of the minority of the directors of the Syndicate to get him out. There is to be a meeting of the directors to-night at the Prince Henry. He was to be in no condition to go. Are you willing to be mixed up in such a scandal?"

Stella Larue was crying into a lace handkerchief. "You—you

are all—against me," she sobbed. "What have I done?"

"Nothing," soothed Constance, patting her shoulder. "As for Charmant and Drummond, they are tied by these proofs," she added, tapping the papers with the prints, then picking them up and handing them to Warrington. "I think if the story were told to the directors at the Prince Henry to-night with reporters waiting downstairs in the lobby, it might produce a quieting effect."

Warrington was speechless. He saw them all against him, Vera, Braden, Stella, Drummond.

"More than that," added Constance, "nothing that you can ever do can equal the patience, the faith of the little woman I saw here to-day, slaving, yes, slaving for beauty. Here in my hand, in these scraps of paper, I hold your old life,—not part of it, but ALL of it," she emphasized. "You have your chance. Will you take it?"

He looked up quickly at Stella Larue. She had risen impulsively and flung her arms about Constance.

"Yes," he muttered huskily, taking the papers, "all of it."

CHAPTER VIII

THE ABDUCTORS

"Take care of me—please—please!"

A slip of a girl, smartly attired in a fur-trimmed dress and a chic little feather-tipped hat, hurried up to Constance Dunlap late one afternoon as she turned the corner below her apartment.

"It isn't faintness or illness exactly—but—it's all so hazy," stammered the girl breathlessly. "And I've forgotten who I am. I've forgotten where I live—and a man has been following me—oh, ever so long."

The weariness in the tone of the last words caused Constance to look more closely at the girl. Plainly she was on the verge of hysterics. Tears were streaming down her pale cheeks and there were dark rings under her eyes, suggestive of a haunting fear of something from which she fled.

Constance was astounded for the moment. Was the girl crazy? She had heard of cases like this, but to meet one so unexpectedly was surely disconcerting.

"Who has been following you!" asked Constance gently,

looking hastily over her shoulder and seeing no one.

"A man," exclaimed the girl, "but I think he has gone now."

"Can't you think of your name!" urged Constance. "Try."

"No," cried the girl, "no, I can't, I can't."

"Or your address?" repeated Constance. "Try—try hard!"

The girl looked vacantly about.

"No," she sobbed, "it's all gone—all."

Puzzled, Constance took her arm and slowly walked her up the street toward her own apartment in the hope that she might catch sight of some familiar face or be able to pull herself together.

But it was of no use.

They passed a policeman who eyed them sharply. The mere sight of the blue-coated officer sent a shudder through the already trembling girl on her arm.

"Don't, don't let them take me to a hospital—don't," pleaded the girl in a hoarse whisper when they had passed the officer.

"I won't," reassured Constance. "Was that the man who was following you?"

"No—oh, no," sobbed the girl nervously looking back.

"Who was he, then?" asked Constance eagerly.

The girl did not answer, but continued to look back wildly

from time to time, although there was no doubt that, if he existed at all, the man had disappeared.

Suddenly Constance realized that she had on her hands a case of aphasia, perhaps real, perhaps induced by a drug.

At any rate, the fear of being sent away to an institution was so strong in the poor creature that Constance felt intuitively how disastrous to her might be the result of disregarding the obsession.

She was in a quandary. What should she do with the girl? To leave her on the street was out of the question. She was now more helpless than ever.

They had reached the door of the apartment. Gently she led the trembling girl into her own home.

But now the question of what to do arose with redoubled force. She hesitated to call a physician, at least yet, because his first advice would probably be to send the poor little stranger to the psychopathic ward of some hospital.

Constance's eye happened to rest on the dictionary in her bookcase. Perhaps she might recall the girl's name to her, if she were not shamming, by reading over the list of women's names in the back of the book.

It meant many minutes, perhaps hours. But then Constance reflected on what might have happened to the girl if she had chanced to appeal to some one who had not felt a true interest in her. It was worth trying. She would do it.

Starting with "A," she read slowly.

"Is your name Abigail?"

Down through Barbara, Camilla, Deborah, Edith, Faith, she read.

"Flora?" she asked.

The girl seemed to apprehend something, appear less blank.

"Florence?" persisted Constance.

"Oh, yes," she cried, "that's it—that's my name."

But as for the last name and the address she was just as hazy as ever. Still, there was now something different about her.

"Florence—Florence what?" reiterated Constance patiently.

There was no answer. But with the continued repetition it seemed as if some depth in her nature had been stirred. Constance could not help feeling that the girl had really found herself.

She had risen and was facing Constance, both hands pressed to her throbbing temples as if to keep her head from bursting. Constance had assisted her off with her coat and hat, and now the sartorial wreck of her masses of blonde hair was apparent.

"I suppose," she cried incoherently, "I'm just one more of the thousands of girls who drop out of sight every year."

Constance listened in amazement. As the spell of her influence seemed to calm the overwrought mind of the girl there succeeded a hardness in her tone that was wholly out of keeping with her youth. There was something that breathed of a past where there should have been nothing but the thought of a future.

"Tell me why," soothed Constance with an air that invited confidence.

The girl looked up and again passed her hand over her white forehead with its mass of tangled fallen hair. Somehow Constance felt a tingling sensation of sympathy in her heart. Impulsively she put out her hand and took the cold moist hand of the girl.

"Because," she hesitated, struggling now with re-flooding consciousness, "because—I don't know. I thought, perhaps—" she added, dropping her eyes, "you could—help me."

She was speaking rapidly enough now, "I think they have employed detectives to trace me. One of them is almost up with me. I'm afraid I can't slip out of the net again. And—I—I won't go back to them. I can't. I won't."

"Go back to whom?" queried her friend. "Detectives employed by whom?"

"My folks," she answered quickly.

Constance was surprised. Least of all had she expected that.

"Why won't you go home?" she prompted as the girl seemed about to lapse into a sort of stolid reticence.

"Home?" she repeated bitterly. "Home? No one would believe my story. I couldn't go home, now. They have made it impossible for me to go home. I mean, every newspaper has published my picture. There were headlines for days, and only by chance I was not recognized."

She was sobbing now convulsively. "If they had only let me alone! I might have gone back, then. But now—after the newspapers and the search—never! And yet I am going to have revenge some day. When he least expects it I am going to tell the truth and—"

She stopped.

"And what?" asked Constance.

"Tell the truth—and then do a cowardly thing. I would—"

"You would not!" blazed Constance.

There was no mistaking the meaning.

"Leave it to me. Trust me. I will help you."

She pulled the girl down on the divan beside her.

"Why talk of suicide?" mused Constance. "You can plead this aphasia I have just seen. I know lots of newspaper women. We could carry it through so that even the doctors would help us. Remember, aphasia will do for a girl nowadays what nothing else can do."

"Aphasia!" Florence repeated harshly. "Call it what you like—weakness—anything. I—I loved that man—not the one who followed me—another. I believed him. But he left me—left me in a place—across in Brooklyn. They said I was a fool, that some other fellow, perhaps better, with more money, would take care of me. But I left. I got a place in a factory. Then some one in the factory became suspicious. I had saved a little. It took me to Boston.

"Again some one grew suspicious. I came back here, here— the only place to hide. I got another position as waitress in the Betsy Ross Tea Room. There I was able to stay until yesterday. But then a man came in. He had been there before. He seemed too interested in me, not in a way that others have been, but in me—my name. Some how I suspected. I put on my hat and coat. I fled. I think he followed me. All night I have walked the streets and ridden in cars to get away from him. At last—I appealed to you."

The girl had sunk back into the soft pillows of the couch beside her new friend and hid her face. Softly Constance patted and smoothed the wealth of golden hair.

"You—you poor little girl," she sympathized.

Then a film came over her own eyes.

"New York took me at a critical time in my own life," she said more to herself than to the girl. "She sheltered me, gave me a new start. What she did for me she will do for any other person who really wishes to make a fresh start in life. I made few acquaintances, no friends. Fortunately, the average New Yorker asks only that his neighbor leave him alone. No hermit could find better and more complete solitude than in the heart of this great city."

Constance looked pityingly at the girl before her.

"Why can't you tell them," she suggested, "that you wanted to be independent, that you went away to make your own living?"

"But—they—my father—is well off. And they have this detective who follows me. He will find me some day—for the reward—and will tell the truth."

"The reward?"

"Yes—a thousand dollars. Don't you remember reading—"

The girl stopped short as if to check herself.

"You—you are Florence Gibbons!" gasped Constance as with a rush there came over her the recollection of a famous unsolved mystery of several months before.

The girl did not look up as Constance bent over and put her arms about her.

"Who was he?" she asked persuasively.

"Preston—Lansing Preston," she sobbed bitterly. "Only the other day I read of his engagement to a girl in Chicago— beautiful, in society. Oh—I could KILL him," she cried, throwing out her arms passionately. "Think of it. He—rich, powerful, respected. I—poor, almost crazy—an outcast."

Constance did not interfere until the tempest had passed.

"What name did you give at the tea room?" asked Constance.

"Viola Cole," answered Florence.

"Rest here," soothed Constance. "Here at least you are safe. I have an idea. I shall be back soon."

The Betsy Ross was still open after the rush of tired shoppers and later of business women to whom this was not only a restaurant but a club. Constance entered and sat down.

"Is the manager in?" she asked of the waitress.

"Mrs. Palmer? No. But, if you care to wait, I think she'll be back directly."

As Constance sat toying absently with some food at one of the snowy white tables, a man entered. A man in a tea room is an anomaly. For the tea room is a woman's institution, run by women for women. Men enter with diffidence, and seldom alone. This man was quite evidently looking for some one.

His eye fell on Constance. Her heart gave a leap. It was her old enemy, Drummond, the detective. For a moment he hesitated, then bowed, and came over to her table.

"Peculiar places, these tea rooms," observed Drummond.

Constance was doing some quick thinking. Could this be the detective Florence Gibbons had mentioned?

"The only thing lacking to make them complete," he rattled on, "is a license. Now, take those places that have a ladies' bar—that do openly what tea rooms do covertly. They don't reckon with the attitude of women. This is New York—not Paris. Such things are years off. I don't say they'll not come or that women won't use them—but not by that name—not yet."

Constance wondered what his cynical inconsequentialities masked.

"I think it adds to the interest," she observed, watching him furtively, "this evasion of the laws."

Drummond was casting about for something to do and, naturally, to a mind like his, a drink was the solution. Evidently, however, there were degrees of brazenness, even in tea rooms. The Betsy Ross not only would not produce a labeled bottle and an obvious glass but stoutly denied their ability to fill such an order, even whispered.

"Russian tea?" suggested Drummond cryptically.

"How will you have it—with Scotch or rye?" asked the waitress.

"Bourbon," hazarded Drummond.

When the "Russian tea" arrived it was in a neat little pot with two others, the first containing real tea and the second hot water. It was served virtuously in tea cups, so opaquely concealed that no one but the clandestine drinker could know what sort of poison was being served.

Mrs. Palmer was evidently later than expected. Drummond fidgeted after the manner of a man out of his accustomed habitat. And yet he did not seem to be interested really in Constance, or even in Mrs. Palmer. For after a few moments, he rose and excused himself.

"How did HE come here?" Constance asked herself over and over.

As far as she could reason it out, there could be only one reason. Drummond was clearly up with Florence. Did he also know that Constance was shielding her?

The more she thought of it, the more she shuddered at the tactless way in which the detective would perform the act of "charity" by discovering the lost girl—and pocketing the reward.

If her family only knew, how eagerly they might let her come back in her own way. She looked up the address of Everett Gibbons while she was waiting, a half-formed plan taking definite shape in her mind.

What—she did must be done quickly. Here at the tea room at least Florence, or rather Viola, was known. Perhaps the best way, after all, was to let her be discovered here. They could not deny that she had been working for them acceptably for some time.

Half an hour later, Mrs. Palmer, a bustling business woman, came in and the waitress pointed her out to Constance.

"Did you have a waitress here named Viola Cole?" began Constance, watching keenly the effect of her inquiry.

"Yes," replied Mrs. Palmer in a tone of interest that reassured Constance that, if there were any connection between Drummond's presence and Mrs. Palmer, it was wholly on his seeking. "But she disappeared last night. A most peculiar girl—but a splendid worker."

"She has been ill," Constance hastened to explain. "I am a friend of hers. I have a business downtown and could not come around until to-night to tell you that she will be back to-morrow if you will take her back."

"Of course I'll take her back. I'm sorry she's ill," and Mrs. Palmer bustled out into the kitchen, not unfeelingly but merely because that was her manner.

Constance paid her check and left the tea room. So far she had succeeded. The next thing she had planned was a visit to Mr. Gibbons. That need not take long, for she was not going to tell anything. Her idea was merely to pave the way.

The Gibbons she found, lived in a large house on one of the numerous side streets from the Park, in a neighborhood that was in fact something more than merely well-to-do.

Fortunately she found Everett Gibbons in and was ushered into his study, where he sat poring over some papers and enjoying an after-dinner cigar.

"Mr. Gibbons," began Constance, "I believe there is a one thousand dollar reward for news of the whereabouts of your daughter, Florence."

"Yes," he said in a colorless tone that betrayed the hopelessness of the long search. "But we have traced down so many false clues that we have given up hope. Since the day she went away, we have never been able to get the slightest trace of her. Still, we welcome outside aid."

"Of detectives?" she asked.

"Official and private—paid and volunteer—anybody," he answered. "I myself have come to the belief that she is dead, for that is the only explanation I can think of for her long silence."

"She is not dead," replied Constance in a low tone.

"Not dead?" he repeated eagerly, catching at even such a straw as an unknown woman might cast out. "Then you know—"

"No," she interrupted positively, "I cannot tell you any more. You must call off all other searchers. I will let you know."

"When?"

"To-morrow, perhaps the next day. I will call you on the telephone."

She rose and made a hasty adieu before the man who had

been prematurely aged might overwhelm her with questions and break down her resolution to carry the thing through as she had seen best.

Cheerily, Constance turned the key in the lock of her door.

There was no light and somehow the silence smote on her ominously.

"Florence!" she called.

There was no answer.

Not a sign indicated her presence. There was the divan with the pillows disarranged as they had been when she left. The furniture was in the same position as before. Hastily she went from one room to another. Florence had disappeared!

She went to the door again. All seemed right there. If any one had entered, it must have been because he was admitted, for there were no marks to indicate that the lock had been forced.

She called up the tea room. Mrs. Palmer was very sympathetic, but there had been no trace of "Viola Cole" there yet.

"You will let me know if you get any word?" asked Constance anxiously.

"Surely," came back Mrs. Palmer's cordial reply.

A hundred dire possibilities crowded through her mind. Might Florence be held somewhere as a "white slave"—not by physical force but by circumstances, ignorant of her rights, afraid to break away again?

Or was it suicide, as she had threatened? She could not believe it. Nothing could have happened in such a short time to change her resolution about revenge.

The recollection of all the stories she had read recently crossed her mind. Could it be a case of drugs? The girl had given no evidence of being a "dope" fiend.

Perhaps some one had entered, after all.

She thought of the so-called "poisoned needle" cases. Might she not have been spirited off in that way? Constance had doubted the stories. She knew that almost any doctor would say that it was impossible to inject a narcotic by a sudden jab of a hypodermic syringe. That was rather a slow, careful and deliberate operation, to be submitted to with patience.

Yet Florence was gone!

Suddenly it flashed over Constance that Drummond might not be seeking the reward primarily, after all. His first object might be shielding Preston. She recollected that Mr. Gibbons had said nothing about Drummond, either one way or the other. And if he were both shielding Preston and working for the reward, he would care little how much Florence suffered. He might be playing both ends to serve himself.

She rang the elevator bell.

"Has anybody called at my apartment while I was out?" she asked.

"Yes'm. A man came here."

"And you let him up?"

"I didn't know you were out. You see I had just come on. He said he was to meet some one at your apartment. And when he pressed the buzzer, the door opened, and I ran the elevator down again. I thought it was all right, ma'am."

"And then what?" inquired Constance breathlessly.

"Well, in about five minutes my bell rang. I ran the elevator up again, and, waiting, was this man with a girl I had never seen before. You understand—I thought it was all right—he told me he was going to meet some one."

"Yes—yes. I understand. Oh, my God, if I had only thought to leave word not to let her go. How did she look?"

"Her clothes, you mean, Ma'am?"

"No—her face, her eyes!"

"Beggin' your pardon, I thought she was—well, er,—acted queer—scared—dazed-like."

"You didn't notice which way they went, I suppose!"

"No ma'am, I didn't."

Constance turned back again into her empty apartment, heart-sick. In spite of all she had planned and done, she was defeated—worse than defeated. Where was Florence! What might not happen to her! She could have sat down and cried. Instead she passed a feverishly restless night.

All the next day passed, and still not a word. She felt her own helplessness. She could not appeal to the police. That might defeat the very end she sought. She was single-handed. For all she knew, she was fighting the almost limitless power of brains and money of Preston. Inquiry developed the fact that Preston himself was reported to be in Chicago with his fiancee. Time and again she was on the point of making the journey to let him know that some one at least was watching him. But, she reflected, if she did that she might miss the one call from Florence for help.

Then she thought bitterly of the false hopes she had raised in the despairing father of Florence Gibbons. It was maddening.

Several times during the day Constance dropped into the Betsy Ross, without finding any word.

Late that night the buzzer on her door sounded. It was Mrs. Palmer herself, with a letter at last, written on rough paper in pencil with a trembling hand.

Constance almost literally pounced on it.

"Will you tell the lady who was so kind to me that while she was out seeing you at the tea room, there was a call at her door? I didn't like to open it, but when I asked who was there, a man said it was the steam-fitter she had asked to call about the heat.

"I opened the door. From that moment when I saw his face until I came to myself here I remember nothing. I would write to her, only I don't know where she lives. One of the bell-boys here is kind enough to smuggle this note out for me addressed to the Betsy Boss.

"Tell her please, that I am at a place in Brooklyn, I think, called Lustgarten's—she can recognize it because it is at a railroad crossing—steam railroads, not trolleys or elevateds.

"I know you think me crazy, Mrs. Palmer, but the other lady

can tell you about it. Oh, it was the same horrible feeling that came over me that night as before. It isn't a dream; it's more like a trance. It comes in a second—usually when I am frightened. I suddenly feel nervous and shaky. I can't tell what is going on around me. I lose my hearing. Part of the time it is as though, I had a paralytic stroke of the tongue. The next day, perhaps, it is gone. But while it lasts it is terrifying. It's like walking into a new world, with everybody, everything strange about me."

The note ended with a most pathetic appeal.

Constance was already nervously putting on her hat.

"You are going to go there?" asked Mrs. Palmer.

"If I can locate the place," she answered.

"Aren't you afraid?" inquired the other.

Constance did not reply. She ostentatiously slipped a little ivory-handled revolver into her handbag.

"It's a new one," she explained finally, "like nothing you ever heard of before, I guess. I bought it only the other day after a friend of mine told me about it."

Mrs. Palmer was watching her closely.

"You—you are a wonderful woman," she burst out finally. "It isn't good business, it isn't good sense."

Constance stopped short in her preparations for the search. "What are business and sense compared to the—the life of—"

She checked herself on the very point of revealing the girl's real name.

"Nothing," replied Mrs. Palmer. "I had already made up my mind to go with you before I spoke—if you will let me."

In a moment the two understood each other better than after years of casual acquaintance.

Back and forth through the mazes of streets and car lines of the city across the river the two women traveled, asking veiled questions of every wearer of a uniform, until at last they found such a place as Florence had described in her note.

There, it seemed, had sprung up a little center of vice. While reformers were trying to clamp down tight the "lid" in New York, all the vicious elements were prying it up here. Crushed in one place, they rose again in another.

There was the electric sign—"Lustgarten." Even a cursory glance told them that it included a saloon on the first floor, with a sort of dance hall and second-rate cabaret. Above that was a hotel. The windows were darkened, with awnings pulled down, even on what must have been in the daytime the shady side.

"Shall we go in? Are you game?" asked Constance of her companion.

"I haven't gone so far without considering that," replied Mrs. Palmer, somewhat reproachfully.

Without a word Constance entered the door down the street followed by her companion.

A negro at the little cubby hole of an office pushed out a

register at them. Constance signed the first names that came into her head, and a moment later they were on their way up to a big double room on the third floor, led by another, younger negro.

"Will you send the bell-boy up?" asked Constance as they entered the room.

"I'm the bell-boy ma'am," was his disconcerting reply.

"I mean the other one," replied Constance, hazarding, "the one who is here in the day time."

"There ain't no other boy, ma'am. There ain't no—"

"Could you deliver a note for me at a tea room in New York to-morrow?" interrupted Constance, striking while the iron seemed hot.

The boy turned around abruptly from his busy occupation of doing something useless that would elicit a tip. He quietly shut the door, and wheeled about with his hand still on the knob.

"Do you want to know what room she's in?" he asked.

Constance opened her handbag. Mrs. Palmer suppressed a little scream. She had expected that ivory-handled thing to appear. Instead there was a treasury note of a size that caused the white part of the boy's eyes to expand beyond all the laws of optics.

"Yes," she said, pressing it into his hand.

"Forty-two-down the hall, around the turn, on the other side," whispered the boy. "And for God's sake, ma'am, don't tell nobody I told you."

His shuffle down the hall had scarcely ceased before the two women were stealthily creeping in the opposite direction, looking eagerly at the numbers.

Constance had stopped abruptly around the turn. Through a transom of one of the rooms they could hear voices but could see no light.

"Well, go back then," growled a gruff voice. "Your family will never believe your story, never believe that you came again and stayed at Lustgarten's against your will. Why," the voice taunted with a harsh laugh, "if they knew the truth, they would turn you from the door, instead of offering a reward."

There was a moment of silence. Then a woman's voice, strangely familiar to Constance, spoke.

"The truth!" she exclaimed bitterly. "He knew it was a case of a girl who liked a good time, liked pretty clothes, a ride in an automobile, theaters, excitement, bright lights, night life—a girl with a romantic disposition in whom all that was repressed at home. He knew it," she repeated, raising the tone to an almost hysterical pitch, "led me on, made me love him because he could give them all to me. And when I began to show the strain of the pace-they all show it more than the men—he cast me aside like a squeezed-out lemon."

As she listened, Constance understood it all now. It was to make Florence Gibbons a piece of property, a thing to be traded in, bartered—that was the idea. Discover her—yes; but first to thrust her into the life if she would not go into it herself—anything to discredit her testimony beforehand, anything to save the precious reputation of one man.

"Well," shouted the other voice menacingly, "do you want to know the truth? Haven't you read it often enough? Instead of hoping you will return, they pray that you are DEAD!"

He hissed the words out, then added, "They prefer to think that you are dead. Why—damn it!—they turn to that belief for COMFORT!"

Constance had seized Mrs. Palmer by the arm, and, acting in concert, they threw both their weights against the thin wooden door.

It yielded with a crash.

Inside the room was dark.

Indistinctly Constance could make out two figures, one standing, the other seated in a deep rocker.

A suppressed exclamation of surprise was followed by a hasty lunge of the standing figure toward her.

Constance reached quickly into her handbag and drew out the little ivory-handled pistol.

"Bang!" it spat almost into the man's face.

Choking, sputtering, the man groped a minute blindly, then fell on the floor and frantically tried to rise again and call out.

The words seemed to stick in his throat.

"You—you shot him?" gasped a woman's voice which Constance now knew was Florence's.

"With the new German Secret Service gun," answered Constance quietly, keeping it leveled to cow any assistance that might be brought. "It blinds and stupefies without killing—a bulletless revolver intended to check and render harmless the criminal instead of maiming him. The cartridges contain several chemicals that combine when they are exploded and form a vapor which blinds a man and puts him out. No one wants to kill such a person as this."

She reached over and switched on the lights.

The man on the floor was Drummond himself.

"You will tell your real employer, Mr. Preston," she added contemptuously, "that unless he agrees to our story of his elopement with Florence, marries her, and allows her to start an undefended action for divorce, we intend to make use of the new federal Mann Act—with a jail sentence—for both of you."

Drummond looked up sullenly, still blinking and choking.

"And not a word of this until the suit is filed. Then WE will see the reporters—not he. Understand?"

"Yes," he muttered, still clutching his throat.

An hour later Constance was at the telephone in her own apartment.

"Mr. Gibbons? I must apologize for troubling you at this late, or rather early, hour. But I promised you something which I could not fulfill until now. This is the Mrs. Dunlap who called on you the other day with a clue to your daughter Florence. I have found her—yes—working as a waitress in the Betsy Ross Tea Boom. No—not a word to anyone—not even to her mother. No—not a word. You can see her tomorrow—at my apartment. She is going to live with me for a few days until—well—until we get a few little matters straightened out."

Constance had jammed the receiver back on the hook hastily.

Florence Gibbons, wild-eyed, trembling, imploring, had flung her arms about her neck.

"No—no—no," she cried. "I can't. I won't."

With a force that was almost masculine, Constance took the girl by both shoulders.

"The one thousand dollar reward which comes to me," said Constance decisively, "will help us—straighten out those few little matters with Preston. Mrs. Palmer can stretch the time which you have worked for her."

Something of Constance's will seemed to be infused into Florence Gibbons by force of suggestion.

"And remember," Constance added in a tense voice, "for anything after your elopement—it's aphasia, aphasia, APHASIA!"

CHAPTER IX

THE SHOPLIFTERS

"Madam, would you mind going with me for a few moments to the office on the third floor?"

Constance Dunlap had been out on a shopping excursion. She had stopped at the jewelry counter of Stacy's to have a ring repaired and had gone on to the leather goods department to purchase something else.

The woman who spoke to her was a quietly dressed young person, quite inconspicuous, with a keen eye that seemed to take in everything within a radius of a wide-angled lens at a glance.

She leaned over and before Constance could express even surprise, added in a whisper, "Look in your bag."

Constance looked hastily, then realized what had happened. The ring was gone!

It gave her quite a shock, too, for the ring, a fine diamond, was a present from her husband, one of the few pieces of jewelry, treasured not only for its intrinsic value but as a remembrance of Carlton and the supreme sacrifice he had made for her.

She had noticed nothing in the crowd, nothing more than she had noticed scores of times before. The woman watched her puzzled look.

"I've been following you," she said. "By this time the other store detectives must have caught the shoplifter and bag-opener who touched you. You see, we don't make any arrests in the store if we can help it, because we don't like to make a scene. It's bad for business. Besides, if she had anything else, we are safer when the case comes to court, if we have caught her actually leaving the store with it. Of course, when we make an arrest on the sidewalk, we bring the shoplifter back, but in a private, back elevator."

Constance was following the young woman mechanically. At least there was a chance of recovering the ring.

"She was standing next to you at the jewelry counter," she continued, "and if you will help identify her the store management will appreciate it—and make it worth your while. Besides," she urged, "It's really your duty to do it, madam."

Constance remembered now the rather simply but richly gowned young woman who had been standing next to her at the counter, seemingly unable to decide which of a number of beautiful rings she really wanted. She remembered because, with her own love of beauty, she had wanted one herself, in fact had thought at the time that she, too, might have difficulty in choosing.

With the added feeling of curiosity, Constance followed the woman detective up in the elevator.

In the office, apart in a little room curiously furnished with a camera, innumerable photographs, cabinets, and filing cases, was a young woman, perhaps twenty-six or seven. On a table before her lay a pile of laces and small trinkets. There, too, was the beautiful diamond ring which she had hidden in her muff. Constance fairly gasped at the sight.

The girl was sitting limply in a chair crying bitterly. She was not a hardened looking creature. In fact, her face bore evident traces of refinement, and her long, slender fingers hinted at a nervous, artistic temperament. It was rather a shock to see such a girl under such distressing circumstances.

"We've lost so much lately," a small ferret-eyed man was saying, "that we must make an example of some one. It's serious for us detectives, too. We'll lose our jobs unless we can stop you boosters."

"Oh—I—I didn't mean to do it. I—I just couldn't help it," sobbed the girl over and over again.

"Yes," drawled the man, "that's what they all say. But you've been caught with the goods, this time, young lady."

A woman entered, and the man turned to her quickly.

"Carr—Kitty Carr. Did you find anything under that name?"

"No, sir," replied the woman store detective. "We've looked all through the records and the photographs. We don't find her. And yet I don't think it is an alias—at least, if it is, not an alias for any one we have any record of. I've a good eye for faces, and there isn't one we have on file as—as good looking," she added, perhaps with a little touch of wistfulness at her own plainness and this beauty gone wrong.

"This is the woman who lost the ring," put in the other woman detective, motioning to Constance, who had accompanied her and was standing, a silent spectator.

The man held up the ring, which Constance had already recognized.

"Is that yours?" he asked.

For a moment, strangely, she hesitated. If it had been any other ring in the world she felt sure that she would have said no. But, then, she reflected, there was that pile of stuff. There was no use in concealing her ownership of the ring. "Yes," she murmured.

"One moment, please," answered the man brusquely. "I must send down for the salesgirl who waited on you to identify you and your check—a mere formality, you know, but necessary to keep things straight."

Constance sat down.

"I suppose you don't realize it," explained the man, turning to Constance, "but the shoplifters of the city get away with a couple of million dollars' worth of stuff every year. It's the price we have to pay for displaying our goods. But it's too high. They are the department store's greatest unsolved problem. Now most of the stores are working together for their common interests, seeing what they can do to root them out. We all keep a sort of private rogue's gallery of them. But we don't seem to have anything on this girl, nor have any of the other stores who exchange photographs and information with us anything on her."

"Evidently, then, it is her first offense," put in Constance, wondering at herself. Strangely, she felt more of sympathy than of anger for the girl.

"You mean the first time she has been caught at it," corrected the head of the store detectives.

"It is my weakness," sobbed the girl. "Sometimes an irresistible impulse to steal comes over me. I just can't help it."

She was sobbing convulsively. As she talked and listened there seemed to come a complete breakdown. She wept as though her heart would break.

"Oh," exclaimed the man, "can it! Cut out the sob stuff!"

"And yet," mused Constance half to herself, watching the girl closely, "when one walks through the shops and sees thousands of dollars' worth of goods lying unprotected on the counters, is it any wonder that some poor woman or girl should be tempted and fall? There, before her eyes and within her grasp, lies the very article above all others which she so ardently craves. No one is looking. The salesgirl is busy with another customer. The rest is easy. And then the store detective steps in—and here she is—captured."

The girl had been listening wildly through her tears. "Oh," she sobbed, "you don't understand—none of you. I don't crave anything. I—I just—can't help it—and then, after-wards—I—I HATE the stuff—and I am so—afraid. I hurry home—and I—oh, what shall I do—what shall I do?"

Constance pitied her deeply. She looked from the wild-eyed, tear-stained face to the miscellaneous pile of material on the table, and the unwinking gaze of the store detectives. True, the girl had taken a very valuable diamond ring, and from herself. But the laces, the trinkets, all were abominably cheap, not worth risking anything for.

Constance's attention was recalled by the man who beckoned her aside to talk to the salesgirl who had waited on her.

"You remember seeing this lady at the counter?" he asked of the girl. She nodded. "And that woman in there?" he motioned. Again the salesgirl nodded.

"Do you remember anything else that happened?" he asked Constance as they faced Kitty Carr and he handed Constance the ring.

Constance looked the detective squarely in the face for a moment.

"I have my ring. You have the other stuff," she murmured. "Besides, there is no record against her. She doesn't even look like a professional bad character. No—I'll not appear to press the charge—I'll make it as hard as I can before I'll do it," she added positively.

The woman, who had overheard, looked her gratitude. The detectives were preparing to argue. Constance hardly knew what she was saying, as she hurried on before any one else could speak.

"No," she added, "but I'll tell you what I will do. If you will let her go I will look after her. Parole her, unofficially, with me."

Constance drew a card from her case and handed it to the detective. He read it carefully, and a puzzled look came over his face. "Charge account—good customer—pays promptly," he muttered under his breath.

For a moment he hesitated. Then he sat down at a desk.

"Mrs. Dunlap," he said, "I'll do it."

He pulled a piece of printed paper from the desk, filled in a few blanks, then turned to Kitty Carr, handing her a pen.

"Sign here," he said brusquely.

Constance bent over and read. It was a form of release:

"I, Kitty Carr, residing at—East—th Street, single, age twenty-seven years, in consideration of the sum of One Dollar, hereby admit taking the following property... without having paid therefor and with intent not to pay therefor, and by reason of the withdrawal of the complaint of larceny, OF WHICH I AM GUILTY, I hereby remise, release, and forever discharge the said Stacy Co. or its representatives from any claims, action, or causes of action which I may have against the Stacy Co. or its representatives or agents by reason of the withdrawal of said charge of larceny and failure to prosecute."

"Signed, Kitty Carr."

"Now, Kitty," soothed Constance, as the trembling signature was blotted and added to a photograph which had quietly been taken, "they are going to let you go this time—with me. Come, straighten your hat, wipe your eyes. You must take me home with you—where we can have a nice long talk. Remember, I am your friend."

On the way uptown and across the city the girl managed to tell most of her history. She came from a family of means in another city. Her father was dead, but her mother and a brother were living. She herself had a small annuity, sufficient to live on modestly, and had come to New York seeking a career as an artist. Her story, her ambitions appealed to Constance, who had been somewhat of an artist herself and recognized even in talking to the girl that she was not without some ability.

Then, too, she found that Kitty actually lived, as she had said, in a cozy little kitchenette apartment with two friends, a man and his wife, both of whom happened to be out when they arrived. As Constance looked about she could see clearly that there was indeed no adequate reason why the girl should steal.

"How do you feel?" asked Constance when the girl had sunk half exhausted on a couch in the living room.

"Oh, so nervous," she replied, pressing her hands to the back of her head, "and I have a terrible headache, although it is a little better now."

They had talked for perhaps half an hour, as Constance soothed her, when there was the sound of a key in the door. A young woman in black entered. She was well-dressed, in fact elegantly dressed in a quiet way, somewhat older than Kitty, but by no means as attractive.

"Why—hello, Kitty," she cried, "what's the matter!"

"Oh, Annie, I'm so unstrung," replied the girl, then recollecting Constance, added, "let me introduce my friend, Mrs. Dunlap. This is Mrs. Annie Grayson, who has taken me in as a lodger and is ever so kind to me."

Constance nodded, and the woman held out her hand frankly.

"Very glad to meet you," she said. "My husband, Jim, is not at home, but we are a very happy little family up here. Why, Kitty, what is the matter?"

The girl had turned her face down in the sofa pillows and was sobbing again. Between sobs she blurted out the whole of the sordid story. And as she proceeded, Annie glanced quickly from her to Constance, for confirmation.

Suddenly she rose and extended her hand to Constance.

"Mrs. Dunlap," she said, "how can I ever thank you for what you have done for Kitty? She is almost like a sister to me. You—you were—too good."

There was a little catch in the woman's voice. But Constance could not quite make out whether it was acted or wholly genuine.

"Did she ever do anything like that before?" she asked.

"Only once," replied Annie Grayson, "and then I gave her such a talking to that I thought she would be able to restrain herself when she felt that way again."

It was growing late and Constance recollected that she had an engagement for the evening. As she rose to go Kitty almost overwhelmed her with embraces.

"I'll keep in touch with Kitty," whispered Constance at the door, "and if you will let me know when anything comes up that I may help her in, I shall thank you."

"Depend on me," answered Mrs. Grayson, "and I want to add my thanks to Kitty's for what you have done. I'll try to help you."

As she groped her way down the as yet unlighted stairs, Constance became aware of two men talking in the hall. As she passed them she thought she recognized one of the voices. She lowered her head, and fortunately her thin veil in the half-light did the rest. She passed unnoticed and reached the door of the apartment.

As she opened it she heard the men turn and mount the stairs. Instinctively she realized that something was wrong. One of the men was her old enemy, Drummond, the detective.

They had not recognized her, and as she stood for a moment with her hand on the knob, she tried to reason it out. Then she crept back, and climbed the stairs noiselessly. Voices inside the apartment told her that she had not been mistaken. It was the apartment of the Graysons and Kitty that they sought.

The hall door was of thin, light wood, and as she stood there she could easily hear what passed inside.

"What—is Kitty ill?" she heard the strange man's voice inquire.

"Yes," replied Mrs. Grayson, then her voice trailed off into an indistinguishable whisper.

"How are you, Kitty?" asked the man.

"Oh, I have a splitting headache, Jim. I've had it all day. I could just get up and—screech!"

"I'm sorry. I hope it gets better soon."

"Oh, I guess it will. They often go away as suddenly as they come. You know I've had them before."

Drummond's voice then spoke up.

"Did you see the Trimble ad. to-night?" he asked, evidently of Annie. "They have a lot of new diamonds from Arkansas, they say,—one of them is a big one, the Arkansas Queen, I believe they call it."

"No, I didn't see the papers," replied Annie.

There was the rustle of a newspaper.

"Here's a picture of it. It must be great. I've heard a good deal about it."

"Have you seen it?" asked Annie.

"No, but I intend to see it."

They had passed into the next room, and Constance, fearing to be discovered, decided to get away before that happened.

Early the next morning she decided to call on Kitty, but by the time Constance arrived at the apartment it was closed, and a neighbor informed her that the two women had gone out together about half an hour before.

Constance was nervous and, as she left the apartment, she did not notice that a man who had been loitering about had quickened his pace and overtaken her.

"So," drawled a voice, "you're traveling with shoplifters now."

She looked up quickly. This time she had run squarely into Drummond. There was no concealment possible now. Her only refuge was silence. She felt the hot tingle of indignation in her cheeks. But she said nothing.

"Huh!" exclaimed Drummond, walking along beside her, and adding contemptuously, "I don't know the young one, but you know who the other is?"

Constance bit her lip.

"No?" he queried. "Then I'll show you."

He had taken from his pocket a bunch of oblong cards. Each bore, she could see from the corner of her eye, a full face and a profile picture of a woman, and on the back of the card was a little writing.

He selected one and handed it to Constance. Instantly she recognized the face. It was Annie Grayson, with half a dozen aliases written after the name.

"There!" he fairly snorted. "That's the sort of people your little friend consorts with. Why, they call Annie Grayson the queen of the shoplifters. She has forgotten more about shoplifting than all the rest will ever know."

Constance longed to ask him what had taken him to the Grayson flat the night before, but thought better of it. There was no use in angering Drummond further. Instead, she let him think that he had succeeded in frightening her off.

She went back to her own apartment to wait and worry. Evidently Drummond was pretty sure of something, or he would not have disclosed his hand to her, even partially. She felt that she must see Kitty before it was too late. Then the thought crossed her mind that perhaps already it was too late. Drummond evidently was working in some way for an alliance of the department stores outside.

Constance had had her own ideas about Kitty. And as she

waited and watched, she tried to reason how she might carry them out if she had a chance.

She had just been insured, and had been very much interested in the various tests that the woman doctor of the insurance company had applied to her. One in particular which involved the use of a little simple instrument that fitted over the forearm had interested her particularly. She had talked to the doctor about it, and as she talked an idea had occurred to her that it might have other uses than those which the doctor made of it. She had bought one. While she was waiting it occurred to her that perhaps it might serve her purpose. She got the instrument out. It consisted of a little arrangement that fitted over the forearm, and was attached by a tube to a dial that registered in millimeters a column of mercury. Would it really show anything, she wondered?

There was a quick call on the telephone and she answered it, her hand trembling, for she felt sure that it was something about the little woman she had befriended.

Somehow or other her voice hardened as she answered the call and found that it was from Drummond. It would never do to betray even nervousness before him.

"Your friend, Miss Carr," shot out Drummond with brutal directness, "has been caught again. She fell into something as neatly as if she had really meant to do it. Yesterday, you know, Trimble's advertised the new diamond, the Arkansas Queen, on exhibition. Well, it was made of paste, anyway. But it was a perfect imitation. But that didn't make any difference. We caught Kitty just now trying to lift it. I'm sorry it wasn't the other one. But small fry are better than none. We'll get her, too, yet. Besides, I find this Kitty has a record already at Stacy's."

Arthur B. Reeve

He added the last words with a taunting sneer. Constance realized suddenly the truth. The whole affair had been a plant of Drummond's!

"You are at Trimble's?" she inquired quickly. "Well, can you wait there just a few minutes? I'd like to see Miss Carr."

Drummond promised. His acquiescence in itself boded no good, but nevertheless she decided to go. As she left her apartment hurriedly she picked up the little instrument and dropped it into her hand-bag.

"You see, it's no use," almost chortled Drummond as Constance stepped off the elevator and opened the door to a little room at Trimble's much like that which she had already seen at Stacy's. "A shoplifter becomes habitual after twenty-five. They get to consorting with others of their kind."

Kitty was sitting rigidly motionless in a chair, staring straight ahead, as Constance entered. She gave a start at the sight of a familiar face, rose, and would almost have fainted if Constance had not caught her. It seemed as if something had snapped in the girl's make-up. For the first time tears came. Constance patted her hand softly. The girl was an enigma. Was she a clever actress—one minute hardened Miss Sophisticated, the next appealing Miss Innocence?

"How did you—catch her?" asked Constance a moment later as she found an opportunity to talk to Drummond alone.

"Oh, she was trying to substitute a paste replica for the alleged Arkansas Queen. The clerk noticed the replica in time, saw a little spot of carbon on it—and she was shadowed and arrested just as she was leaving the store. Yes, they found the other paste jewel on her. She was caught with the goods."

"Replica?" repeated Constance, thinking of the picture that had appeared in the papers the night before. "How could she get a replica of it?"

"How do I know?" shrugged Drummond coldly.

Constance looked him squarely in the eyes.

"What about Annie Grayson?" she asked pointblank.

"I have taken care of that," he replied harshly. "She is already under arrest, and from what I have heard we may get something on her now. We have a record against the Carr girl. We can use it against her friend. We're just about taking her to the flat to identify the Grayson woman. Would you like to come along?" he added in a spirit of bravado. "I think you are a material witness in the Stacy case, anyhow."

Constance felt bitterly her defeat. Still she went with them. There was always a chance that something might turn up.

As they entered the door of the kitchenette loud voices told them that some one was disputing inside.

Drummond strode in.

The sight of a huge pile of stuff that two strange men had drawn out of drawers and closets and stacked on the table riveted Constance's eyes. Only dimly she could hear that Annie Grayson was violently threatening Drummond, who stood coolly surveying the scene.

The stuff on the table was, in fact, quite enough to dazzle the eyes. There were articles of every sort and description there—silks, laces, jewelry and trinkets, little antiques, even rare books—everything small and portable, some of the richest and most exquisite, others of the cheapest and most tawdry. It was a truly remarkable collection, which the raiding detectives had brought to light.

As Constance took in the scene—the raiding detectives holding the stormy Annie Grayson at bay, Drummond, cool, supercilious, Kitty almost on the edge of collapse—she wondered how Jim Grayson had managed to slip through the meshes of the net.

She had read of such things. Annie Grayson was to all appearances a "fence" for stolen goods. This was, perhaps, a school for shoplifters. In addition to her other accomplishments, the queen of the shoplifters was a "Fagin," educating others to the tricks of her trade, taking advantage of their lack of facility in disposing of the stolen goods.

Just then the woman caught sight of Constance standing in the doorway.

In an instant she had broken loose and ran toward her.

"What are you," she hissed, "one of these department store Moll Dicks, too?"

Quick as a flash Kitty Carr had leaped to her feet and placed herself between them.

"No, Annie, no. She was a real friend of mine. No—if your own friends had been as loyal as she was to me this would never have happened—I should never have been caught again, for I should never have given them a chance to get it on me."

"Little fool!" ground out Annie Grayson, raising her arm.

"Here—here—LADIES!" interposed Drummond, protruding an arm between the two, and winking sarcastically to the two other men. "None of that. We shall need both of you in our business. I've no objection to your talking; but cut out the rough stuff."

Constance had stepped back. She was cool, cool as Drummond, although she knew her heart was thumping like a sledge-hammer. There was Kitty Carr, in a revulsion of feeling, her hands pressed tightly to her head again, as if it were bursting. She was swaying as if she would faint.

Constance caught her gently about the waist and forced her down on the couch where she had been lying the night before. With her back to the others, she reached quickly into her hand-bag and pulled out the little instrument she had hastily stuffed into it. Deftly she fastened it to Kitty's wrist and forearm.

She dropped down on her knees beside the poor girl, and gently stroked her free hand, reassuring her in a low tone.

"There, there," she soothed. "You are not well, Kitty. Perhaps, after all, there may be something—some explanation."

In spite of all, however, Kitty was on the verge of the wildest hysterics. Annie Grayson sniffed contemptuously at such weakness.

Drummond came over, an exasperating sneer on his face. As he looked down he saw what Constance was doing, and she rose, so that all could see now.

"This girl," she said, speaking rapidly, "is afflicted with a nervous physical disorder, a mania, which is uncontrollable, and takes this outlet. It is emotional insanity—not loss of control of the will, but perversion of the will."

"Humph!" was Drummond's sole comment with a significant glance at the pile of goods on the table.

"It is not the articles themselves so much," went on Constance, following his glance, "as it is the pleasure, the excitement, the satisfaction—call it what you will—of taking them. A thief works for the benefit he may derive from objects stolen after he gets them. Here is a girl who apparently has no further use for an article after she gets it, who forgets, perhaps hates it."

"Oh, yes," remarked Drummond; "but why are they all so careful not to get caught? Every one is responsible who knows the nature and consequences of his act."

Constance had wheeled about.

"That is not so," she exclaimed. "Any modern alienist will tell you that. Sometimes the chief mark of insanity may be knowing the nature and consequences, craftily avoiding detection with an almost superhuman cunning. No; the test is whether knowing the nature and consequences, a person suffers under such a defect of will that in spite of everything, in the face of everything, that person cannot control that will."

As she spoke, she had quickly detached the little instrument and had placed it on Annie Grayson's arm. If it had been a Bertillon camera, or even a finger-print outfit, Annie Grayson would probably have fought like a tigress. But this thing was a new one. She had a peculiar spirit of bravado.

"Such terms as kleptomania," went on Constance, "are often regarded as excuses framed up by the experts to cover up plain ordinary stealing. But did you wiseacres of crime ever stop to think that perhaps they do actually exist?

"There are many things that distinguish such a woman as I have described to you from a common thief. There is the insane desire to steal—merely for stealing's sake—a morbid craving. Of course in a sense it is stealing. But it is persistent, incorrigible, irrational, motiveless, useless.

"Stop and think about it a moment," she concluded, lowering her voice and taking advantage of the very novelty of the situation she had created. "Such diseases are the product of civilization, of sensationalism. Naturally enough, then, woman, with her delicately balanced nervous organization, is the first and chief offender—if you insist on calling such a person an offender under your antiquated methods of dealing with such cases."

She had paused.

"What did you say you called this thing?" asked Drummond as he tapped the arrangement on Annie Grayson's arm.

He was evidently not much impressed by it, yet somehow instinctively regarded it with somewhat of the feelings of an elephant toward a mouse.

"That?" answered Constance, taking it off Annie Grayson's wrist before she could do anything with it. "Why, I don't know that I said anything about it. It is really a sphygmomanometer—the little expert witness that never lies—one of the instruments the insurance companies use now to register blood pressure and discover certain diseases. It occurred to me that it might be put to other and equally practical uses. For no one can conceal the emotions from this instrument, not even a person of cast-iron nerves."

She had placed it on Drummond's arm. He appeared fascinated.

"See how it works?" she went on. "You see one hundred and twenty-five millimeters is the normal pressure. Kitty Carr is absolutely abnormal. I do not know, but I think that she suffers from periodical attacks of vertigo. Almost all kleptomaniacs do. During an attack they are utterly irresponsible."

Drummond was looking at the thing carefully. Constance turned to Annie Grayson.

"Where's your husband?" she asked offhand.

"Oh, he disappeared as soon as these department store dicks showed up," she replied bitterly. She had been watching Constance narrowly, quite nonplussed, and unable to make anything out of what was going on.

Constance looked at Drummond inquiringly.

He shook his head slowly. "I'm afraid we'll never catch him," he said. "He got the jump on us—although we have our lines out for him, too."

She had glanced down quickly at the little innocent-looking but telltale sphygmomanometer.

"You lie!" she exclaimed suddenly, with all the vigor of a man.

She was pointing at the quivering little needle which registered a sudden, access of emotion totally concealed by the sang-froid of Drummond's well-schooled exterior.

She wrenched the thing off his wrist and dropped it into her bag. A moment later she stood by the open window facing the street, a bright little police whistle gleaming in her hand, ready for its shrill alarm if any move were made to cut short what she had to say.

She was speaking rapidly now.

"You see, I've had it on all of you, one after another, and each has told me your story, just enough of it for me to piece it together. Kitty is suffering from a form of vertigo, an insanity, kleptomania, the real thing. As for you, Mr. Drummond, you were in league with the alleged husband—your own stool pigeon—to catch Annie Grayson."

Drummond moved. So did the whistle. He stopped.

"But she was too clever for you all. She was not caught, even by a man who lived with her as her own husband. For she was not operating."

Annie Grayson moved as if to face out her accusers at this sudden turn of fortune.

"One moment, Annie," cut in Constance.

"And yet, you are the real shoplifter, after all. You fell into the trap which Drummond laid for you. I take pleasure, Mr. Drummond, in presenting you with better evidence than even your own stool pigeon could possibly have given you under the circumstances."

She paused.

"For myself," she concluded, "I claim Kitty Carr. I claim the right to take her, to have her treated for her—her disease. I claim it because the real shoplifter, the queen of the shoplifters, Annie Grayson, has worked out a brand-new scheme, taking up a true kleptomaniac and using her insanity to carry out the stealings which she suggested—and safely, to this point, has profited by!"

CHAPTER X

THE BLACKMAILERS

"They're late this afternoon."

"Yes. I think they might be on time. I wish they had made the appointment in a quieter place."

"What do you care, Anita? Probably somebody else is doing the same thing somewhere else. What's sauce for the gander is sauce for the goose."

"I know he has treated me like a dog, Alice, but—"

There was just a trace of a catch in the voice of the second woman as she broke off the remark and left it unfinished.

Constance Dunlap had caught the words unintentionally above the hum of conversation and the snatches of tuneful music wafted from the large dining-room where day was being turned into night.

She had dropped into the fashionable new Vanderveer Hotel, not to meet any one, but because she liked to watch the people in "Peacock Alley," as the corridor of the hotel was often popularly called.

Somehow, as she sat inconspicuously in a deep chair in an angle, she felt that very few of the gaily chatting couples or of the waiting men and women about her were quite what they seemed on the surface.

The conversation from around the angle confirmed her opinion. Here, apparently at least, were two young married women with a grievance, and it was not for those against whom they had the grievance, real or imagined, that they were waiting so anxiously.

Constance leaned forward to see them better. The woman nearest her was a trifle the elder of the two, a very attractive-looking woman, tastefully gowned and carefully groomed. The younger, who had been the first speaker, was, perhaps, the more dashing. Certainly she appeared to be the more sophisticated. And as Constance caught her eye she involuntarily thought of the old proverb, "Never trust a man who doesn't look you in the eye or a woman who does."

Two men sauntered down the long corridor, on the way from a visit to the bar. As they caught sight of the two ladies, there was a smile of recognition, an exchange of remarks between each pair, and the men hurried in the direction of the corner.

They greeted the two ladies in low, bantering, familiar terms—"Mr. Smith," "Mrs. Jones," "Mr. White" and "Mrs. Brown."

"You got my card!" asked one of the men of the woman nearest Constance. "Sorry we're late, but a business friend ran into us as we were coming in and I had to shunt him off in the other direction."

He nodded toward the opposite end of the corridor with a laugh.

"You've been bad boys," pouted the other woman, "but we forgive you—this time."

"Perhaps we may hope to be reinstated after a little—er—tea—and a dance?" suggested the other man.

The four were all moving in the direction of the dining-room and the gay music.

They had disappeared in the crush about the door before Constance noticed that the woman who had been sitting nearest her had dropped an envelope. She picked it up. It was on the stationery of another fashionable hotel, evidently written by one of those who lounge in, and on the strength of a small bill in the cafe use the writing room. In a man's hand was the name, "Mrs. Anita Douglas, The Melcombe Apartments, City"

Before she realized it, Constance had pulled out the card inside and glanced at it. It read:

MY DEAREST A—:

Can you meet us in the Vanderveer to-morrow afternoon at four? Bring along your little friend.

With many * * * *

Yours,

?????

Mechanically Constance crumpled the card and the envelope in her hand and held them as she regarded the passing throng, intending to throw them away when she passed a scrap basket on the way out.

Still, it was a fascinating scene, this of the comedy and tragedy of human weaknesses, and she stayed much longer than she had intended. One by one the people had either gone to dinner in the main dining-room or elsewhere and Constance had nearly decided on going, too.

She was looking down the corridor toward the desk when she saw something that caused her to change her mind. There was the young lady who had been talking so flippantly to the woman with a grievance, and she was now talking, of all people, to Drummond!

Constance shrank back into her wicker chair in the protecting angle. What did it mean? If Drummond had anything to do with it, even remotely, it boded no good, at least.

Suddenly a possible explanation crossed her mind. Was it a side-light upon that peculiar industry of divorce as practiced in no place except New York?

It was not only that Constance longed for, lived by excitement. She felt a sense of curiosity as to what the detective was up to now. And, somehow, she felt a duty in the case. She determined to return the envelope and card, and meet the woman. And the more she thought of it the more imperative became the idea.

So it came about that the following forenoon Constance sought out the Melcombe Apartments, a huge stone and brick affair on a street which the uptown trend of population was transforming.

Anita Douglas, she had already found out by an inquiry or two, was the wife of a well-known business man. Yet, as she entered the little apartment, she noticed that there was no evidence about it of a man's presence.

Mrs. Douglas greeted her unexpected visitor with an inquiring look.

"I was passing through the corridor of the Vanderveer yesterday afternoon," began Constance, leaping into the middle of her errand, "and I happened to see this envelope lying on the carpet. I thought first of destroying it; then that perhaps you would rather destroy it yourself."

Mrs. Douglas almost pounced on the letter as Constance handed it to her. "Thank you," she exclaimed. "It was very thoughtful of you."

For a moment or two they chatted of inconsequential things.

"Who was your friend?" asked Constance at length.

The woman caught her breath and flushed a bit, evidently wondering just how much Constance really knew.

"The young lady," added Constance, who had put the question in this form purposely.

"Why do you ask?" Mrs. Douglas inquired in a tone that betrayed considerable relief.

"Because I can tell you something of her, I think."

"A friend of mine—a Mrs. Murray. Why?"

"Aren't you just a little bit afraid of—er—friends that you may chance to make in the city?" queried Constance.

"Afraid?" repeated the other.

"Yes," said Constance, coming gradually to the point. "You

know there are so many detectives about."

Mrs. Douglas laughed half nervously. "Oh, I've been shadowed," she replied confidently. "I know how to shake them off. If you can't do anything else, you can always take a taxi. Besides, I think I can uncover almost any shadow. All you have to do, if you think you're being shadowed, is to turn a corner and stop. That uncovers the shadow as soon as he comes up to the corner, and after that he is useless. You know him."

"That's all right," nodded Constance; "but you don't know these crooked detectives nowadays as I do. They can fake up evidence to order. That is their business, you know, to manufacture it. You may uncover a six-dollar operative, Mrs. Douglas, but are you the equal of a twenty-dollar-a-day investigator?"

The woman looked genuinely scared. Evidently Constance knew some things she didn't know, at least about detectives.

"You—you don't think there is anything like that, do you?" she asked anxiously.

"Well," replied Constance slowly to impress her, "I saw your friend, Mrs. Murray, after you had left the Vanderveer, talking to a detective whom I have every reason to fear as one of the most unscrupulous in the game."

"Oh, that is impossible!" persisted Mrs. Douglas.

"Not a bit of it," pursued Constance. "Think it over for a moment. Who would be the last person a man or woman would suspect of being a detective? Why, just such an attractive young woman, of course. You see, it is just this way. They reason that if they can only get acquainted with people the rest is easy. For, people, under the right circumstances, will tell everything they know."

The woman was staring at Constance.

"For example," urged Constance, "I'm talking to you now as if I had known you for years. Why, Mrs. Douglas, men tell their most important business secrets to chance luncheon and dinner companions whom they think have no direct or indirect interest in them. Over tea-tables women tell their most intimate personal affairs. In fact, all you have to do is to keep your ears open."

Mrs. Douglas had risen and was nervously watching Constance, who saw that she had made an impression and that all that was necessary was to follow it up.

"Now, for instance," added Constance quickly, "you say she is a friend of yours. How did you meet her?"

Mrs. Douglas did not raise her eyes to Constance's now. Yet she seemed to feel that Constance was different from other chance acquaintances, to feel a sort of confidence, and to want to meet frankness with frankness.

"One day I was with a friend of mine at the new Palais de Maxixe," she answered in a low voice as if making a confession. "A woman in the dressing-room borrowed a cigarette. You know they often do that. We got talking, and it seemed that we had much in common in our lives. Before I went back to him—"

She bit her lip. She had evidently not intended to admit that she knew any other men. Constance, however, appeared not to notice the slip.

Arthur B. Reeve

"I had arranged to meet her at luncheon the next day," she continued hastily. "We have been friends ever since."

"You went to luncheon with her, and—" Constance prompted.

"Oh, she told me her story. It was very much like my own— a husband who was a perfect bear, and then gossip about him that so many people, besides his own wife, seemed to know, and—"

Constance shook her head. "Really," she observed thoughtfully, "it's a wonder to me how any one stays married these days. Somebody is always mixing in, getting one or the other so wrought up that they get to thinking there is no possibility of happiness. That's where the crook detective comes in."

Anita Douglas, confidence established now, poured out her story unreservedly, as there was little reason why she should not, a story of the refined brutality and neglect and inhumanity of her husband.

She told of her own first suspicions of him, of a girl who had been his stenographer, a Miss Helen Brett.

But he was careful. There had never been any direct, positive evidence against him. Still, there was enough to warrant a separation and the payment to her of an allowance.

They had lived, she said, in a pretty little house in the suburb of Glenclair, near New York. Now that they were separated, she had taken a little kitchenette apartment at the new Melcombe. Her husband was living in the house, she believed, when he was not in the city at his club, "or elsewhere," she added bitterly.

"But," she confided as she finished, "it is very lonely here in a big city all alone."

"I know it is," agreed Constance sympathetically as they parted. "I, too, am often very lonely. Call on me, especially if you find anything crooked going on. Call on me, anyhow. I shall be glad to see you any time."

The words, "anything crooked going on," rang in Mrs. Douglas's ears long after the elevator door had clanged shut and her new friend had gone. She was visibly perturbed. And the more she thought about it the more perturbed she became.

She had carried on a mild, then an ardent, flirtation with the man who had introduced himself as "Mr. White"—really Lynn Munro. But she relied on her woman's instinct in her judgment of him. No, she felt sure that he could not be other than she thought. But as for Alice Murray and her friend whom she had met at the Palais de Maxixe—well, she was forced to admit that she did not know, that Constance's warning might, after all, be true.

Munro had had to run out of town for a few days on a business trip. That she knew, for it had been the reason why he had wanted to see her before he went.

He had, in fact, spent the evening in her company, after the other couple had excused themselves on one pretext or another.

She called up Alice Murray at the number she had given. She was not there. In fact, no one seemed to know when she would be there. It was strange, because always before it had seemed possible to get her at any moment, almost instantly. That, too, worried her.

She tried to get the thing out of her mind, but she could not. She had a sort of foreboding that her new friend had not spoken without reason, a feeling of insecurity as though something were impending over her.

The crisis came sooner than even Constance had anticipated when she called on Anita Douglas. It was early in the afternoon, while Anita was still brooding, that a strange man called on her. Instinctively she seemed to divine that he was a detective. He, at least, had the look.

"My name," he introduced himself, "is Drummond."

Drummond paused and glanced about as if to make sure that he could by no possibility be overheard.

"I have called," he continued, "on a rather delicate matter."

He paused for effect, then went on:

"Some time ago I was employed by Mr. Douglas to—er—to watch his wife."

He was watching her narrowly to see what effect his sudden remark would have on her. She was speechless.

"Since then," he added quietly, "I have watched, I have seen—what I have seen."

Drummond had faced her. Somehow the effect of his words was more potent on her than if he had not accused her by indirection. Still she said nothing.

"I can suppress it," he insinuated.

Her heart was going like a trip-hammer.

"But it will cost something to do that."

Here was a straw—she caught at it eagerly.

"Cost something?" she repeated, facing him. "How much?"

Drummond never took his eyes from her anxious face.

"I was to get a fee of one thousand dollars if I obtained some letters that had passed from her to a man named Lynn Munro. He has gone out of town—has left his rooms unguarded. I have the letters."

She felt a sinking sensation. One thousand dollars!

Suddenly the truth of the situation flashed over her. He had come with an offer that set her bidding against her husband for the letters. And in a case of dollars her husband would win. One thousand dollars! It was blackmail.

"I—I can't afford it," she pleaded weakly. "Can't you make it—less?"

Drummond shook his head. Already he had learned what he had come to learn. She did not have the money.

"No," he replied positively, adding, by way of inserting the knife and turning it around, "I shall have to turn the letters over to him to-day."

She drew herself up. At least she could fight back.

"But you can't prove anything," she cut in quickly.

"Can't I?" he returned. "The letters don't speak for them-selves, do they? You don't realize that this interview helps to prove it, do you? An innocent woman wouldn't have considered my offer, much less plead with me. Bah! can't prove anything. Why, it's all in plain black and white!"

Drummond flicked the ashes from his cigar into the fireplace as he rose to go. At the door he turned for one parting shot.

"I have all the evidence I need," he concluded. "I've got the goods on you. To-night it will be locked in his safe— documentary evidence. If you should change your mind— you can reach me at his office. Call under an assumed name—Mrs. Green, perhaps."

He was gone, with a mocking smile at the parting shot.

Anita Douglas saw it all now. Things had not been going fast enough to suit her new friend, Mrs. Murray. So, after a time, she had begun to tell of her own escapades and to try to get Anita to admit that she had had similar adventures. It was a favorite device of detectives, working under the new psychological method by use of the law of suggestion.

She had introduced herself, had found out about Lynn Munro, and in some way, after he had left town, had got the letters. Was he in the plot, too? She could not believe it.

Suddenly the thought came to her that the blackmailers might give her husband material that would look very black if a suit for divorce came up in court.

What if he were able to cut off her little allowance? She trembled at the thought of being thus cast adrift on the world.

Anita Douglas did not know which way to turn. In her dilemma she thought only of Constance. She hurried to her.

"It was as you said, a frame-up," she blurted out, as she entered Constance's apartment, then in the same breath added, "That Mrs. Murray was just a stool pigeon."

Constance received her sympathetically. She had expected such a visit, though not so soon.

"Just how much do they—know?" she asked pointedly.

Anita had pressed her hands together nervously. "Really—I confess," she murmured, "indiscretions—yes; misconduct— no!"

She spoke the last words defiantly. Constance listened eagerly, though she did not betray it.

She had found out that it was a curious twist in feminine psychology that the lie under such circumstances was a virtue, that it showed that there was hope for such a woman. Admission of the truth, even to a friend, would have shown that the woman was hopelessly lost. Lie or not, Constance felt in her inmost heart that she approved of it.

"Still, it looks badly," she remarked.

"Perhaps it does—on the surface," persisted Anita.

"You poor dear creature," soothed Constance. "I don't say I blame you for your—indiscreet friendships. You are more sinned against than sinning."

Sympathy had its effect. Anita was now sobbing softly, as Constance stole her arm about her waist.

"The next question," she reasoned, considering aloud, "is, of course, what to do? If it was just one of these blackmailing detective cases it would be common, but still very hard to deal with. There's a lot of such blackmailing going on in New York. Next to business and political cases, I suppose, it is the private detective's most important graft. Nearly everybody has a past—although few are willing to admit it. The graft lies in the fact that people talk so much, are so indiscreet, take such reckless chances. It's a wonder, really, that there isn't more of it."

"Yet there is the—evidence, as he called it—my letters to Lynn—and the reports that that woman must have made of our—our conversations," groaned Anita. "How they may distort it all!"

Constance was thinking rapidly.

"It is now after four o'clock," she said finally, looking at her wrist watch. "You say it was not half an hour ago that Drummond called on you. He must be downtown about now. Your husband will hardly have a chance more than to glance over the papers this afternoon."

Suddenly an idea seemed to occur to her. "What do you suppose he will do with them?" she asked.

Mrs. Douglas looked up through her tears, calmer. "He is very methodical," she answered slowly. "If I know him rightly, I think he will probably go out to Glenclair with them to-night, to look them over."

"Where will he keep them?" broke in Constance suddenly.

"He has a little safe in the library out there where he keeps all such personal papers. I shouldn't be surprised if he looked them over and locked them up there until he intends to use them at least until morning."

"I have a plan," exclaimed Constance excitedly. "Are you game?"

Anita Douglas looked at her friend squarely. In her face Constance read the desperation of a woman battling for life and honor.

"Yes," replied Anita in a low, tense tone, "for anything."

"Then meet me after dinner in the Terminal. We'll go out to Glenclair."

The two looked deeply into each other's eyes. Nothing was said, but what each read was a sufficient answer to a host of unspoken questions.

A moment after Mrs. Douglas had gone, Constance opened a cabinet. From the false back of a drawer she took two little vials of powder and a small bottle with a sponge.

Then she added a long steel bar, with a peculiar turn at the end, to her paraphernalia for the trip.

Nothing further occurred until they met at the Terminal, or, in fact, on the journey out. On most of the ride Mrs. Douglas kept her face averted, looking out of the window into the blackness of the night. Perhaps she was thinking of other journeys out to Glenclair, perhaps she was afraid of meeting the curious gaze of any late sojourners who might suffer from acute suburban curiosity.

Quietly the two women alighted and quickly made their way from the station up the main street, then diverged to a darker and less frequented avenue.

"There's the house," pointed out Mrs. Douglas, halting

Constance, with a little bitter exclamation.

Evidently she had reasoned well. He had gone out there early and there was a light in the library.

"He isn't much of a reader," whispered Mrs. Douglas. "Oh—it's clear to me that he has the stuff all right. He's devouring it, gloating over it."

The sound of footsteps approaching down the paved walk came to them. Loitering on the streets of a suburban town always occasions suspicion, and instinctively Constance drew Anita with her into the shadow of a hedge that set off the house from that next to it.

There was no fence cutting it off from the sidewalk, but at the corner of the plot a large bush stood. In this bower they were perfectly hidden in the shadow.

Hour after hour they waited, watching that light in the library, speculating what it was he was reading, while Anita, half afraid to talk, wondered what it was that Constance had in mind.

Finally the light in the library winked out and the house was in darkness.

Midnight passed, and with it the last belated suburbanite.

At last, when the moon had disappeared under some clouds, Constance pulled Anita gently along up the lawn.

There was no sign of life about the house, yet Constance observed all the caution she would have if it had been well guarded.

Quickly they advanced over the open space to the cottage, approaching in the shadow as much as possible.

Tiptoeing over the porch, Constance tried a window, the window through which had shown the tantalizing light. It was fastened.

Without hesitation she pulled out the long steel bar with the twisted head, and began to insert the sharp end between the sashes.

"Aren't—you—afraid?" chattered her companion.

"No," she whispered, not looking up from her work. "You know, most persons don't know enough about jimmies. Against them an ordinary door lock or window catch is no protection at all. Why, with this jimmy, even a woman can exert a pressure of a ton or so. Not one catch in a thousand can stand it—certainly not this one."

Constance continued to work, muffling the lever as much as possible in a piece of felt.

At last a quick wrench and the catch yielded.

The only thing wrong about it was the noise. There had been no wind, no passing trolley, nothing to conceal it.

They shrank back into the shadow, and waited breathless. Had it been heard? Would a window open presently and an alarm be sounded?

There was not a sound, save the rustle of the leaves in the night wind.

A few minutes later Constance carefully raised the lower

sash and they stepped softly into the house—once the house over which Anita Douglas had been mistress.

Cautiously Constance pressed the button on a little pocket storage-battery lamp and flashed it slowly about the room.

All was quiet in the library. The library table was disordered, as if some one in great stress of mind had been working at it. Anita wondered what had been the grim thoughts of the man as he pondered on the mass of stuff, the tissue of falsehoods that the blackmailing detective had handed to him at such great cost.

At last the cone of light rested on a little safe at the opposite end.

"There it is," whispered Anita, pointing, half afraid even of the soft tones of her own voice.

Constance had pulled down all the shades quietly, and drew the curtains tightly between the room and the foyer.

On the top of the safe she was pouring some of the powder in a neat pile from one of the vials.

"What is that?" asked Anita, bending close to her ear.

"Some powdered metallic aluminum mixed with oxide of iron," whispered Constance in return. "I read of this thing in a scientific paper the other day, and I determined to get some of it. But I didn't think I'd ever really have occasion to use it."

She added some powder from the other vial.

"And that?"

"Magnesium powder."

Constance had lighted a match.

"Stand back, Anita," she whispered, "back, Anita," she whispered, "back in the farthest corner of the room, and keep quiet. Shut your eyes—turn your face away!"

There was a flash, blinding, then a steady, brilliant burst of noiseless, penetrating, burning flame.

Anita had expected an explosion. Instead she found that her eyes hurt. She had not closed them tightly quick enough.

Still, Constance's warning had been sufficient to prevent any damage to the sight, and she slowly recovered.

Actually, the burning powder seemed to be sinking into the very steel of the safe itself, as if it had been mere ice!

Was it an optical illusion, a freak of her sight?

"Wh-what is it!" she whispered in awe, drawing closer to her friend.

"Thermit," whispered Constance in reply, as the two watched the glowing mass fascinated, "an invention of a German chemist named Goldschmidt. It will burn a hole right through steel—at a terrific temperature, three thousand or more degrees."

The almost burned out mass seemed to fall into the safe as if it had been a wooden box instead of chrome steel.

They waited a moment, still blinking, to regain control over their eyes in spite of the care they had used to shield them.

Then they tiptoed across the floor.

In the top of the safe yawned a hole large enough to stick one's hand and arm through!

Constance reached into the safe and drew out something on which she flashed the pocket light.

There was bundle after bundle of checks, the personal checks of a methodical business man, carefully preserved.

Hastily she looked them over. All seemed to be perfectly straight—payments to tradesmen, to real estate agents, payments of all sorts, all carefully labeled.

"Oh, he'd never let anything like that lie around," remarked Anita, as she began to comprehend what Constance was after.

Constance was scrutinizing some of the checks more carefully than others. Suddenly she held one up to the light. Apparently it was in payment of legal services.

Quickly she took the little bottle of brownish fluid which she had brought with the sponge.

She dipped the sponge in it lightly and brushed it over the check. Then she leaned forward breathlessly.

"Eradicating ink is simply a bleaching process," she remarked, "which leaves the iron of the ink as a white oxide instead of a black oxide. The proper reagent will restore the original color—partially and at least for a time. Ah—yes—it is as I thought. There have been erasures in these checks. Other names have been written in on some of them in place of those that were originally there. The sulphide of ammonia ought to bring out anything that is hidden here."

There, faintly, was the original writing. It read, "Pay to the order of—Helen Brett—"

Mrs. Douglas with difficulty restrained an exclamation of anger and hatred at the mere sight of the name of the other woman.

"He was careful," remarked Constance. "Reckless at first in giving checks-he has tried to cover it up. He didn't want to destroy them, yet he couldn't have such evidence about. So he must have altered the name on the canceled vouchers after they were returned to him paid by the bank. Very clever—very."

Constance reached into the safe again. There were some personal and some business letters, some old check books, some silver and gold trinkets and table silver.

She gave a low exclamation. She had found a packet of letters and a sheaf of typewritten flimsy tissue paper pages.

Mrs. Douglas uttered a little cry, quickly suppressed. The letters were those in her own handwriting addressed to Lynn Munro.

"Here are Drummond's reports, too," Constance added.

She looked them hastily over. The damning facts had been massed in a way that must inevitably have prejudiced any case for the defense that Mrs. Douglas might set up.

"There—there's all the evidence against you," whispered Constance hoarsely, handing it over to Anita. "It's all yours again. Destroy it"

In her eagerness, with trembling hands, Anita had torn up the whole mass of incriminating papers and had cast them into the fireplace. She was just about to strike a match.

Suddenly there came a deep voice from the stairs.

"Well—what's all this?"

Anita dropped the match from her nerveless hands. Constance felt an arm grasp her tightly. For a moment a chill ran over her at being caught in the nefarious work of breaking and entering a dwelling-house at night. The hand was Anita's, but the voice was that of a man.

Lights flashed all over the house at once, from a sort of electric light system that could be instantly lighted and would act as a "burglar expeller."

It was Douglas himself. He was staring angrily at his wife and the stranger with her.

"Well!" he demanded with cold sarcasm. "Why this—this burglary?"

Before he could quite take in the situation, with a quick motion, Constance struck a match and touched it to the papers in the fireplace.

As they blazed up he caught sight of what they were and almost leaped across the floor.

Constance laid her hand on his arm. "One moment, Mr. Douglas," she said quietly. "Look at that!"

"Who—who the devil are you?" he gasped. "What's all this?"

"I think," remarked Constance slowly and quietly, "that your wife is now in a position to prove that you—well, don't come into court with clean hands, if you attempt to do so. Besides, you know, the courts rather frown on detectives that practice collusion and conspiracy and frame up evidence, to say nothing of trying to blackmail the victims. I thought perhaps you'd prefer not to say anything about this—er—visit to-night—after you saw that."

Constance had quietly laid one of the erased checks on the library table. Again she dipped the sponge into the brownish liquid. Again the magic touch revealed the telltale name. With her finger she was pointing to the faintly legible "Helen Brett" on the check as the sulphide had brought it out.

Douglas stared-dazed.

He rubbed his eyes and stared again as the last of the flickering fire died away. In an instant he realized that it was not a dream, that it was all a fact.

He looked from one to the other of the women.

He was checkmated.

Constance ostentatiously folded up the erased vouchers.

"I—I shall not—make any—contest," Douglas managed to gasp huskily.

CHAPTER XI

THE DOPE FIENDS

"I have a terrible headache," remarked Constance Dunlap to her friend, Adele Gordon, the petite cabaret singer and dancer of the Mayfair, who had dropped in to see her one afternoon.

"You poor, dear creature," soothed Adele. "Why don't you go to see Dr. Price? He has cured me. He's splendid—splendid."

Constance hesitated. Dr. Moreland Price was a well-known physician. All day and even at night, she knew, automobiles and cabs rolled up to his door and their occupants were, for the most part, stylishly gowned women.

"Oh, come on," urged Adele. "He doesn't charge as highly as people seem to think. Besides, I'll go with you and introduce you, and he'll charge only as he does the rest of us in the profession."

Constance's head throbbed frantically. She felt that she must have some relief soon. "All right," she agreed, "I'll go with you, and thank you, Adele."

Dr. Price's office was on the first floor of the fashionable Recherche Apartments, and, as she expected, Constance noted a line of motor cars before it.

They entered and were admitted to a richly furnished room, in mahogany and expensive Persian rugs, where a number of patients waited. One after another an attendant summoned them noiselessly and politely to see the doctor, until at last the turn of Constance and Adele came.

Dr. Price was a youngish, middle-aged man, tall, with a sallow countenance and a self-confident, polished manner which went a long way in reassuring the patients, most of whom were ladies.

As they entered the doctor's sanctum behind the folding doors, Adele seemed to be on very good terms indeed with him.

They seated themselves in the deep leather chairs beside Dr. Price's desk, and he inclined his head to listen to the story of their ailments.

"Doctor," began Constance's introducer, "I've brought my friend, Mrs. Dunlap, who is suffering from one of those awful headaches. I thought perhaps you could give her some of that medicine that has done me so much good."

The doctor bowed without saying anything and shifted his eyes from Adele to Constance. "Just what seems to be the difficulty?" he inquired.

Constance told him how she felt, of her general lassitude and the big, throbbing veins in her temples.

"Ah—a woman's headaches!" he smiled, adding, "Nothing

Arthur B. Reeve

serious, however, in this case, as far as I can see. We can fix this one all right, I think."

He wrote out a prescription quickly and handed it to Constance.

"Of course," he added, as he pocketed his fee, "it makes no difference to me personally, but I would advise that you have it filled at Muller's—Miss Gordon knows the place. I think Muller's drugs are perhaps fresher than those of most druggists, and that makes a great deal of difference."

He had risen and was politely and suavely bowing them out of another door, at the same time by pressing a button signifying to his attendant to admit the next patient.

Constance had preceded Adele, and, as she passed through the other door, she overheard the doctor whisper to her friend, "I'm going to stop for you to-night to take a ride. I have something important I want to say to you."

She did not catch Adele's answer, but as they left the marble and onyx, brass-grilled entrance, Adele remarked: "That's his car—over there. Oh, but he is a reckless driver—dashes along pell-mell—but always seems to have his eye out for everything—never seems to be arrested, never in an accident."

Constance turned in the direction of the car and was startled to see the familiar face of Drummond across the street dodging behind it. What was it now, she wondered—a divorce case, a scandal—what?

The medicine was made up into little powders, to be taken until they gave relief, and Constance folded the paper of one, poured it on the back of her tongue and swallowed a glass of water afterward.

Her head continued to throb, but she felt a sense of well-being that she had not before. Adele urged her to take another, and Constance did so.

The second powder increased the effect of the first marvelously. But Constance noticed that she now began to feel queer. She was not used to taking medicine. For a moment she felt that she was above, beyond the reach of ordinary rules and laws. She could have done any sort of physical task, she felt, no matter how difficult. She was amazed at herself, as compared to what she had been only a few moments before.

"Another one?" asked Adele finally.

Constance was by this time genuinely alarmed at the sudden unwonted effect on herself. "N-no," she replied dubiously, "I don't think I want to take any more, just yet."

"Not another?" asked Adele in surprise. "I wish they would affect me that way. Sometimes I have to take the whole dozen before they have any effect."

They chatted for a few minutes, and finally Adele rose.

"Well," she remarked with a nervous twitching of her body, as if she were eager to be doing something, "I really must be going. I can't say I feel any too well myself."

"I think I'll take a walk with you," answered Constance, who did not like the continued effect of the two powders. "I feel the need of exercise—and air."

Adele hesitated, but Constance already had her hat on. She

had seen Drummond watching Dr. Price's door, and it interested her to know whether he could possibly have been following Adele or some one else.

As they walked along Adele quickened her pace, until they came again to the drug store.

"I believe I'll go in and get something," she remarked, pausing.

For the first time in several minutes Constance looked at the face of her friend. She was amazed to discover that Adele looked as if she had had a spell of sickness. Her eyes were large and glassy, her skin cold and sweaty, and she looked positively pallid and thin.

As they entered the store Muller, the druggist, bowed again and looked at Adele a moment as she leaned over the counter and whispered something to him. Without a word he went into the arcana behind the partition that cuts off the mysteries of the prescription room in every drug store from the front of the store.

When Muller returned he handed her a packet, for which she paid and which she dropped quickly into her pocketbook, hugging the pocketbook close to herself.

Adele turned and was about to hurry from the store with Constance. "Oh, excuse me," she said suddenly as if she had just recollected something, "I promised a friend of mine I'd telephone this afternoon, and I have forgotten to do it. I see a pay station here." Constance waited.

Adele returned much quicker than one would have expected she could call up a number, but Constance thought nothing of it at the time. She did notice, however, that as her friend emerged from the booth a most marvelous change had taken place in her. Her step was firm, her eye clear, her hand steady. Whatever it was, reasoned Constance, it could not have been serious to have disappeared so quickly.

It was with some curiosity as to just what she might expect that Constance went around to the famous cabaret that night. The Mayfair occupied two floors of what had been a wide brownstone house before business and pleasure had crowded the residence district further and further uptown. It was a very well-known bohemian rendezvous, where under-, demi- and upper-world rubbed elbows without friction and seemed to enjoy the novelty and be willing to pay for it.

Adele, who was one of the performers, had not arrived yet, but Constance, who had come with her mind still full of the two unexpected encounters with Drummond, was startled to see him here again. Fortunately he did not see her, and she slipped unobserved into an angle near the window overlooking the street.

Drummond had been engrossed in watching some one already there, and Constance made the best use she could of her eyes to determine who it was. The outdoor walk and a good dinner had checked her headache, and now the excitement of the chase of something, she knew not what, completed the cure.

It was not long before she discovered that Drummond was watching intently, without seeming to do so, a nervous-looking fellow whose general washed-out appearance of face was especially unattractive for some reason or other. He was very thin, very pale, and very stary about the eyes. Then, too, it seemed as if the bone in his nose was going, due perhaps to the shrinkage of the blood vessels from some cause.

Constance noticed a couple of girls whom she had seen Adele speak to on several other occasions approaching the young man.

There came an opportune lull in the music and from around the corner of her protecting angle Constance could just catch the greeting of one of the girls, "Hello, Sleighbells! Got any snow!"

It was a remark that seemed particularly malapropos to the sultry weather, and Constance half expected a burst of laughter at the unexpected sally.

Instead, she was surprised to hear the young man reply in a very serious and matter-of-fact manner, "Sure. Got any money, May?"

She craned her neck, carefully avoiding coming into Drummond's line of vision, and as she did so she saw two silver quarters gleam momentarily from hand to hand, and the young man passed each girl stealthily a small white paper packet.

Others came to him, both men and women. It seemed to be an established thing, and Constance noted that Drummond watched it all covertly.

"Who is that?" asked Constance of the waiter who had served her sometimes when she had been with Adele, and knew her.

"Why, they call him Sleighbells Charley," he replied, "a coke fiend."

"Which means a cocaine fiend, I suppose!" she queried.

"Yes. He's a lobbygow for the grapevine system they have now of selling the dope in spite of this new law."

"Where does he get the stuff!" she asked.

The waiter shrugged his shoulders. "Nobody knows, I guess. I don't. But he gets it in spite of the law and peddles it. Oh, it's all adulterated—with some white stuff, I don't know what, and the price they charge is outrageous. They must make an ounce retail at five or six times the cost. Oh, you can bet that some one who is at the top is making a pile of money out of that graft, all right."

He said it not with any air of righteous indignation, but with a certain envy.

Constance was thinking the thing over in her mind. Where did the "coke" come from? The "grapevine" system interested her.

"Sleighbells" seemed to have disposed of all the "coke" he had brought with him. As the last packet went, he rose slowly, and shuffled out. Constance, who knew that Adele would not come for some time, determined to follow him. She rose quietly and, under cover of a party going out, managed to disappear without, as far as she knew, letting Drummond catch a glimpse of her. This would not only employ her time, but it was better to avoid Drummond as far as possible, at present, too, she felt.

At a distance of about half a block she followed the curiously shuffling figure. He crossed the avenue, turned and went uptown, turned again, and, before she knew it, disappeared in a drug store. She had been so engrossed in following the lobbygow that it was with a start that she realized that he had entered Muller's.

What did it all mean? Was the druggist, Muller, the man higher up? She recalled suddenly her own experience of the afternoon. Had Muller tried to palm off something on her? The more she thought of it the more sure she was that the powders she had taken had been doped.

Slowly, turning the matter over in her mind, she returned to the Mayfair. As she peered in cautiously before entering she saw that Drummond had gone. Adele had not come in yet, and she went in and sat down again in her old place.

Perhaps half an hour later, outside, she heard a car drive up with a furious rattle of gears. She looked out of the window and, as far as she could determine in the shadows, it was Dr. Price. A woman got out, Adele. For a moment she stopped to talk, then Dr. Price waved a gay good-bye and was off. All she could catch was a hasty, "No; I don't think I'd better come in to-night," from him.

As Adele entered the Mayfair she glanced about, caught sight of Constance and came and sat down by her.

It would have been impossible for her to enter unobserved, so popular was she. It was not long before the two girls whom Constance had seen dealing with "Sleighbells" sauntered over.

"Your friend was here to-night," remarked one to Adele.

"Which one?" laughed Adele.

"The one who admired your dancing the other night and wanted to take lessons."

"You mean the young fellow who was selling something?" asked Constance pointedly.

"Oh, no," returned the girl quite casually. "That was Sleighbells," and they all laughed.

Constance thought immediately of Drummond. "The other one, then," she said, "the thick-set man who was all alone!"

"Yes; he went away afterward. Do you know him?"

"I've seen him somewhere," evaded Constance; "but I just can't quite place him."

She had not noticed Adele particularly until now. Under the light she had a peculiar worn look, the same as she had had before.

The waiter came up to them. "Your turn is next," he hinted to Adele.

"Excuse me a minute," she apologized to the rest of the party. "I must fix up a bit. No," she added to Constance, "don't come with me."

She returned from the dressing room a different person, and plunged into the wild dance for which the limited orchestra was already tuning up. It was a veritable riot of whirl and rhythm. Never before had Constance seen Adele dance with such abandon. As she executed the wild mazes of a newly imported dance, she held even the jaded Mayfair spellbound. And when she concluded with one daring figure and sat down, flushed and excited, the diners applauded and even shouted approval. It was an event for even the dance-mad Mayfair.

Constance did not share in the applause. At last she understood. Adele was a dope fiend, too. She felt it with a sense of pain. Always, she knew, the fiends tried to get away alone somewhere for a few minutes to snuff some of their favorite nepenthe. She had heard before of the cocaine "snuffers" who took a little of the deadly powder, placed it on the back of the hand, and inhaled it up the nose with a quick intake of breath. Adele was one. It was not Adele who danced. It was the dope.

Constance was determined to speak.

"You remember that man the girls spoke of?" she began.

"Yes. What of him?" asked Adele with almost a note of defiance.

"Well, I really DO know him," confessed Constance. "He is a detective."

Constance watched her companion curiously, for at the mere word she had stopped short and faced her. "He is?" she asked quickly. "Then that was why Dr. Price—"

She managed to suppress the remark and continued her walk home without another word.

In Adele's little apartment Constance was quick to note that the same haggard look had returned to her friend's face.

Adele had reached for her pocketbook with a sort of clutching eagerness and was about to leave the room.

Constance rose. "Why don't you give up the stuff?" she asked earnestly. "Don't you want to?"

For a moment Adele faced her angrily. Then her real nature seemed slowly to come to the surface. "Yes," she murmured frankly.

"Then why don't you?" pleaded Constance.

"I haven't the power. There is an indescribable excitement to do something great, to make a mark. It's soon gone, but while it lasts, I can sing, dance, do anything—and then—every part of my body begins crying for mere of the stuff again."

There was no longer any necessity of concealment from Constance. She took a pinch of the stuff, placed it on the back of her wrist and quickly sniffed it. The change in her was magical. From a quivering wretched girl she became a self-confident neurasthenic.

"I don't care," she laughed hollowly now.

"Yes, I know what you are going to tell me. Soon I'll be 'hunting the cocaine bug,' as they call it, imagining that in my skin, under the flesh, are worms crawling, perhaps see them, see the little animals running around and biting me."

She said it with a half-reckless cynicism. "Oh, you don't know. There are two souls in the cocainist—one tortured by the pain of not having the stuff, the other laughing and mocking at the dangers of it. It stimulates. It makes your mind work—without effort, by itself. And it gives such visions of success, makes you feel able to do so much, and to forget. All the girls use it."

"Where do they get it?" asked Constance "I thought the new law prohibited it."

"Get it?" repeated Adele. "Why, they get it from that fellow they call 'Sleighbells.' They call it 'snow,' you know, and the girls who use it 'snowbirds.' The law does prohibit its sale, but—"

She paused significantly.

"Yes," agreed Constance; "but Sleighbells is only a part of the system after all. Who is the man at the top?"

Adele shrugged her shoulders and was silent. Still, Constance did not fail to note a sudden look of suspicion which Adele shot at her. Was Adele shielding some one?

Constance knew that some one must be getting rich from the traffic, probably selling hundreds of ounces a week and making thousands of dollars. Somehow she felt a sort of indignation at the whole thing. Who was it? Who was the man higher up?

In the morning as she was working about her little kitchenette an idea came to her. Why not hire the vacant apartment cross the hall from Adele? An optician, who was a friend of hers, in the course of a recent conversation had mentioned an invention, a model of which he had made for the inventor. She would try it.

Since, with Constance, the outlining of a plan was tantamount to the execution, it was not many hours later before she had both the apartment and the model of the invention.

Her wall separated her from the drug store and by careful calculation she determined about where came the little prescription department. Carefully, so as to arouse no suspicion, she began to bore away at the wall with various tools, until finally she had a small, al-most imperceptible opening. It was tedious work, and toward the end needed great care so as not to excite suspicion. But finally she was rewarded. Through it she could see just a trace of daylight, and by squinting could see a row of bottles on a shelf opposite.

Then, through the hole, she pushed a long, narrow tube, like a putty blower. When at last she placed her eye at it, she gave a low exclamation of satisfaction. She could now see the whole of the little room.

It was a detectascope, invented by Gaillard Smith, adapter of the detectaphone, an instrument built up on the principle of the cytoscope which physicians use to explore internally down the throat. Only, in the end of the tube, instead of an ordinary lens, was placed what is known as a "fish-eye" lens, which had a range something like nature has given the eyes of fishes, hence the name. Ordinarily cameras, because of the flatness of their lenses, have a range of only a few degrees, the greatest being scarcely more than ninety. But this lens was globular, and, like a drop of water, refracted light from all directions. When placed so that half of it caught the light it "saw" through an angle of 180 degrees, "saw" everything in the room instead of just that little row of bottles on the shelf opposite.

Constance set herself to watch, and it was not long before her suspicions were confirmed, and she was sure that this was nothing more than a "coke" joint. Still she wondered whether Muller was the real source of the traffic of which Sleighbells was the messenger. She was determined to find out.

All day she watched through her detectascope. Once she saw Adele come in and buy more dope. It was with difficulty that she kept from interfering. But, she reflected, the time was not ripe. She had thought the thing out. There was no use in trying to get at it through Adele. The only way was to stop the whole curse at its source, to dam the stream. People came and went. She soon found that he was selling them packets from a box hidden in the woodwork. That much she had learned, anyhow.

Constance watched faithfully all day with only time enough taken out for dinner. It was after her return from this brief interval that she felt her heart give a leap of apprehension, as she looked again through the detectascope. There was Drummond in the back of the store talking to Muller and a woman who looked as if she might be Mrs. Muller, for both, seemed nervous and anxious.

As nearly as she could make out, Drummond was alternately threatening and arguing with Muller. Finally the three seemed to agree, for Drummond walked over to a typewriter on a table, took a fresh sheet of carbon paper from a drawer, placed it between two sheets of paper, and hastily wrote something.

Drummond read over what he had written. It seemed to be short, and the three apparently agreed on it. Then, in a trembling hand, Muller signed the two copies which Drummond had made, one of which Drummond himself kept and the other he sealed in an envelope and sent away by a boy. Drummond reached into his pocket and pulled out a huge roll of bills of large denomination. He counted out what seemed to be approximately half, handed it to the woman, and replaced the rest in his pocket. What it was all about Constance could only vaguely guess. She longed to know what was in the letter and why the money had been paid to the woman.

Perhaps a quarter of an hour after Drummond left Adele appeared again, pleading for more dope. Muller went back of the partition and made up a fresh paper of it from a bottle also concealed.

Constance was torn by conflicting impulses. She did not want to miss anything in the perplexing drama that was being enacted before her, yet she wished to interfere with the deadly course of Adele. Still, perhaps the girl would resent interference if she found out that Constance was spying on her. She determined to wait a little while before seeing Adele. It was only after a decided effort that she tore herself away from the detectascope and knocked on Adele's door as if she had just come in for a visit. Again she knocked, but still there was no answer. Every minute something might be happening next door. She hurried back to her post of observation.

One of the worst aspects of the use of cocaine, she knew, was the desire of the user to share his experience with some one else. The passing on of the habit, which seemed to be one of the strongest desires of the drug fiend, made him even more dangerous to society than he would otherwise have been. That thought gave Constance an idea.

She recalled also now having heard somewhere that it was a common characteristic of these poor creatures to have a passion for fast automobiling, to go on long rides, perhaps even without having the money to pay for them. That, too, confirmed the idea which she had.

As the night advanced she determined to stick to her post. What could it have been that Drummond was doing? It was no good, she felt positive.

Suddenly before her eye, glued to its eavesdropping aperture, she saw a strange sight. There was a violent commotion in the store. Blue-coated policemen seemed to swarm in from nowhere. And in the rear, directing them, appeared Drummond, holding by the arm the unfortunate Sleighbells, quaking with fear, evidently having been picked up already elsewhere by the wily detective.

Muller put up a stout resistance, but the officers easily seized him and, after a hasty but thorough search, unearthed his cache of the contraband drug.

As the scene unfolded, Constance was more and more bewildered after having witnessed that which preceded it, the signing of the letter and the passing of the money. Muller evidently had nothing to say about that. What did it mean?

The police were still holding Muller, and Constance had not noted that Drummond had disappeared.

"It's on the first floor—left, men," sounded a familiar voice outside her own door. "I know she's there. My shadow saw her buy the dope and take it home."

Her heart was thumping wildly. It was Drummond leading his squad of raiders, and they were about to enter the apartment of Adele. They knocked, but there was no answer.

A few moments before Constance would have felt perfectly safe in saying that Adele was out. But if Drummond's man had seen her enter, might she not have been there all the time, be there still, in a stupor? She dreaded to think of what might happen if the poor girl once fell into their hands. It would be the final impulse that would complete her ruin.

Constance did not stop to reason it out. Her woman's intuition told her that now was the time to act—that there was no retreat.

She opened her own door just as the raiders had forced in the flimsy affair that guarded the apartment of Adele.

"So!" sneered Drummond, catching sight of her in the dim light of the hallway. "You are mixed up in these violations of the new drug law, too!"

Constance said nothing. She had determined first to make Drummond display his hand.

"Well," he ground out, "I'm going to get these people this time. I represent the Medical Society and the Board of Health. These men have been assigned to me by the Commissioner as a dope squad. We want this girl. We have others who will give evidence; but we want this one, too."

He said it with a bluster that even exaggerated the theatrical character of the raid itself. Constance did not stop to weigh the value of his words, but through the door she brushed quickly. Adele might need her if she was indeed there.

As she entered the little living-room she saw a sight which almost transfixed her. Adele was there—lying across a divan, motionless.

Constance bent over. Adele was cold. As far as she could determine there was not a breath or a heart beat!

What did it mean? She did not stop to think. Instantly there flashed over her the recollection of an instrument she had read about at one of the city hospitals, It might save Adele. Before any one knew what she was doing she had darted to the telephone in the lower hall of the apartment and had called up the hospital frantically, imploring them to hurry. Adele must be saved.

Constance had no very clear idea of what happened next in the hurly-burly of events, until the ambulance pulled up at the door and the white-coated surgeon burst in carrying a heavy suitcase.

With one look at the unfortunate girl he muttered, "Paralysis of the respiratory organs—too large a dose of the drug. You did perfectly right," and began unpacking the case.

Constance, calm now in the crisis, stood by him and helped as deftly as could any nurse.

It was a curious arrangement of tubes and valves, with a large rubber bag, and a little pump that the doctor had brought. Quickly he placed a cap, attached to it, over the nose and mouth of the poor girl, and started the machine.

"Wh-what is it?" gasped Drummond as he saw Adele's hitherto motionless breast now rise and fall.

"A pulmotor," replied the doctor, working quickly and carefully, "an artificial lung. Sometimes it can revive even the medically dead. It is our last chance with this girl."

Constance had picked up the packet which had fallen beside Adele and was looking at the white powder.

"Almost pure cocaine," remarked the young surgeon, testing it. "The hydrochloride, large crystals, highest quality. Usually it is adulterated. Was she in the habit of taking it this way?"

Constance said nothing. She had seen Muller make up the packet—specially now, she recalled. Instead of the adulterated dope he had given Adele the purest kind. Why? Was there some secret he wished to lock in her breast forever?

Mechanically the pulmotor pumped. Would it save her?

Constance was living over what she had already seen through the detectascope. Suddenly she thought of the strange letter and of the money.

She hurried into the drug store. Muller had already been taken away, but before the officer left in charge could interfere she picked up the carbon sheet on which the letter had been copied, turned it over and held it eagerly to the light.

She read in amazement. It was a confession. In it Muller admitted to Dr. Moreland Price that he was the head of a sort of dope trust, that he had messengers out, like Sleighbells, that he had often put dope in the prescriptions sent him by the doctor, and had repeatedly violated the law and refilled such prescriptions. On its face it was complete and convincing.

Yet it did not satisfy Constance. She could not believe that Adele had committed suicide. Adele must possess some secret. What was it?

"Is—is there any change?" she asked anxiously of the young surgeon now engrossed in his work.

For answer he merely nodded to the apparently motionless form on the bed, and for a moment stopped the pulmotor.

The mechanical movement of the body ceased. But in its place was a slight tremor about the lips and mouth.

Adele moved—was faintly gasping for breath!

"Adele!" cried Constance softly in her ear. "Adele!"

Something, perhaps a far-away answer of recognition, seemed to flicker over her face. The doctor redoubled his efforts.

"Adele—do you know me?" whispered Constance again.

"Yes," came back faintly at last. "There—there's some-thing—wrong with it—They—they—"

"How? What do you mean?" urged Constance. "Tell me, Adele."

The girl moved uneasily. The doctor administered a stimulant and she vaguely opened her eyes, began to talk hazily, dreamily. Constance bent over to catch the faint words which would have been lost to the others.

"They—are going to—double cross the Health Department," she murmured as if to herself, then gathering strength she went on, "Muller and Sleighbells will be arrested and take the penalty. They have been caught with the goods, anyhow. It has all been arranged so that the detective will get his case. Money—will be paid to both of them, to Muller and the detective, to swing the case and protect him. He made me do it. I saw the detective, even danced with him and he agreed to do it. Oh, I would do anything—I am his willing tool when I have the stuff. But—this time—it was—" She rambled off incoherently.

"Who made you do it? Who told you?" prompted Constance. "For whom would you do anything?"

Adele moaned and clutched Constance's hand convulsively. Constance did not pause to consider the ethics of questioning a half-unconscious girl Her only idea was to get at the truth.

"Who was it?" she reiterated.

Adele turned weakly.

"Dr. Price," she murmured as Constance bent her ear to catch even the faintest sound. "He told me—all about it—last night—in the car."

Instantly Constance understood. Adele was the only one outside who held the secret, who could upset the carefully planned frame-up that was to protect the real head of the dope trust who had paid liberally to save his own wretched skin.

She rose quickly and wheeled about suddenly on Drummond.

"You will convict Dr. Price also," she said in a low tone. "This girl must not be dragged down, too. You will leave her alone, and both you and Mr. Muller will hand over that money to her for her cure of the habit."

Drummond started forward angrily, but fell back as Constance added in a lower but firmer tone, "Or I'll have you all up on a charge of attempting murder."

Drummond turned surlily to those of his "dope squad," who remained:

"You can go, boys," he said brusquely.

"There's been some mistake here."

CHAPTER XII

THE FUGITIVES

"Newspaper pictures seldom look like the person they represent," asserted Lawrence Macey nonchalantly.

Constance Dunlap looked squarely at the man opposite her at the table, oblivious to the surroundings. It was a brilliant sight in the great after-theater rendezvous, the beautiful faces and gowns, the exquisite music, the bright lights and the gayety. She had chosen this time and place for a reason. She had hoped that the contrast with what she had to say would be most marked in its influence on the man.

"Nevertheless," she replied keenly, "I recognize the picture—as though you were Bertillon's new 'spoken portrait' of this Graeme Mackenzie."

She deliberately folded up a newspaper clipping and shoved it into her hand-bag on a chair beside the table.

Lawrence Macey met her eye unflinchingly.

"Suppose," he drawled, "just for the sake of argument, that you are right. What would you do?"

Constance looked at the unruffled exterior of the man. With her keen perception she knew that it covered just as calm an interior. He would have said the same thing if she had been a real detective, had walked up behind him suddenly in the subway crush, had tapped his shoulder, and whispered, "You're wanted."

"We are dealing with facts, not suppositions," she replied evasively.

Momentarily, a strange look passed over Macey's face. What was she driving at—blackmail? He could not think so, even though he had only just come to know Constance. He rejected the thought before it was half formed.

"Put it as you please," he persisted. "I am, then, this Graeme Mackenzie who has decamped from Omaha with half a million—it is half a million in the article, is it not?—of cash and unregistered stocks and bonds. Now what would you do?"

Constance felt unconsciously the shift which he had skilfully made in their positions. Instead of being the pursuer, she was now the pursued, at least in their conversation. He had admitted nothing of what her quick intuition told her.

Yet she felt an admiration for the sang-froid of Macey. She felt a spell thrown over her by; the magnetic eyes that seemed to search her own. They were large eyes, the eyes of a dreamer, rather than of a practical man, eyes of a man who goes far and travels long with the woman on whom he fixes them solely.

"You haven't answered my hypothetical question," he reminded her.

She brought herself back with a start. "I was only thinking," she murmured.

"Then there is doubt in your mind what you would do?"

"N—no," she hesitated.

He bent over nearer across the table. "You would at least recall the old adage, 'Do unto others as you would that they should do unto you'?" he urged.

It was uncanny, the way this man read her thoughts.

"You know whom they say quotes scripture," she avoided.

"And am I a—a devil?"

"I did not say so."

"You hinted it."

She had. But she said, "No, nor hinted it."

"Then you did not MEAN to hint it?"

She looked away a moment at the gay throng. "Graeme Mackenzie," she said, slowly, "what's the use of all this beating about? Why cannot we be frank with one another?"

She paused, then resumed, meditatively, "A long time ago I became involved with a man in a scheme to forge checks. I would have done anything for him, anything."

A cloud passed over his face. She saw it, had been watching for it, but appeared not to do so. His was a nature to brook no rivalry.

"My husband had become involved in extravagances for which I was to blame," she went on.

The cloud settled, and in its place came a look of intense relief. He was like most men. Whatever his own morals, he demanded a high standard in her.

"We formed an amateur partnership in crime," she hurried on. "He lost his life, was unable to stand up against the odds, while he was alone, away from me. Since then I have been helping those who have become involved, on the wrong side, with the law. There," she concluded simply, "I have put myself in your power. I have admitted my part in something that, try as they would, they could never connect me with. I have done it because—because I want to help you. Be as frank with me."

He eyed her keenly again. The appeal was irresistible.

"I can tell you Graeme Mackenzie's story," he began carefully. "Six months ago there was a young man in Omaha who had worked faithfully for a safe deposit company for years. He was getting eighty-five dollars a month. That is more than it seems to you here in New York. But it was very little for what he did. Why, as superintendent of the safe deposit vaults he had helped to build up that part of the trust company's business to such an extent that he knew he deserved more.

"Now, a superintendent of a safe deposit vault has lots of chances. Sometimes depositors give him their keys to unlock their boxes for them. It is a simple thing to make an impression in wax or chewing gum palmed in the hand. Or he has access to a number of keys of unrented boxes; he can, as opportunity offers, make duplicates, and then when the boxes are rented, he has a key. Even if the locks of unrented boxes are blanks, set by the first insertion of the key chosen at random, he can still do the same thing. And even if it takes two to get at the idle keys, himself and another trusted employe, he can get at them, if he is clever, without the other officer knowing it, though it may be done almost before his eyes. You see, it all comes down to the honesty of the man."

He paused. Constance was fascinated at the coolness with which this man had gone to work, and with which he told of it.

"This superintendent earned more than he received. He deserved it. But when he asked for a raise, they told him he was lucky to keep the job,—they reduced him, instead, to seventy-five dollars. He was angry at the stinging rebuke. He determined to make them smart, to show them what he could do.

"One noon he went out to lunch and—they have been looking for him ever since. He had taken half a million in cash, stocks, and bonds, unregistered and hence easily hypothecated and traded on."

"And his motive?" she asked.

He looked at her long and earnestly as if making up his mind to something. "I think," he replied, "I wanted revenge quite as much as the money."

He said it slowly, measured, as if realizing that there was now nothing to be gained by concealment from her, as if only he wanted to put himself in the best light with the woman who had won from him his secret. It was his confession!

Acquaintances with Constance ripened fast into friendships.

She had known Macey, as he called himself, only a fortnight. He had been introduced to her at a sort of Bohemian gathering, had talked to her, direct, as she liked a man to talk. He had seen her home that night, had asked to call, and on the other nights had taken her to the theater and to supper.

Delicately unconsciously, a bond of friendship had grown up between them. She felt that he was a man vibrating with physical and mental power, long latent, which nothing but a strong will held in check, a man by whom she could be fascinated, yet of whom she was just a little bit afraid.

With Macey, it would have been difficult to analyze his feelings. He had found in Constance a woman who had seen the world in all its phases, yet had come through unstained by what would have drowned some in the depths of the under-world, or thrust others into the degradation of the demi-monde, at least. He admired and respected her. He, the dreamer, saw in her the practical. She, an adventurer in amateur lawlessness saw in him something kindred at heart.

And so when a newspaper came to her in which she recognized with her keen insight Lawrence Macey's face under Graeme Mackenzie's name, and a story of embezzlement of trust company and other funds from the Omaha Central Western Trust of half a million, she had not been wholly surprised. Instead, she felt almost a sense of elation. The man was neither better nor worse than herself. And he needed help.

Her mind wandered back to a time, months before, when she had learned the bitter lesson of what it was to be a legal outcast, and had determined always to keep within the law, no matter how close to the edge of things she went.

Mackenzie continued looking at her, as if waiting for the

answer to his first question.

"No," she said slowly, "I am not going to hand you over. I never had any such intention. We are in each other's power. But you cannot go about openly, even in New York, now. Some one besides myself must have seen that article."

Graeme listened blankly. It was true. His fancied security in the city was over. He had fled to New York because there, in the mass of people, he could best sink his old identity and take on a new.

She leaned her head on her hand and her elbow on the table and looked deeply into his eyes. "Let me take those securities," she said. "I will be able to do safely what you cannot do."

Graeme did not seem now to consider the fortune for which he had risked so much. The woman before him was enough.

"Will you?" he asked eagerly.

"I will do with them as I would for myself, better, because—because it is a trust," she accepted.

"More than a trust," he added, as he leaned over in turn and in spite of other diners in the restaurant took her hand.

There are times when the rest of the critical world and its frigid opinions are valueless. Constance did not withdraw her hand. Rather she watched in his eyes the subtle physical change in the man that her very touch produced, watched and felt a response in herself.

Quickly she withdrew her hand. "I must go," she said rather hurriedly, "it is getting late."

"Constance," he whispered, as he helped her on with her wraps, brushing the waiter aside that he might himself perform any duty that involved even touching her, "Constance, I am in your hands—absolutely."

It had been pleasant to dine with him. It was more pleasant now to feel her influence and power over him. She knew it, though she only half admitted it. They seemed for the moment to walk on air, as they strolled, chatting, out to a taxicab.

But as the cab drew up before her own apartment, the familiar associations of even the entrance brought her back to reality suddenly. He handed her out, and the excitement of the evening was over. She saw the thing in its true light. This was the beginning, not the end.

"Graeme," she said, as she lingered for a moment at the door. "To-morrow we must find a place where you can hide."

"I may see you, though?" he asked anxiously.

"Of course. Ring me up in the morning, Graeme. Good-night," and she was whisked up in the elevator, leaving Mackenzie with a sense of loss and loneliness.

"By the Lord," he muttered, as he swung down the street in preference to taking a cab, "what a woman that is!"

Together the next day they sought out a place where he could remain hidden. Mackenzie would have been near her, but Constance knew better. She chose a bachelor apartment where the tenants never arose before noon and where night was turned into day. Men would not ask questions. In an apartment like her own there was nothing but gossip.

In the daytime he stayed at home. Only at night did he go forth and then under her direction in the most unfrequented ways.

Every day Constance went to Wall Street, where she had established confidential relations with a number of brokers. Together they planned the campaigns; she executed them with consummate skill and adroitness.

Constance was amazed. Here was a man who for years had been able to earn only eighty-five dollars a month and had not seemed to show any ability. Yet he was able to speculate in Wall Street with such dash that he seemed to be in a fair way, through her, to accumulate a fortune.

One night as they were hurrying back to Graeme's after a walk, they had to pass a crowd on Broadway. Constance saw a familiar face hurrying by. It gave her a start. It was Drummond, the detective. He was not, apparently, looking for her. But then that was his method. He might have been looking. At any rate it reminded her unpleasantly of the fact that there were detectives in the world.

"What's the matter?" asked Graeme, noticing the change in her.

"I just saw a man I know."

The old jealousy flushed his face. Constance laughed in spite of her fears. Indeed, there was something that pleased her in his jealousy.

"He was the detective who has been hounding me ever since that time I told you about."

"Oh," he subsided. But if Drummond had been there,

Mackenzie could have been counted on to risk all to protect her.

"We must be more careful," she shuddered.

Constance was startled one evening just as she was going out to meet Graeme and report on the progress of the day at hearing a knock at her door.

She opened it.

"I suppose you think I am your Nemesis," introduced Drummond, as he stepped in, veiling the keenness of his search by an attempt to be familiar.

She had more than half expected it. She said nothing, but her coldness was plainly one of interrogation.

"A case has been placed in my hands by some western clients of ours," he said by way of swaggering explanation, "of an embezzler who is hiding in New York. It required no great reasoning power to decide that the man's trail would sooner or later cross Wall Street. I believe it has done so— not directly, but indirectly. The trail, I think, has brought me back to the proverbial point of 'CHERCHEZ LA FEMME.' I am delighted," he dwelt on the word to see what would be its effect, "to see in the Graeme Mackenzie case my old friend, Constance Dunlap."

"So," she replied quietly, "you suspect ME, now. I suppose *I* am Graeme Mackenzie."

"No," Drummond replied dubiously, "you are not Graeme Mackenzie, of course. You may be Mrs. Graeme Mackenzie, for all I know. But I believe you are the receiver of Graeme Mackenzie's stolen goods!"

"You do?" she answered calmly. "That remains for you to prove. Why do you believe it? Is it because you are ready to believe anything of me!"

"I have noticed that you are more active downtown than—"

"Oh, it is because I speculate. Have I no means of my own?" she asked pointedly.

"Where is he? Not here, I know. But where?" insinuated Drummond with a knowing look.

"Am I my brother's keeper?" she laughed merrily. "Come, now. Who is this wonderful Graeme Mackenzie? First show me that I know him. You know the rule in a murder case— you must prove the CORPUS DELICTI."

Drummond was furious. She was so baffling. That was his weak point and she had picked it out infallibly. Whatever his suspicions, he had been able to prove nothing, though he suspected much in the buying and selling of Constance.

A week of bitterness, of a constant struggle against the wiles of one of the most subtle sleuths followed, avoiding hidden traps that beset her on every side. Was this to be the end of it all? Was Drummond's heroic effort to entangle her to succeed at last?

She felt that a watch of the most extraordinary kind was set on her, an invisible net woven about her. Eyes that never slept were upon her; there was no minute in her regular haunts that she was not guarded. She knew it, though she could not see it.

It was a war of subtle wits. Yet from the beginning Constance was the winner of every move. She was on her mettle. They would not, she determined, find Graeme through her.

Days passed and the detectives still had no sign of the missing man. It seemed hopeless, but, like all good detectives, Drummond knew from experience that a clue might come to the surface when it was least expected. Constance on her part never relaxed.

One day it was a young woman dressed in most inconspicuous style who followed close behind her, a woman shadow, one of the shrewdest in the city.

A tenant moved into the apartment across the hall from Constance, and another hired an apartment in the next house, across the court. There was constant espionage. She seemed to "sense" it. The newcomer was very neighborly, explaining that her husband was a traveling salesman, and that she was alone for weeks at a time.

The lines tightened. The next door neighbor always seemed to be around at mail time, trying to get a look at the postmarks on the Dunlap letters. She had an excuse in the number of letters to herself. "Orders for my husband," she would smile. "He gets lots of them personally here."

All their ingenuity went for naught. Constance was not to be caught that way.

They tried new tricks. If it was a journey she took, some one went with her whom she had to shake off sooner or later. There were visits of peddlers, gas men, electric light and telephone men. They were all detectives, also, always seeking a chance to make a search that might reveal her secret. The janitor who collected the waste paper found that it had a ready sale at a high price. Every stratagem that

Drummond's astute mind could devise was called into play. But nothing, not a scrap of new evidence did they find.

Yet all the time Constance was in direct communication with Mackenzie.

Graeme, in his enforced idleness, was more deeply in love with Constance now than ever. He had eyes for nothing else. Even his fortunes would have been disregarded, had he not felt that to do that would have been the surest way to condemn himself before her.

They had cut out the evening trips now, for fear of recognition. She was working faithfully. Already she had cleaned up something like fifty thousand dollars on the turn over of the stuff he had stolen. Another week and it would be some thousands more.

Yet the strain was beginning to show.

"Oh, Graeme," she cried, one night after she had a parti- cularly hard time in shaking Drummond's shadows in order to make her unconventional visit to him, "Graeme, I'm so tired of it all—tired."

He was about to pour out what was in his own heart when she resumed, "It's the lonesomeness of it. We are having success. But, what is success—alone?"

"Yes," he echoed, thinking of his feeling that night when she had left him at the elevator, of the feeling now every moment of the time she was away from him, "yes, alone!"

With the utmost difficulty he restrained the wildly surging emotions within him. He could not know with what effort Constance held her poise so admirably, keeping always that barrier of reserve beyond which now and then he caught a glimpse.

"Let us cut out and bury ourselves in Europe," he urged.

"No," she replied firmly. "Wait. I have a plan. Wait. We could never get away. They would find us and extradite us surely."

She was coming out of a broker's office one day after the close of the market, only to run full tilt into Drummond, who had been waiting for her, cat-like. Evidently he had a purpose.

"You will be interested to know," remarked the detective, watching her narrowly, "that District Attorney Wickham, who had the case in charge out there, is in New York, with the president of the Central Western Trust."

"Yes?" she said non-committally.

"I told them I was on the trail, through a woman, and they have come here to aid me."

Why had he told her that? Was it to put her on her guard or was it in a spirit of bravado? She could not think so. It was not his style to bluster at this stage of the game. No, there was a deep-laid purpose. He expected her to make some move to extricate herself that would display her hand and betray all. It was clever and a less clever person than Constance would have fallen before the onslaught.

Constance was thinking rapidly, as he told her where and how the new pursuers were active. Here, she felt, was the crisis, her opportunity.

Scarcely had Drummond gone, than she, too, was hurrying down the street on her way to see Mackenzie's pursuers face to face.

She found Wickham registered at the Prince Henry, a new hotel and sent up her card. A few moments later he received her, with considerable restraint as if he knew about her and had not expected so soon to have to show his own hand.

"I understand," she began quickly, "that you have come to New York because Mr. Drummond claims to be able to clear up the Graeme Mackenzie case."

"Yes?" he replied quizzically.

"Perhaps," she continued, coming nearer to the point of her self-imposed mission, "perhaps there may be some other way to settle this case than through Mr. Drummond."

"We might hold you," he shot out quickly.

"No," she replied, "you have nothing on me. And as for Mr. Mackenzie, I understand, you don't even know where he is— whether he is in New York, London, Paris, or Berlin, or whether he may not go from one city to another at any moment you take open action."

Wickham bit his lip. He knew she was right. Even yet the case hung on the most slender threads.

"I have been wondering," she continued, "if there is not some way in which this thing can be compromised."

"Never," exclaimed Wickham positively. "He must return the whole sum, with interest to date. Then and only then can we consider his plea for clemency."

"You would consider it?" she asked keenly.

"Of course. We should have to consider it. Voluntary surrender and reparation would be something like turning state's witness—against himself."

Constance said nothing.

"Can you do it?" he asked, watching craftily to see whether she might not drop a hint that might prove valuable.

"I know those who might try," she answered, catching the look.

Wickham changed.

"What if we should get him without your aid!" he blustered.

"Try," she shrugged.

Arguments and threats were of no avail with her. She would say nothing more definite. She was obdurate.

"You must leave it all to me," she repeated. "I would not betray him. You cannot prove anything on ME."

"Bring the stuff up here yourself, then," he insinuated.

"But I don't trust you, either," she replied frankly.

The two faced each other. Constance knew in her heart that it was going to be a battle royal with this man, that now she had taken a step even so far in the open it was every one for himself and the devil take the hindmost.

"I can't help it," he concluded. "Those are the terms. It is as far as I can trust a—a thief."

"But I will keep my word," she said quietly. "When you prove to me that you are absolutely on the level, that Mackenzie can make restitution in full with interest, and in return be left as free a man as he is at this moment—why,—I can have him give up."

"Mrs. Dunlap," said Wickham with an air of finality, "I will make one concession. I will adopt any method of restitution he may prefer. But it must be by direct dealing between Mackenzie and myself, with Drummond present as well as Mr. Taylor, president of the Trust Company, who is now also in New York. That is my ultimatum. Good-afternoon."

Constance left the room with flushed face and eyes that glinted with determination. Over and over she thought out methods to accomplish what she had planned. When they complied with all the conditions that would safeguard Mackenzie, she had determined to act. But Graeme must be master of the situation.

Cautiously she went through her usual elaborate precautions to shake off any shadows that might be following her, and an hour later found her with Mackenzie.

"What has happened!" he asked eagerly, surprised at her early visit.

Briefly she ran over the events of the afternoon. "Would you be willing," she asked, "to go to District Attorney Wickham, hand over the half million with, say, twelve thousand dollars interest, in return for freedom?"

Graeme looked at Constance a moment doubtfully.

"I would not do that," he measured slowly. "How do I know what they will do, the moment they get me in their power? No. Almost, I would say that I would not go there under any guarantee they might give. I do not trust them. The indictment must be dismissed first."

"But they won't do that. The ultimatum was personal restitution."

Constance was faced by an apparently insurmountable dilemma. She saw and agreed with the reasonableness of Graeme's position. But there was the opposition and obstinacy of Wickham, the bitterness and unscrupulousness of Drummond. Here was a tremendous problem. How was she to meet it?

For perhaps half an hour they sat in silence. One plan after another she rejected.

Suddenly an idea occurred to her. Somewhere, in a bank, she had seen a method which might meet the difficulty.

"To-morrow—I will arrange it—to suit both of you," she cried confidently.

"How?" he asked.

"Trust it all to me," she appealed.

"All," replied Graeme, rising and standing before her. "All. I will do anything you say."

He was about to take her hand, but she rose. "No, Graeme. Not now. There is work—the crisis. No, I must go. Trust me."

It was not until noon of the next day that he saw Constance again. There was an air of suppressed excitement about her as she entered the apartment and placed on a table before him a small oblong box of black enameled metal, beneath which was a roll of paper. Above was another somewhat similar box with another roll of paper.

Constance attached the instrument to the telephone, an enigmatical conversation followed, and she hung up the receiver.

A few minutes later, she took the stylus that was in the lower box. Hastily across the blank paper she wrote the words, "We are ready."

Mackenzie was too fascinated to ask questions. Suddenly, out of the corner of his eye, he saw something in the upper box move, as if of itself. It was a similar, self-inking stylus.

"Watch!" exclaimed Constance.

"Do you get this?" wrote the spirit hand.

"Perfectly," she scrawled in turn. "Go ahead, as you promised."

The upper stylus was now moving freely at the ends of its two rigid arms, counterparts of those holding the lower stylus.

"We promise," it wrote, "that in consideration of the return..."

"What is it?" interrupted Graeme, as the meaning of the words even now began to dawn on him.

"A telautograph," she replied simply, "a long distance writer which I have had installed over a leased wire from the hotel room of Wickham to meet the demands of you two. With it you write over wires just as with the telephone you talk over wires. It is as though you took one of the old pantagraphs, split it in half, and had each half connected only by the telephone wires. While you write on this transmitter, their receiver records for them what you write. Look!"

"... of $500,000," it continued to write, "in cash, stocks and bonds, with interest to date, all proceedings against Graeme Mackenzie will be dropped and the indictment quashed.

"Marshall Taylor, Pres. Central Western Trust."

"Maxwell Wickham, District Att'y."

"Riley Drummond, Detective."

"It is even broader than I had hoped," cried Constance in delight. "Does that satisfy you, Graeme?"

"Y-yes," he murmured, not through hesitation, but from the suddenness and surprise of the thing.

"Then sign this."

She wrote quickly: "In consideration of the dropping of all charges against me, I agree to tell the number and location of the safe deposit box in New York where the stocks and bonds I possess are located and to hand over a key and written order to the same. I now agree immediately to pay by check the balance of the half million, including interest."

She stepped aside from the machine. With a tremor of eagerness he seized the stylus and underneath what she had written wrote boldly the name, "Graeme Mackenzie."

Next Constance herself took the stylus. "Place in the telautograph a blank check," she wrote. "He will write in the name of the bank, the amount, and the signature."

She did the same. "Now, Graeme, sign this cheek on the Universal Bank as Lawrence Macey," she said, writing in the amount.

Mechanically he took the stylus. His fingers trembled as he held it, but with an effort he controlled himself. It was too weird, too uncanny to be true. Here he was, without stirring forth from the security of his hiding place; there were his pursuers in their hotel. With the precautions taken by Constance, neither party knew where the other was. Yet they were in instant touch, not by the ear alone, but by handwriting itself.

He placed the stylus on the paper. She had already written in the number of the check, the date, the bank, the amount, and the payee, Marshall Taylor. Hastily Graeme signed it, as though in fear that they might rescind their action before he could finish.

"Now the securities," she said. "I have withdrawn already the amount we have made trading—it is a substantial sum. Write out an order to the Safe Deposit Company to deliver the key and the rest of the contents of the box to Taylor. I have fixed it with them after a special interview this morning. They understand."

Again Graeme wrote, feverishly.

"I—we—are entirely free from prosecution of any kind?" he asked eagerly.

"Yes," Constance murmured, with just a catch in her throat, as now that the excitement was over, she realized that he was free, independent of her again.

The telautograph had stopped. No, it was starting again. Had there been a slip! Was the dream at last to turn to ashes? They watched anxiously.

"Mrs. Dunlap," the words unfolded, "I take my hat off to you. You have put it across again.

"DRUMMOND."

Constance read it with a sense of overwhelming relief. It was a magnanimous thing in Drummond. Almost she forgave him for many of the bitter hours he had caused in the discharge of his duty.

As they looked at the writing they realized its import. The detective had abandoned the long search. It was as though he had put his "O.K." on the agreement.

"We are no longer fugitives!" exclaimed Graeme, drawing in a breath that told of the weight lifted from him.

For an instant he looked down into her upturned face and read the conflict that was going on in her. She did not turn away, as she had before. It flashed over him that once, not long ago, she had talked in a moment of confidence of the loneliness she had felt since she had embarked as the rescuer of amateur criminals.

Graeme bent down and took her hand, as he had the first night when they had entered their strange partnership.

"Never—never can I begin to pay you what I owe," he said

Arthur B. Reeve

huskily, his face near hers.

He felt her warm breath almost on his cheek, saw the quick color come into her face, her breast rise and fall with suppressed emotion. Their eyes met.

"You need not pay," she whispered, "I am yours."

THE END

Other books by this author

The Gold of the Gods

The Master Mystery

Choose from Thousands of 1stWorldLibrary Classics By

A. M. Barnard
Ada Leverson
Adolphus William Ward
Aesop
Agatha Christie
Alexander Aaronsohn
Alexander Kielland
Alexandre Dumas
Alfred Gatty
Alfred Ollivant
Alice Duer Miller
Alice Turner Curtis
Alice Dunbar
Allen Chapman
Alleyne Ireland
Ambrose Bierce
Amelia E. Barr
Amory H. Bradford
Andrew Lang
Andrew McFarland Davis
Andy Adams
Angela Brazil
Anna Alice Chapin
Anna Sewell
Annie Besant
Annie Hamilton Donnell
Annie Payson Call
Annie Roe Carr
Annonaymous
Anton Chekhov
Archibald Lee Fletcher
Arnold Bennett
Arthur C. Benson
Arthur Conan Doyle
Arthur M. Winfield
Arthur Ransome
Arthur Schnitzler
Arthur Train
Atticus
B.H. Baden-Powell
B. M. Bower
B. C. Chatterjee
Baroness Emmuska Orczy
Baroness Orczy
Basil King
Bayard Taylor
Ben Macomber
Bertha Muzzy Bower
Bjornstjerne Bjornson

Booth Tarkington
Boyd Cable
Bram Stoker
C. Collodi
C. E. Orr
C. M. Ingleby
Carolyn Wells
Catherine Parr Traill
Charles A. Eastman
Charles Amory Beach
Charles Dickens
Charles Dudley Warner
Charles Farrar Browne
Charles Ives
Charles Kingsley
Charles Klein
Charles Hanson Towne
Charles Lathrop Pack
Charles Romyn Dake
Charles Whibley
Charles Willing Beale
Charlotte M. Braeme
Charlotte M. Yonge
Charlotte Perkins Stetson
Clair W. Hayes
Clarence Day Jr.
Clarence E. Mulford
Clemence Housman
Confucius
Coningsby Dawson
Cornelis DeWitt Wilcox
Cyril Burleigh
D. H. Lawrence
Daniel Defoe
David Garnett
Dinah Craik
Don Carlos Janes
Donald Keyhoe
Dorothy Kilner
Dougan Clark
Douglas Fairbanks
E. Nesbit
E. P. Roe
E. Phillips Oppenheim
E. S. Brooks
Earl Barnes
Edgar Rice Burroughs
Edith Van Dyne
Edith Wharton

Edward Everett Hale
Edward J. O'Biren
Edward S. Ellis
Edwin L. Arnold
Eleanor Atkins
Eleanor Hallowell Abbott
Eliot Gregory
Elizabeth Gaskell
Elizabeth McCracken
Elizabeth Von Arnim
Ellem Key
Emerson Hough
Emilie F. Carlen
Emily Bronte
Emily Dickinson
Enid Bagnold
Enilor Macartney Lane
Erasmus W. Jones
Ernie Howard Pie
Ethel May Dell
Ethel Turner
Ethel Watts Mumford
Eugene Sue
Eugenie Foa
Eugene Wood
Eustace Hale Ball
Evelyn Everett-green
Everard Cotes
F. H. Cheley
F. J. Cross
F. Marion Crawford
Fannie E. Newberry
Federick Austin Ogg
Ferdinand Ossendowski
Fergus Hume
Florence A. Kilpatrick
Fremont B. Deering
Francis Bacon
Francis Darwin
Frances Hodgson Burnett
Frances Parkinson Keyes
Frank Gee Patchin
Frank Harris
Frank Jewett Mather
Frank L. Packard
Frank V. Webster
Frederic Stewart Isham
Frederick Trevor Hill
Frederick Winslow Taylor

Friedrich Kerst
Friedrich Nietzsche
Fyodor Dostoyevsky
G.A. Henty
G.K. Chesterton
Gabrielle E. Jackson
Garrett P. Serviss
Gaston Leroux
George A. Warren
George Ade
Geroge Bernard Shaw
George Cary Eggleston
George Durston
George Ebers
George Eliot
George Gissing
George MacDonald
George Meredith
George Orwell
George Sylvester Viereck
George Tucker
George W. Cable
George Wharton James
Gertrude Atherton
Gordon Casserly
Grace E. King
Grace Gallatin
Grace Greenwood
Grant Allen
Guillermo A. Sherwell
Gulielma Zollinger
Gustav Flaubert
H. A. Cody
H. B. Irving
H. C. Bailey
H. G. Wells
H. H. Munro
H. Irving Hancock
H. R. Naylor
H. Rider Haggard
H. W. C. Davis
Haldeman Julius
Hall Caine
Hamilton Wright Mabie
Hans Christian Andersen
Harold Avery
Harold McGrath
Harriet Beecher Stowe
Harry Castlemon
Harry Coghill
Harry Houidini

Hayden Carruth
Helent Hunt Jackson
Helen Nicolay
Hendrik Conscience
Hendy David Thoreau
Henri Barbusse
Henrik Ibsen
Henry Adams
Henry Ford
Henry Frost
Henry James
Henry Jones Ford
Henry Seton Merriman
Henry W Longfellow
Herbert A. Giles
Herbert Carter
Herbert N. Casson
Herman Hesse
Hildegard G. Frey
Homer
Honore De Balzac
Horace B. Day
Horace Walpole
Horatio Alger Jr.
Howard Pyle
Howard R. Garis
Hugh Lofting
Hugh Walpole
Humphry Ward
Ian Maclaren
Inez Haynes Gillmore
Irving Bacheller
Isabel Cecilia Williams
Isabel Hornibrook
Israel Abrahams
Ivan Turgenev
J. G.Austin
J. Henri Fabre
J. M. Barrie
J. M. Walsh
J. Macdonald Oxley
J. R. Miller
J. S. Fletcher
J. S. Knowles
J. Storer Clouston
J. W. Duffield
Jack London
Jacob Abbott
James Allen
James Andrews
James Baldwin

James Branch Cabell
James DeMille
James Joyce
James Lane Allen
James Lane Allen
James Oliver Curwood
James Oppenheim
James Otis
James R. Driscoll
Jane Abbott
Jane Austen
Jane L. Stewart
Janet Aldridge
Jens Peter Jacobsen
Jerome K. Jerome
Jessie Graham Flower
John Buchan
John Burroughs
John Cournos
John F. Kennedy
John Gay
John Glasworthy
John Habberton
John Joy Bell
John Kendrick Bangs
John Milton
John Philip Sousa
John Taintor Foote
Jonas Lauritz Idemil Lie
Jonathan Swift
Joseph A. Altsheler
Joseph Carey
Joseph Conrad
Joseph E. Badger Jr
Joseph Hergesheimer
Joseph Jacobs
Jules Vernes
Julian Hawthrone
Julie A Lippmann
Justin Huntly McCarthy
Kakuzo Okakura
Karle Wilson Baker
Kate Chopin
Kenneth Grahame
Kenneth McGaffey
Kate Langley Bosher
Kate Langley Bosher
Katherine Cecil Thurston
Katherine Stokes
L. A. Abbot
L. T. Meade

L. Frank Baum
Latta Griswold
Laura Dent Crane
Laura Lee Hope
Laurence Housman
Lawrence Beasley
Leo Tolstoy
Leonid Andreyev
Lewis Carroll
Lewis Sperry Chafer
Lilian Bell
Lloyd Osbourne
Louis Hughes
Louis Joseph Vance
Louis Tracy
Louisa May Alcott
Lucy Fitch Perkins
Lucy Maud Montgomery
Luther Benson
Lydia Miller Middleton
Lyndon Orr
M. Corvus
M. H. Adams
Margaret E. Sangster
Margret Howth
Margaret Vandercook
Margaret W. Hungerford
Margret Penrose
Maria Edgeworth
Maria Thompson Daviess
Mariano Azuela
Marion Polk Angellotti
Mark Overton
Mark Twain
Mary Austin
Mary Catherine Crowley
Mary Cole
Mary Hastings Bradley
Mary Roberts Rinehart
Mary Rowlandson
M. Wollstonecraft Shelley
Maud Lindsay
Max Beerbohm
Myra Kelly
Nathaniel Hawthrone
Nicolo Machiavelli
O. F. Walton
Oscar Wilde

Owen Johnson
P.G. Wodehouse
Paul and Mabel Thorne
Paul G. Tomlinson
Paul Severing
Percy Brebner
Percy Keese Fitzhugh
Peter B. Kyne
Plato
Quincy Allen
R. Derby Holmes
R. L. Stevenson
R. S. Ball
Rabindranath Tagore
Rahul Alvares
Ralph Bonehill
Ralph Henry Barbour
Ralph Victor
Ralph Waldo Emmerson
Rene Descartes
Ray Cummings
Rex Beach
Rex E. Beach
Richard Harding Davis
Richard Jefferies
Richard Le Gallienne
Robert Barr
Robert Frost
Robert Gordon Anderson
Robert L. Drake
Robert Lansing
Robert Lynd
Robert Michael Ballantyne
Robert W. Chambers
Rosa Nouchette Carey
Rudyard Kipling
Saint Augustine
Samuel B. Allison
Samuel Hopkins Adams
Sarah Bernhardt
Sarah C. Hallowell
Selma Lagerlof
Sherwood Anderson
Sigmund Freud
Standish O'Grady
Stanley Weyman
Stella Benson
Stella M. Francis

Stephen Crane
Stewart Edward White
Stijn Streuvels
Swami Abhedananda
Swami Parmananda
T. S. Ackland
T. S. Arthur
The Princess Der Ling
Thomas A. Janvier
Thomas A Kempis
Thomas Anderton
Thomas Bailey Aldrich
Thomas Bulfinch
Thomas De Quincey
Thomas Dixon
Thomas H. Huxley
Thomas Hardy
Thomas More
Thornton W. Burgess
U. S. Grant
Upton Sinclair
Valentine Williams
Various Authors
Vaughan Kester
Victor Appleton
Victor G. Durham
Victoria Cross
Virginia Woolf
Wadsworth Camp
Walter Camp
Walter Scott
Washington Irving
Wilbur Lawton
Wilkie Collins
Willa Cather
Willard F. Baker
William Dean Howells
William le Queux
W. Makepeace Thackeray
William W. Walter
William Shakespeare
Winston Churchill
Yei Theodora Ozaki
Yogi Ramacharaka
Young E. Allison
Zane Grey